BRIGHTON
BELLE

BRIGHTON BELLE

Sara Sheridan

KENSINGTON BOOKS
http://www.kensingtonbooks.com

KENSINGTON BOOKS are published by

Kensington Publishing Corp.
119 West 40th Street
New York, NY 10018

Library of Congress Card Catalogue Number: 2015958695

Kensington and the K logo Reg. U.S. Pat. & TM Off.

ISBN-13: 978-1-4967-0118-3
ISBN-10: 1-4967-0118-6
First Kensington Hardcover Edition: April 2016

eISBN-13: 978-1-4967-0119-0
eISBN-10: 1-4967-0119-4
First Kensington Electronic Edition: April 2016

10 9 8 7 6 5 4 3 2 1

Printed in the United States of America

Suspicion: a feeling that something may be possible.

PROLOGUE

April 10, 1951

London was glossy—the pavements shone with a slick of rain now the sun had broken through the clouds. It felt like spring at last. At the gates of Victoria Station newsboys scurried with bundles of papers—the early evening editions were hitting the stands. An old man carefully pasted the headline to a thin strip of wood. NAZI WAR CRIMINALS TO HANG AT LAST. Romana Laszlo turned toward the platform. Inside, the station seemed gloomy compared to the blaze of spring sunshine on the street. She stared down the murky platform, her first-class ticket clasped firmly between kid-gloved fingers. She wished they'd stop going on about the Germans. The war had been over for years and Romana, on principle, never took sides about anything. The smell of frying bacon wafted from the direction of the station café as she smoothed her sea-green taffeta coat, checked in case she was being followed, and then, satisfied that she was safe, set off for the Brighton train. In her wake a porter wheeled a large leather suitcase on a trolley. Her stilettos clicked delicately on the concrete.

A small huddle had formed beside the open door of the carriage. The passengers had all arrived at once and there was a flurry of porters handing up luggage and people trying to board the train.

"Do you want me to put this into the luggage compartment?" the porter asked Romana hopefully. It would be easier.

Romana shook her head. "No, here. I prefer to keep it close to hand," she said coldly, with only a hint of an accent.

The porter nodded and resigned himself to waiting.

The little group of passengers hovered on the platform. A man with thick spectacles and a briefcase, a tweed-suited lawyer with a bristling mustache and a gray-haired woman who might be his wife. Romana found her interest held by a tiny corner of cardboard protruding from the older woman's pocket. It was a ration book. She honed in immediately and contrived to stumble against the woman, then, like lightning, skillfully removed the book, straight into her own pocket.

"Oh, my dear, you poor thing," the old woman said, helping Romana to steady herself.

"So sorry," Romana smiled.

"Not at all, quite understandable."

The jam at the carriage door had dissipated and the old woman gestured. "Please, you first."

"You need a hand there, young lady?" the porter offered when Romana hesitated, looking both wide-eyed and vague, as if she didn't understand. Then, collecting herself, she gracefully proffered her hand. It was best to be careful while boarding. The porter loaded the leather case and hovered as she searched her handbag for a coin. It was a gold one. He smiled broadly. "Home soon, eh?" he said cheerily.

Brighton was not her home, but that was none of the fellow's business. Romana handed over the tip and gave an elegant shrug that made her sleek dark bob catch what little light there was. Then she turned her back and stalked into a compartment. As she sat down she slipped the ration book into her handbag. Nestling inside, had anyone bothered to look, there were three more ration books and four passports (none in Mrs. Laszlo's name). It was good to keep her hand in. Stations were excellent for that, Romana thought as she drew an enamel cigarette case from the inside pocket. At once a dark-suited man offered her a light. She stared steadily as she popped the cigarette into an amber holder and leaned into the flame. It seemed her entire concentration was focused on lighting that cigarette, although she was scanning him, of course, for any opportunity or, indeed, danger. Satisfied, she took a deep draw. "Thank you," she breathed.

Normally she would have fluttered her eyelashes to great effect and the nameless man would offer her a drink, but she couldn't expect that now. Romana Laszlo was accustomed to being troubled by men. No longer. Her hand came to rest on her swollen stomach. She was looking forward to Brighton. London had been damp and cold for months. All winter the fog had strangled the city like a filthy shroud. Everything smelled of vinegar—cafés, restaurants and even the flat where she had been staying. Romana had heard good things about the attractions of the Sussex coast and the fresh air at the seaside would surely do her good.

As the train moved off she glanced back, just to be sure no one had followed her. The receding platform was completely clear and she settled back again, noticing the man staring at her stomach as he shifted in his seat.

"Not long now," he said. "Your baby will be born in Brighton, won't it?"

"It will be like a little holiday," she replied, turning toward the window to make it clear she did not want to chat.

Romana Laszlo had never been on a holiday in her life.

1

Better a diamond with a flaw than a pebble without.

Mirabelle Bevan surveyed Brighton's beachfront from her deck chair. The weather had been so fine the last few days she was picking up a golden tan.

Well put-together and in her prime, Mirabelle always ate her lunch on Brighton beach if the weather was in any way passable, but out of sheer principle she never paid tuppence for a chair. We did not win the war to have to pay to sit down, she frequently found herself thinking. Mirabelle's stance against the deck chair charges was one of the few things that kept her going these days. In an act of personal defiance, she carefully timed the coming and goings of Ron, the deck chair attendant, and concluded that it was perfectly possible to sneak enough time to enjoy her sandwich while he tended the other end of his pitch. By selecting the right chair she could have an average of twenty-five undisturbed minutes, which was perfect. Mirabelle's life these days revolved around small victories, little markers in her day that got her through until it was time for bed.

She loved the beach. There was something soothing about the expanse of gray and cream pebbles, the changing color of the sea and the movement of the clouds. Mirabelle didn't mind if it was cold or if there was a spot of rain and it was only during a full-blown downpour or a gale-force wind that she retreated to the steamy interior of the Pier Café. Now she ate her fish paste sandwich with her large hazel eyes on the ocean and her sixth sense switched on in case Ron returned early.

While the nation complained about rationing, Mirabelle found the limited range of foods available comforting. These days she never had much of an appetite and her favorite whiskey was in easy supply as long as she swapped her meat coupons on a regular basis and paid slightly over the odds. A nice bottle of Islay malt was all Mirabelle Bevan really wanted—though Glenlivet was fine at a push. When she had finished her sandwich she brushed the crumbs from her tweed skirt, checked right and left, and slipped a small leather-bound flask from her crocodile-skin handbag to wash down the sandwich with a tiny swig. Back at the office she always made herself a strong cup of tea and sipped it with a cracker so that if her boss came in he would be none the wiser. The whiskey was the only outward sign that Mirabelle Bevan was in mourning. It reminded her of Jack.

As she negotiated the steps in her vertiginous heels and glided back onto the Promenade, Ron came into view, his hands deep in his apron pockets, chatting to two girls. It was always easier to avoid paying the tuppence when the sun was out and a stream of pretty girls occupied the deck chairs on the pebbles. Mirabelle smiled as she cut away from the front and made her way back to the office, in a grubby white stone building on the corner of East Street and Brill Lane. She climbed the dark stairway to the second floor, passed the sign that said MCGUIGAN & MCGUIGAN DEBT RECOVERY and opened the frosted-glass door with every intention of putting on the kettle to boil, but the sight that greeted her stopped Mirabelle in her tracks. Big Ben McGuigan was sitting at his desk. That, in itself, was unusual. Big Ben was what one might call a man of action and, much to Mirabelle's relief, was rarely in his office. But it wasn't only his presence that lent a perturbing air to the office that spring afternoon. Mirabelle's boss was sitting under a grimy blue towel with a cloud of menthol steam emanating from above his head. The place smelled like a hammam.

"Mr. McGuigan." Mirabelle coughed.

Big Ben emerged with his chubby face flushed. He had been out all morning collecting money from what he referred to as "his friends in the slums." He had seemed in perfectly good health when he left.

"Mirabelle, Mirabelle, not so great," he said, and disappeared back under the towel from where he mumbled, "Put on the kettle. I need a hot drink."

Mirabelle complied. She made two cups of strong milky tea and laid one on Big Ben's desk. It was most unlike him to ask for anything. In the eighteen months since Mirabelle had taken the job she hadn't had a single request. Unbidden she opened the mail, dealt with the ledger, the files, the banking and the invoices. She answered the telephone, leaving accurate and detailed messages that required no further explanation on Big Ben's tidy desk. Occasionally a client might come to the office in pursuit of their money. Most days there was a visit from at least one debtor, either ready to pay or to give their excuses, which they seemed to clutch to their chests and then let out, too quickly, like machine-gunfire. Mirabelle Bevan dealt with everything briskly. Big Ben appreciated her efficiency and she appreciated his absence or, on his fleeting visits to the office, his silence. After everything she had been through, it was the perfect job.

"Are you ill?" Mirabelle inquired gently.

One of Big Ben's rheumy blue eyes peered through a crack in the towel. He removed the tea from the desktop and disappeared back beneath the swathe of material. The sound of him drinking ensued.

"Cold. Influenza. Maybe pneumonia," he said.

A shadow of amusement passed across Mirabelle's face. Big Ben was six feet two inches in height and he weighed two hundred pounds. An ex-professional boxer, he had been a sergeant major during the war. The thousands of conscripts who had passed through his capable hands had endowed him with a highly honed capacity for judging human nature and a complete inability to accept any form of excuse. He had set up McGuigan & McGuigan after he demobbed and quickly gained a good reputation for chasing other people's money, on commission. Big Ben, it transpired, was the only McGuigan—the sole employee of the firm until Mirabelle arrived—but he thought that the dual name sounded more professional, so he'd doubled up. It was all very businesslike, which was something both Ben McGuigan and Mirabelle Bevan had recognized in each other from the first moment they'd met. The interview for the job lasted two minutes—exactly long enough to establish that he knew what he wanted and she knew what to do. Until today Mirabelle had never seen Big Ben display any kind of weakness.

"Do you think it might be a good idea to go home?" she suggested tentatively.

Big Ben emerged from under the towel and took a sip of tea. "Seventy-two-hour job," he said.

"I can keep things ticking along," Mirabelle assured him.

"Right," Big Ben said without moving. "Sleep's the best cure."

"And perhaps some Beecham's powders might help," Mirabelle suggested.

Big Ben shrugged his shoulders and the blue towel dropped to the faded linoleum floor. He ignored it and got up from the chair, reaching automatically for his hat. "Seventy-two hours," he repeated, and walked through the door without a backward glance.

Mirabelle cleared Big Ben's desk and took his notebook

over to the ledger to transcribe the payments he had picked up that morning at the Albion Hill estate. Whole streets there were still rubble. The locals used the bombed-out floorboards as firewood, she'd heard—it had been a mild winter, but the houses were damp. There were plans now for rebuilding, of course. About time, too, she thought—it was almost six years since VE Day.

With the ledger up to date, Mirabelle checked her watch and went to stand by the window. It suddenly seemed like it might be a long afternoon. She absentmindedly poked her finger into the dry compost of the half-dead geranium on her desk and wondered if it was better for the soil to be wet. Despite her efficiency there were some areas of life that remained incomprehensible to Mirabelle and care of household plants was one of them. Perhaps I should water it, she thought. Or maybe it needs more light—cut flowers were so much easier, she deliberated, because you knew they were going to die. She moved the plant onto the windowsill. Then, just as she was considering boiling the kettle again and making more tea there was the hammering sound of someone coming up the stairs and Mirabelle hurriedly returned to her chair and appeared busy by reading a file.

The man who burst through the door was dapper. He was short, about forty years of age and sported a brown suit with very wide shoulders. "Well, aren't you a glamour puss?" he said with a London accent.

Mirabelle did not smile. "Can I help you?" she asked, crossing her long legs away from him, beneath the table.

"I'm looking for Big Ben McGuigan."

"Your name?"

"Bert." The man smiled and winked.

Mirabelle hesitated. "I'm afraid Mr. McGuigan is out, Mr. Bert."

Bert grinned. "Well, I could see that for myself, sweetheart," he said and sank into the chair on the other side of Mirabelle's desk. He showed no sign of volunteering any information so, after a short silence, Mirabelle tried to prompt him.

"Did you have a job for Mr. McGuigan?"

"Yeah, yeah. Bit of a tricky situation. But I bet you've seen them all in 'ere, love."

Mirabelle primly pushed her sleek chestnut-brown hair off her face. Many of the people Big Ben pursued for money were in dire straits. In general she didn't tend to feel sorry for them, but, still, she didn't want to laugh at their expense or take their difficulties lightly.

"I can take the inquiry," she said as she turned over a fresh page on her notepad. "What is your full name?"

"Awful formal, aren't you?" Bert smiled.

"He won't be back today. He's out on business."

Bert looked out of the window past the wilting geranium. "Know where he's gone, do you?" he tried.

Mirabelle shook her head. "Mr. McGuigan is working."

"Right," Bert sighed.

Mirabelle kept her pen poised.

"Well, I was hoping to get back on the four thirty anyway," he conceded. "My name's Albert Jennings. Best place to get me is the Red Lion in Notting Hill—though Big Ben knows that already."

"And your case, Mr. Jennings?"

"It's a tricky one, like I said. Slightly delicate. Woman borrowed four hundred quid. And now she's in the family way, if you see what I mean. Come down to Brighton all of a sudden to have the little blighter and there's no sign of my money. Six weeks overdue—that's the payment, not the baby—and plenty of interest. She said she had money coming from her uncle's will. I want Ben to find her and see what he can do—it's a tidy sum now. Piles up when it's overdue, dunnit? Got no address for the lady down here."

"Her name?" Mirabelle asked.

"Foreign bird. Widow. Name of Laszlo," Bert smiled.

"Romana Laszlo. Think she's Polish or something." He sniffed. "She's got a sister, but she's done a bunk and all."

"Romana Laszlo. Well, from the name, she is Hungarian, I imagine," Mirabelle said, without thinking. "Do you have a written contract?"

Bert leaned forward and pulled a paper from the inside pocket of his jacket. He laid it on the desk.

Mirabelle peered at the signature. "Yes. Hungarian," she pronounced. "The Poles don't spell it like that. It's an interesting combination—ethnic Hungarian surname with a Catholic given name. She's a Magyar girl, I should think."

"Know a lot of Hungarians, do you, Miss?" Bert asked.

Mirabelle bit her lip, smearing cherry-red lipstick along her incisor. She really ought to be more careful. "I read a book about Hungary. Very interesting," she said lamely.

"Right. Well, do you think Ben might get onto it for me?"

"Yes. I'll give him the details. Of course."

Mr. Jennings punctuated his next remark by tapping his forefinger on the desk. "You tell him ten percent."

Mirabelle shook her head. "The normal rate is twenty," she said briskly.

"Yeah, but this is more than he picks up on any of those calls he makes down the coast. This is real money." He sat back.

Mirabelle considered for a moment. Mr. Jennings had a point. "He'll do it for fifteen," she said.

Bert sighed. "Twelve and a half, an even eighth?" he tried.

"You know I'm not going to budge from fifteen percent," Mirabelle replied. "Fifteen percent is fair."

Bert hesitated for a moment. Then he shrugged and offered his hand.

Mirabelle shook it. "Didn't catch your name," he remarked.

"I'm Mirabelle Bevan, Mr. Jennings."

"French name, Mirabelle. But you sound good and English."

"Indeed."

Bert smiled. "Well," he said, "expect I'll make the three thirty now."

"Sign here and here, Mr. Jennings." Mirabelle pushed a contract over the table. Bert picked up the pen and scribbled his name onto the sheet in the appropriate places.

"Tell me, sweetheart, what did you do during the war, then? Have a good one?" he asked as he got up to leave.

"Oh," Mirabelle replied, as she always did when people inquired, "I was a Land Girl."

2

There are a thousand ways to go home.

At five o'clock precisely Mirabelle left the office and
locked the door. With Big Ben out of commission for
the next three days, she decided to take a detour on her
way home past the Church of the Sacred Heart in Hove.
She might as well get a head start on Bert Jennings's case,
she rationalized, and if a Hungarian-Catholic woman had
a baby in Brighton, the Sacred Heart was the most likely
place for a christening. There were other Catholic churches
in town of course but Mirabelle happened to know that
one of the pastors there was Hungarian, and she knew that
because she had helped Jack to get Father Sandor the job
after the war.

Jack had been happy to pull strings for Sandor. The department owed him for bringing what—with typical Allied
understatement—had been called "highly sensitive" information out of France when most other channels were
closed and every radio transmission on the continent was
being monitored. The priest had access to the Vatican and
had used the Catholic Church's own lines of communica-
tion to do what he thought was right. He was trusted by
the Nazi junta and ministered to several senior SS men sta-

tioned in Paris. Sandor had put his life on the line every day for years.

When he turned up in London after the war Jack shook the priest's hand warmly and slapped him on the back. "You deserve any help we can give you," he promised. "I take it you don't want to go home."

"Well," Sandor said with a twinkle in his eye, "I've come all this way now . . ."

By then the Soviets had closed the Hungarian border in any case. Jack was always generous to his operatives and he was happy to sort out entry papers and get onto the diocese to see what they could come up with. Encouraged by the department's glowing report of the man's character and despite his disappearance from church duty for what was, by then, several months, they suggested a vacant position at the Sacred Heart.

"A ministry by the sea!" The priest had been delighted. "Thank you, Jack. Thank you so much."

Now, years later and with a lot of water under the bridge, Mirabelle hovered uncomfortably on Norton Road in front of the wooden gate that led to the entrance. She glanced at the row of small shops farther up the main road. Two women with brightly-colored net shopping bags were gossiping outside the greengrocers. Mirabelle brought her eyes back to the Church. It felt no better. The Victorian building reared up in front of her like a pale sleeping monster. Her hands were trembling and her fingers were cold. But the truth was that she was drawn here and had been for a while. Romana Laszlo was only an excuse. Jack was buried in the small graveyard behind the building. It was ironic, really. He had given up his faith years before he died.

Mirabelle had never visited the grave. By now, she realized, there would probably be a headstone or a plaque. The thought made her queasy and she wasn't sure she could face it. Besides, there was no point in causing embarrassment or trouble for Jack's wife or his girls—that would be spiteful. Better by far to remain Jack's most covert operation. At least that's what she'd believed for almost two years. Now, though, despite her longstanding rationale for staying away she was here at the door, and the truth was she loved Jack as much as ever.

"Damn it, damn it," she whispered as she paced along the paving stones. Finally Mirabelle drew up her courage, took a deep breath and walked slowly through the gate, keeping her eyes straight ahead. The clicking of her heels echoed across the tiled floor. The Church was deserted. Her vision adjusted to the gloom as she moved down the aisle. Tentatively she peered into the enclaves on either side but there was no one at prayer. Then, from a door near the altar, a stocky man in a cassock with the face of a rugby player emerged into the heavy atmosphere like a cannonball.

"My daughter," he nodded. His accent was Irish. "Have you come for confession?"

Mirabelle shook her head. "I'm looking for Father Sandor," she said, her voice suddenly croaky.

"Can I not help you? I'm Father Grogan." He gripped her hand in a firm shake and Mirabelle felt rather glad she was wearing gloves.

"I'm afraid it's Father Sandor I need to speak to," she said.

"Ah well, I'll fetch him." Father Grogan disappeared back through the door.

Mirabelle sat in a pew and stared at the altar where Jack's coffin would have lain.

Suddenly she heard the heavy iron handle of the door creak and then, looking up, it seemed as if Father Sandor's smile lit up the whole church.

"Mirabelle!" he shouted, his accent as strong as ever. He rushed forward and flung his arms around her. "What are you doing in Brighton?"

Mirabelle's heart sank. Like everyone else, Sandor didn't have a clue about what had happened. He probably thought she was still beetling away in Whitehall. The priest grinned, waiting for Mirabelle to reply. She didn't want to lie—and no matter what her personal convictions, she especially didn't want to lie to a man of God.

"I'm looking for a Hungarian girl called Romana Laszlo," she said. "She is having a baby. She came to Brighton recently and I wondered if you'd heard of her. I thought she'd be bound to come here—for a christening."

Sandor shrugged his shoulders expansively. "No, I don't have a parishioner of that name. Come. Come with me. It's so good to see you. I will put on the kettle and make us a cup of tea."

Father Sandor's tea had quite a kick. He had developed a fondness for brandy. Mirabelle sat at the vestry table and sipped silently as the priest made conversation, fussing over her and saying how happy he was in the parish. Brighton suited him, he said, and Hove was like a village.

"So what have you been doing?" he asked eventually. "Still sorting out everyone's problems?"

Mirabelle shrugged. She had thought about going back to the department and taking up the threads of her old life without Jack. They would have had her back in London like a shot but leaving Brighton meant leaving so much behind—the memory of the little time they'd had together, the shadow of the life that could have been. She shook her head.

Father Sandor tried again. "What did this Romana Laszlo do, Mirabelle? Why are you looking for her?"

At least this was a question Mirabelle could answer easily. "She borrowed a lot of money in London. Four hundred pounds." It seemed so trifling now.

"I see. But that's not what I mean," he persisted. "What did she do in the war?"

Mirabelle couldn't stand it. "I don't know."

"But . . ." Sandor hesitated and then decided not to pursue the matter. "Well, now that you're here, would you like to visit Jack's grave?"

Mirabelle sprang to her feet with her heart racing. Bile rose in her throat. She couldn't. It was a daily haunting as it was. Seeing his name carved in stone would only make things worse. It had been a mistake to come here. "No. Thank you. I have to be going." She felt panicky. "Sandor, if you find out anything about Romana Laszlo, will you call me? Here." She wrote down the office number on a scrap of paper from her bag.

Sandor took it. "This is a Brighton number. Are you on an operation? You can tell me, Mirabelle. Are you undercover?"

Mirabelle's eyes sank to the floor. She wished the stone slabs would swallow her. "I've never been in the field, Sandor. I was intelligence, not operations, remember. And I don't even do that any more. I'm not here to do anything good or worthwhile. I'm simply looking for Romana Laszlo because she owes someone some money. Please just let me have any information that comes your way."

"And now you think you shouldn't have come at all," he said with a smile, still trying to engage her. The priest's blue eyes were like pools. Those eyes had seen a lot over the years. "I'm sorry. It was clumsy of me. My nose always bothers me. But I don't need my nose to see you are upset, no?" Silence. Sandor laid his hand on her arm. He knew that if she didn't want to talk, he couldn't make her. It was only that, in his experience, talking usually helped people who looked as tortured as the wide-eyed elegant near-widow before him.

"I'm sorry," Mirabelle excused herself. She felt horribly ashamed. "I shouldn't have come."

Walking home Mirabelle stopped at the newsagent on the main street and bought her *Evening Argus* without even glancing at the headline. She found herself unable to make small talk with the man on the till and was grateful that the shop was busy. On autopilot, she strolled toward the front door of her building and let herself in, climbing the airy staircase to the first floor. Inside the view was wonderful. It was always wonderful. The sea. The sky. The changing panorama of the light as the clouds moved. Mirabelle laid the paper on the pile. Since August 11, 1949, the day of Jack's death, she had found herself unable to throw away a copy of the *Evening Argus*. Now there were over five hundred of them piled up against the wall with the edition containing the worst possible news at the bottom. Buried for one year, seven months and two days now.

No one had come to tell her that sunny day. No one had offered her sympathy or sent flowers. Jack had covered their tracks very carefully. So when she'd sat by the window to read her evening paper the news had come as a complete shock. "Prominent local businessman, forty-nine years of age," the article said, "recently returned to Brighton after being demobbed. Mr. Duggan died suddenly of a heart attack this morning in the street outside his family home. He had a distinguished war record." It didn't say a word about the fact that he'd bought this flat for her and he was planning to divorce his wife and live there that autumn when his girls went up to Oxford. He had twin girls, you see, and he loved them very much.

"It's 1949 and after all we've been through, why shouldn't we have each other?" he'd said. "It's only making it happen gently. I can see the lawyer when the girls have left for college. I'll arrange everything. But, Belle, will you have me? A divorced man more than ten years older than you?"

Mirabelle had been so happy she'd run around the flat half-naked, scattering pillows in her wake, whooping for joy. "Yes, I'll have you! Yes! Yes!"

They had shared a gin and tonic in celebration and made love on the floor.

Two months later poor Jack was buried in the Church of the Sacred Heart by a wife he scarcely spoke to any more, who had no idea that after what Jack had seen and done during the war the idea of a God or a church was beyond him.

It had been a long day. Seeing Sandor had brought it all back—memories that she had pushed down now surfaced in a flood. Mirabelle removed her shoes, poured herself a glass of whiskey and sniffed it. She took a sip and then, with shaking hands, she sank down on the pale blue sofa and finally let the tears stream down her cheeks.

3

HA HU HI: I am going to Paris
(radio code used by double agent Eddie Chapman)

It was colder today. The spring weather was always un-predictable. Mirabelle stared out of the office window. Two men dressed for a dance were heading home after a long night at the Palais. Their laughter floated up as they sheltered out of the drizzle to light their cigarettes. Pulling her brown cashmere cardigan around her slim frame, Mirabelle closed the window. She hadn't slept well. She put the notes she had taken about Romana Laszlo's debt on Big Ben's desk. Then she wondered whether to throw out the dying geranium and be done with it. The mail sat unopened. Clicking back into work mode, as if she had taken a painkiller, Mirabelle slit open the first envelope with the small dagger she kept on her desk. She removed the check. She'd go to the bank later. Then, as she picked up the second envelope, the phone rang.

"McGuigan & McGuigan Debt Recovery."

"Is that you, Mirabelle?" The priest's voice was distinctive.

"Hello, Sandor." Her heart sank.

"I have something for you," Sandor said.

"My boss is going to deal with this one," Mirabelle replied crisply, "but I take it she's turned up, then?"

"Romana Laszlo? Hmmm, yes." There was an awkward pause and then Sandor sighed. "She is dead."

"Dead?"

"Both she and the baby. She was in labor and there were complications. It was late last night. I'm sorry."

Mirabelle felt her fingers tingle. She felt inexplicably responsible. "That's dreadful," she said quietly. "Poor girl."

"She died with only her doctor in attendance so she did not receive the last rites. I will officiate at the funeral tomorrow. She has a sister coming from London and they want it to be quick. Often this is the case and I understand she was widowed recently so there is no husband to mourn her or the baby. Mirabelle, there is something troubling me. Something strange. I talked to her friend, the doctor. She was staying with him, and I said I also am Hungarian and where was she from, Romana? And he told me Izsak."

"Yes?"

"I know Izsak. I know every Catholic family in the area. I probably know every non-Catholic family, too. It's a small place and I ministered there—it was my first job when I came from the seminary. Four little villages and Izsak one of them. Two years I lived there and I never heard of anyone with a daughter called Romana. This girl was twenty-two, this Romana—she would have been twenty-three next month. Before the war, if she came from a family in Izsak she would have been the age of a schoolgirl. I should know her. But I don't."

Mirabelle's curiosity was pricked, a tantalizing flashback of her former life echoing down from London to her sequestered existence by the sea. It felt as if Jack was calling her. Still, she fought against her instinct. Sandor's information was interesting, but, telling herself she had to be practical, she dismissed it immediately. If a debtor died it was Big Ben's job to claim the money from the estate. That made what she had to do purely administrative and therefore rather easy. Nothing else mattered. Not these days.

"Thank you, Sandor. Tell me," she moved on calmly, "do you know who the executor is?"

"There is a lawyer. Peters. I should think he must be the one."

"Thank you."

Sandor sounded eager. "Will you come to the funeral, Mirabelle? Will you send someone?"

Mirabelle sighed. After the way she'd felt yesterday, she wasn't going back to the church ever.

"No, that won't be necessary, Sandor. I have everything I need now. Thank you."

Sandor hesitated. "You know where I am," he said at last, "if you want to talk." Then he rang off.

Mirabelle pushed all thoughts of Jack from her mind. This was her job now. It might not be the important job to which she had been accustomed but it still had to be done. She retrieved Romana Laszlo's file, looked up Peters in the Brighton directory and found the number of the solicitor's practice on Ship Street. The receptionist transferred her immediately.

"Ralph Peters," the lawyer said briskly.

"Hello," Mirabelle said, "this is Mirabelle Bevan of McGuigan & McGuigan Debt Recovery. I understand you are handling the execution of a recent estate—one Romana Laszlo."

"Yes, Miss Bevan."

"We have an outstanding debt I would like to register with you. Mrs. Laszlo owed our client four hundred pounds to date."

"You are rather quick off the mark."

"Yes, I know. I apologize for that. Can you tell me, please, are there funds?"

"I imagine so. There is a considerable life insurance policy as I understand it. I don't envisage a problem. I'll know the ins and outs in a few days."

"I see."

The solicitor took down Mirabelle's details and she agreed to send over the original contract with Bert Jennings.

"I will inform you of the time scale when I know it, Miss Bevan."

"Yes, that would be very helpful. There are obviously issues with the interest." Mirabelle hesitated. The ministry had gathered enormous amounts of information by simply training people to ask the right questions. Now that she had Peters on the phone, Mirabelle found it almost impossible not to try. "Mr. Peters, may I ask if you knew Mrs. Laszlo?"

"Not at all. I am simply her friend's solicitor. He brought over her papers this morning and instructed me. She had only recently arrived in England, as I understand it, and did not have a solicitor of her own."

"I see. Where did she come from?"

"I have no idea. Is it important?"

"No, no. I only wondered. Unusual name, Romana. Pretty."

"Well, I expect it's Dutch. She had a Dutch passport, I notice."

"I see."

"If that's all, Miss Bevan, I must be getting on. I will keep you informed, but I don't expect it will take too long."

"Yes, of course. Goodbye."

As she put down the phone Mirabelle wondered why she'd pushed. Still, there was no harm in it. Now she had the information she needed to make good on Bert Jennings's debt, though she also had an uncomfortable feeling in the pit of her stomach. Perhaps, she thought, when Big Ben came back she would see about taking a holiday. Things had been going so well. Mirabelle smoothed the cuff of her cardigan and straightened the belt that was cinching her waist. Then she heard steps on the stairs. It was certainly turning out to be a very eventful morning and she did not want to appear to be dallying. She had just picked up her pen but had not yet had time to put it to paper when a man walked into the office without even knocking. He had an extraordinary look on his face, as if he had seen an angel—a cross, Mirabelle thought, between wonder and disbelief. Debtors often arrived first thing in the morning. They were almost always dressed like this man— in shabby demob suits—though his expression marked him out from the normally subdued clientele at McGuigan & McGuigan who invariably arrived with a shameful look on their faces, apologizing as they handed over their coins.

"Come in, I'll only be a minute."

Mirabelle motioned the man to a chair and slipped her note inside the file marked ROMANA LASZLO and then wrote on the buff cover DECEASED in brackets.

"Is that the foreign bird over at Dr. Crichton's then?" the man asked jovially, peering at what she was doing from his chair.

Mirabelle nodded. Somewhere, she thought, Jack is laughing at me. I can practically hear him.

"I suppose all sorts need money now and then," he mused. "I delivered her coffin there this morning. Thought it was the same name. Well, I never. Weird lot, them for-eigners. Don't want an undertaker, oh no. Just a coffin. Basic model. Didn't even want me to lay her in it. Poor soul. Must be a foreign custom. Nice, really, to look after the body yourself, I suppose. Keep it in the family, like. Used to be that way here though people don't bother now."

Mirabelle sighed. There was nothing for it. The details were too intriguing.

"And you are?" she started.

"Michael Smith. Come to make a payment."

Mirabelle reached for the ledger. "And you work at the undertakers?" she inquired casually.

"That's right. Cobb's of Patcham."

Mirabelle scanned through the entries—ten debts on each page. Michael Smith had been running this loan for eighteen months, though it looked as if Big Ben normally made a call once a month to get a little money. Most of the time the man barely covered the interest.

"I'm paying the lot off today," he announced. "I want to clear it."

Mirabelle put her finger on the appropriate entry and read across. "Five pounds, two shillings and sixpence."

Mr. Smith reached into his pocket. He proudly withdrew a large white five-pound note and laid it on the desk with a half-crown piece. Mirabelle indicated where he had to sign for completion.

"Good tipper, that Dr. Crichton," Smith said, his face showing clear delight at being out of the red. "Wanted to give me a gold coin and I said 'Oh, sir, I can't take that.' Just laughed, he did, and gave me one of those." He nodded toward the paper money. "That's for you,' he said. 'Now hop it!' Well, I got out of there quick, I don't mind telling you, before he changed his mind."

It was an outrageous tip, probably worth more than the coffin.

"Gosh, it is your lucky day," Mirabelle said. "Do you have Dr. Crichton's address, Mr. Smith? I need it for this file."

"Course I do," Smith grinned, far too elated to question why. "Twenty-two Second Avenue. Easy to remember. Two, two, two, you see."

When the man left the office, Mirabelle sat back in her chair. There was clearly something going on. She pushed a lock of hair behind her ear with a determined expression. Nothing as intriguing as this had happened in almost two years—not since she left the ministry. It felt comforting in a way—familiar. The best ones started this way—hammering on the door, refusing to be ignored. The devil was always in the detail. And here the detail was certainly devilish—a dead woman and her child, a case of, if not mistaken identity, then some kind of mix-up at best and a very great deal of money.

Mirabelle decided to take a trip along to Second Avenue and have a look for herself.

4

*Chickenfeed: information intended to attract
and puzzle the recipient.*

Mirabelle buttoned her coat and pinned her hat in
place. Then she caught a bus. Second Avenue was
only a few blocks from her flat on the Lawns and she was
familiar with the area, especially Adelaide Crescent with its
majestic white Georgian terrace. Sometimes on the weekend
she liked to walk round the Crescent and enjoy the view of
the sea. A couple of streets along, Second Avenue was
residential—a series of fine Victorian pale brick houses
with ornate architectural features—and today Mirabelle
scanned both sides of the road as she turned the corner
and strode toward the sea. In the old days at the department they would have sent a car on this kind of stake-out.
A car was the best cover, or a van, if you couldn't get into
one of the houses nearby. Stopping at number 22, she hovered on the opposite side of the street, trying to look as if
she was waiting for a cab to pick her up, or a friend to
come home.

There was little remarkable about the house and, ex-
cepting the black crepe bow attached to the brass door-
bell, there was not much to see. You have to be patient if
you're fishing, Mirabelle thought, and settled against a
low wall opposite. She had read several handbooks on sur-

veillance and knew what to do though she had no practical experience—her role had always been supportive and, for that matter, strategic. She had buzzed around the office at the department, always busy, for almost eight years, all told. As the cold stone penetrated her clothes and numbed her buttocks she reminded herself that surveillance was about staying still. This was not in her nature. After about twenty minutes the front door opened and a smart older woman walked down the tiled path. She was carrying a prescription. It looked as if the doctor was consulting. Mirabelle approached, formulating a plan as she smiled in greeting.

"Excuse me," she said. "I was wondering if this is Dr. Crichton's house?"

"Yes."

"And do you mind me asking, is the doctor consulting today? Only I heard there was a bereavement."

"Well, I've just been to see him," the woman said. "I know he had a friend of the family staying. Poor soul. Both she and the baby were taken, I understand."

"Is the doctor in good spirits?" Mirabelle inquired.

"Seemed fine to me. Mind you, doctors must see that sort of thing all the time, I expect."

"Yes, of course. I wasn't sure whether to disturb him. Thank you."

The woman disappeared up the road and Mirabelle continued to hover. Several vans passed to deliver groceries farther up the street. In the bay window she thought she caught a fleeting glimpse of a woman but she couldn't make her out. Waiting for something to turn up was a time-consuming business. Mirabelle knew a successful stake-out could take days or even weeks and she felt frustrated because she couldn't leave the office unmanned much longer than lunchtime—it wouldn't be fair to Ben. Going by the book, she knew that she should monitor the pattern of life in the house for at least a day or two before even attempting to gain entry. But it was clear that if she wanted to make progress quickly she might have to take some chances. This, however, wasn't a war and Mirabelle assured herself that her life wasn't at risk. It was a doctor's surgery, for heaven's sake! The best plan, she decided, was to simply wing it and go in. There would probably be an explanation for everything, the minute she got inside. Resolve hardened, she climbed the steps.

The bell was answered by a housemaid dressed in a black uniform with a white apron. She looked tearful.

"Excuse me," Mirabelle said, casting her gaze over the dark red hallway behind the girl. "I am very sorry to bother you, but I wondered if the doctor might see me."

"Surgery is over at eleven," the maid said promptly. "And he's not NHS today. That's Thursdays and Fridays only."

Mirabelle checked her wristwatch again though she knew the time. It was ten minutes past.

"I see," she said. "Gosh, my watch is running slow. It's taken me a while to get here. I'm happy to be a private patient, only I wonder if you might ask the doctor if he would possibly be able to see me even if I am running a bit late. I'd be ever so grateful."

"It's busy today. What with . . ."

"I know. I'm so sorry. Did you know the lady?" Mirabelle took the opportunity.

"We was all off, Miss," the maid said quickly, her eyes clouding. "I only met her when she arrived. I unpacked for her and that. Then we was dismissed. The doctor said he wanted the house quiet for the labor. Bless her soul. She was due—you could see it!"

"I'll quite understand if he is too busy, only I have come a long way," Mirabelle insisted. "If he could squeeze me in it would be marvelous. Would you ask him?"

The maid relented with an apologetic smile. She stepped

back and allowed Mirabelle to enter. The girl gestured toward an oak chair against the wall. "Who shall I say?" she asked, casting a glance at the silver salver on the hall table.

Mirabelle did not carry cards. Not any more.

"My name is Miss Bevan," she said and sat down.

The maid waited a moment and then turned and knocked on one of the doors leading off the hallway. As she entered, Mirabelle could see that the room was pale green. The doctor's house seemed well furnished with antiques, which made it feel as if he had been living there for a while, but, she noticed, the soft furnishings were all new. Cushions on the chairs were still stiff from the shop and the tie-back on one of the curtains had a small label. Things were not worn in. And it all looked a little too perfect. Either the owner had only just moved or there had been some influx of new money to an already established household. Mirabelle heard voices from behind the study door and the maid returned.

"That's fine, Miss. He'll see you. This way, please," she said.

This, Mirabelle thought, was easier than it had seemed in all those reports she'd read. It was going like a dream. She glided into the study.

Dr. Crichton was not alone. A slight man with a mustache, he snapped to his feet as soon as the door opened. Mirabelle thought he had a cheerful demeanor for someone who had lost not one patient but technically two the night before. He was not wearing mourning dress. On the contrary he was sporting a tweed jacket and a pair of buff trousers. By the fireplace there was a beautiful woman in her twenties. She had short dark hair and was wearing red lipstick and far too much jewelery for eleven o'clock in the morning. Her tiny waist was set off by a flared skirt in white chiffon that moved behind her in what seemed like a three-second time lag as she came forward to greet Mirabelle. Her stiletto heels clicked on the dark wooden floor.

"Miss Bevan," the doctor shook Mirabelle's hand, "this is my house guest—her name is Lisabetta."

To see another resident of the house was definitely a bonus.

"I am so sorry," the girl said breathlessly. Her accent was Eastern European—not heavy but still there. Mirabelle tried to place it as Lisabetta continued. "I thought the surgery was over so I came to see if Eric wanted to come out for some drinks."

"How do you do?" Mirabelle smiled. She couldn't quite tell whether the girl's vowels were Eastern or Northern. "Dr. Crichton kindly gave me an appointment even though I was late. Oh, I say, I do like your skirt."

Lisabetta smiled and an air of triumph came over her. "I bought it in Paris," she said with delight. "I love the gypsy style! It's all the rage!"

"Paris is wonderful for clothes. My mother was French. Where are you from? You have a smashing accent."

"I come from Hungary."

Dr. Crichton cut in. "When you ladies have quite finished with your comments on the fashions of the day . . . Lisabetta, you have to leave now. Miss Bevan is a patient and this is a consultation. I shan't be accompanying you."

Lisabetta gave the doctor a look as if she distrusted his motives and felt that somehow she was being cut out of the fun. "I see," she said petulantly. "Well, Manni and I are going and we won't be back for a while. We'll take your car—the Jag." She flounced through the door, her sharp thin heels pockmarking the wide wooden boards in her wake.

The doctor either didn't notice or didn't care.

"Please, sit down, Miss Bevan," he said, taking his place behind the desk. "I apologize. Among other things Lisabetta is here to help me buy some things for the house. She is not accustomed to . . ."

"Oh, I quite understand. Hungary seems such an exotic place. Have you ever visited?" Mirabelle continued smoothly.

Dr. Crichton shook his head. "No. Never."

Mirabelle had seen and heard enough to give her reason to doubt that Lisabetta had been there either. The vowel sounds were entirely wrong. And the girl's air of jollity didn't fool her one bit—there was a dangerous flash of steel behind those pretty eyes.

"I'm sure it has been a trying day," she said. "I heard of your bereavement last night. In fact, I should pay my respects, shouldn't I? Out of politeness. If you have a body lying in wake in the house."

"That's quite unnecessary, Miss Bevan. We don't stand on such old-fashioned customs here, and in any case the casket is closed. It was a difficult birth."

"The poor lady was another Hungarian, was she not?"

Dr. Crichton nodded curtly. "Yes. Very sad. Lisabetta's sister."

"Her sister?" Mirabelle felt the color draining from her face. An uneasy feeling crept across her heart. Lisabetta could not be bereaved. It was simply impossible. What kind of person could enforce such gaiety in the face of an unexpected death—two deaths, in fact—her sister and her sister's stillborn child. Mirabelle realized that far from allaying her worries, so far her trip to Second Avenue had only made them worse. She looked around the study. The walls were lined with scientific volumes—not, Mirabelle noted, only medical books. She spotted *A History of Trigonometry* and several on the subject of physics as well as one elderly volume on the science of alchemy.

"You're all being dreadfully brave. Her sister helping with the house, too . . ."

"She's spending a fortune." The doctor seemed glad to be moving the conversation along. "A fortune of *my* money! Chap needs help of course—antiques and so forth. It's almost there. Terribly distressing, what happened, goes without saying. Now . . ." Dr. Crichton picked up his stethoscope from a drawer, and leaned forward, getting down to business. "Tell me, Miss Bevan, what seems to be the trouble?"

Outside in the hallway Lisabetta hesitated. She opened her bag and checked the tiny gun inside.

"Problem?" a middle-aged man asked as he came downstairs.

Lisabetta shrugged her shoulders nonchalantly. "Nothing I can't handle if I have to. Come along."

Manni didn't doubt it. "Well, if you need me . . ."

Lisabetta shook her head. "No, I don't. You have done quite enough this week! It's funny, Manni. England is so . . ." She searched for the word. ". . . provincial. Come, I've told them to bring round the car." She checked the diamond watch on her slender wrist and clicked her patent clutch bag closed with an air of decision.

5

Curiosity is one of the forms of feminine bravery.

It must have taken Dr. Crichton's man a while to bring the car round because Mirabelle left 22 Second Avenue a few minutes later, just in time to see a racing-green convertible Jaguar pull away from the front of the house. Inside Lisabetta was sitting in the passenger seat with the flounces of her skirt billowing while a middle-aged man with gray hair perfectly matching his suit took the wheel.

Mirabelle paused for a moment to digest everything. There were a lot of reasons that someone from Eastern Europe, or for that matter any of the Germanic states, might decide to lie about where they had come from. Of course women died in childbirth all the time—babies, too. Despite that, something felt very amiss. The household showed no real signs of mourning. The maid who answered the door was more distressed than the people who had really known the poor dead girl. Mirabelle was transfixed. Her pulse quickened and it was as if the blood was pumping properly round her system for the first time in ages. She had to admit it was invigorating, even slightly addictive.

She might not have walked into a Nazi café to try to overhear the details of a conversation or bluffed her way into SS headquarters in search of a strategic plan but Mirabelle decided that her first stab at what Jack would have called fieldwork hadn't been as difficult as she might have expected. She liked it. Running on instinct, like a dog with a scent for the chase, Mirabelle raised her hand to hail a passing cab. In for a penny, in for a pound, she decided, as the Jaguar reached the bottom of the road and turned left toward Brighton. Mirabelle hopped gracefully into the back of the taxi and told the driver to continue along the front as fast as possible. It didn't take long to catch up. Manni and Lisabetta were taking their cruise along the shore at a leisurely pace. After a couple of minutes the Jaguar swung into the entrance of the Grand—Brighton's poshest hotel. At eight stories it towered over the nearby buildings and as a result it was afforded impressive views right along the beach and out to sea. It would, Mirabelle decided instantly, be a mistake to be seen on the hotel's flashy driveway. "Drop me farther up on the right," she directed the driver, straining to see the Jaguar as she passed.

A safe hundred yards farther along the street she slipped discreetly onto the pavement of King's Road. The Grand had been a wartime billet for hundreds of soldiers but nowadays its luxurious interior was once more the preserve of the well-heeled. It was turning into quite some morning. Mirabelle checked her hat and smoothed her hair. Then she slipped up the steps at the entrance and through the double glass doors, which were held open by a man in a maroon and gold uniform. She couldn't quite believe she was doing this as she passed across the threshold. It was fun. Inside the vast hallway there was no sign of Manni or Lisabetta.

Mirabelle walked confidently past the busy reception desk and into a glass conservatory decorated in the Oriental fashion, which included several enormous palms in large glazed pots. The conservatory was quiet so she quickly moved on to the bar. Several couples whom Big Ben McGuigan would no doubt have designated "smart London types" were smoking and sipping cocktails. One older lady swathed in a thick fur wrap was drinking an espresso and eating a sliver of cake. There was still no sign of Lisabetta and Manni. Mirabelle glanced up at the mezzanine level. Perhaps they had taken a room. She decided to sit in the lounge and wait. She had never been inside the Grand before and there was, after all, plenty to think about. It seemed to Mirabelle that a great deal of trouble might come from the lies that were being told—about where Lisabetta and her sister came from, for a start, and of course about whatever had happened to the poor pregnant girl and her baby. People didn't lie without cause and she could think of no good reason for the selection of falsehoods she had uncovered so far—or at least there was no explanation that fitted together in a satisfying fashion.

It was impossible to station herself somewhere she could be sure to see everything but Mirabelle decided that a central chair would at least allow her to look around. If she had been working for the department she would have rung in and by now another agent would have been dispatched to try to wring information from the staff at Second Avenue. A friendly man from the electricity board might arrive to read the meter and strike up a conversation with the housemaid. A twenty-four-hour watch would be put in place. Mirabelle smiled at the thought. It wasn't wartime anymore. These people weren't the enemy. But nonetheless her brain was buzzing. The details didn't stand. Poor Romana Laszlo. Even in her days at the department Mirabelle had rarely dealt in cold-blooded murder but things here seemed so strange that the possibility now crossed her mind. Why had the girl borrowed money from Bert? What had she been like? Had her sister and the doctor wanted rid of her for some reason and, if so, what was it?

Mirabelle ordered a pot of Earl Grey and when it arrived she nibbled meditatively on a thin wafer biscuit. In wartime, she thought to herself, you don't call a death murder. Still, an investigation might operate in the same fashion to uncover a crime and would start, she knew, by noting anything that didn't fit. The troublesome details knocked around inside her head—a false passport, a strange coincidence, a household that didn't care, a rushed funeral without a proper undertaker, a body at home that wasn't laid in wake—for what could happen in labor that the poor woman might need a closed casket, she wondered. And of course all the money—Dr. Crichton's household renovations and his generous tip.

After a few minutes she was called back to consciousness by a woman laughing in a familiar tone. The sound came from behind. Taking out her compact Mirabelle checked discreetly with the little mirror. Sure enough, Manni and Lisabetta were taking seats on two lavishly upholstered armchairs near the door. They were not alone. Another older man was comfortably ensconced on a sofa beside a very pretty, if somewhat younger, woman, who had, Mirabelle noticed, excellent deportment. The waiter was fussing and laying out glasses for the party of four, in readiness for the two bottles of champagne, one opened and one in a silver ice bucket beside the table. Mirabelle couldn't hear what language they were speaking but she knew it wasn't English or, indeed, Hungarian, the sound of which was distinctive. Lisabetta's body language was dominant—she had brought this little group together. And there was more. Mirabelle examined the slender female figure on the sofa carefully. She clicked her compact closed and sank back into the comfortable cushions of the wingback chair.

She might have only worked in the back office in intelligence, she might never have ventured into the field, and she might appear demure on occasion, but she wasn't stupid. Mirabelle Bevan knew a prostitute when she saw one, even one who could sit up perfectly straight and wear her well-tailored dress like a lady. It was unmistakeable. Not Lisabetta—the other one. The group was at home with it, too, you could see. Mirabelle understood the body language. Jack hadn't protected her from the realities that British agents had to face or indeed indulge in.

I expect they will go upstairs soon in one combination or another, Mirabelle thought with what closely resembled scientific interest. She shifted her chair slightly so she could see the group out of the corner of her eye while still shielded by the high sides of the armchair. Sure enough, just after midday the champagne was all drunk, the waiter was tipped rather generously, Mirabelle noted, and the old man disappeared with the young girl in the direction of the lift while Lisabetta and Manni called for the car.

Careful not to be seen Mirabelle paid her bill and sloped back to the main door just in time to see the green Jaguar leave in the direction of Hove. She checked her watch. It was fifteen minutes past twelve: time to get back to the office. She decided to walk rather than take the bus. It had been an eventful morning and a breath of sea air would do her the power of good.

6

All war is deception.

After the war all the suites at the Grand had been refur-
bished. The whole building was Italian in style and
the interior decorator, fired up by optimism in the wake of
the Allied victory, really went to town when it came to the
more upmarket bedrooms. The color scheme was muted—
a pale dove gray complemented by touches of white. A few
subtle pieces of gilded furniture set off the rooms perfectly
without taking away from the stunning views over the
ocean to the south of the building. The suite smelled fresh
and everything was perfectly placed, from the crisp linen
to the white lilies displayed ostentatiously in cut crystal
vases. It had the feeling of being at once both elegant and
lavish.

Delia had hardly drunk any of the champagne. She needed
to stay sober. She knew that as long as she held a glass in her
manicured fingers, smiled and batted the extraordinarily long
eyelashes that framed her huge blue eyes, nobody seemed to
notice if she actually took a sip or not. Delia had a great
deal of experience in drinking champagne while retaining
her composure. By contrast the old man had downed almost
a whole bottle and was clearly feeling the worse for wear.
When they were downstairs Delia had counted the glasses

carefully while he talked business with Lisabetta. It was not Lisabetta who had to deal with him now—not that Delia minded. Generally drink made the clients easier to handle. She draped herself along the carved wooden sofa at the end of the bed while the old man checked the view from the window.

"This is nice," he said.

"There's a huge tub. Would you like to take a bath?" Delia suggested—down to the nub of things straight away. "We could slip in together," she smiled.

His face lit up. The men loved that kind of thing—champagne and back rubs, baths and room service. Delia knew how to string out the experience for hours and, besides, if she could get a customer into the bath at least he'd be clean. This customer, like many before him, was more than willing to succumb to the ritual.

"Yes. A bath. I'd like that," he said.

Delia cast her eyes shyly to the ground. She read him exactly right—better than he knew himself. This man liked a curious mixture of whore and flirtatious innocent. He'd probably have preferred a naughty girlfriend, if he could find one, though Delia knew how to play that part. It was a show. A pretense. Such negotiations always were.

"Will you wash my back?" she asked.

"Yes," he laughed.

Delia had never heard him laugh before—at least not like that—without a hint of cruelty. She caught his eyes and licked her lips. She had become very good at appearing to be slightly helpless and naive. In reality Delia was neither of these things, and she knew it. Her mother had been a doctor and her father a psychiatrist. Between them they had unwittingly endowed their beautiful daughter with a plethora of useful information that informed all her relationships with other people. Everyone from clients to cleaners, landladies to shop girls and policemen to rent boys.

Delia knew that most of the prostitutes she met were crazy. Even at the more polished and cosmopolitan upper end, where she now found herself working, it was the same. The girls craved money as their only measure of self-worth and shamelessly manipulated the men who paid for them. This man, however, was not just another open wallet to Delia and she was very far from crazy. She had waited a long time and worked very hard to find herself in this suite at the Grand Hotel in Brighton in his company. And now she was here she intended to enjoy herself.

"I hope they have bath foam," she said lightly and disappeared into the bathroom to turn on the taps.

A waiter came to the door with another bottle of champagne, a pot of coffee, a bowl of fruit and some sandwiches. The old man had thought of everything.

"Open the bottle," he told the waiter and then tipped the boy as he left.

He hadn't been looking forward to coming to Brighton but Lisabetta had insisted. The old man hated the sea—it was too powerful. But, he had important business here and although Lisabetta had proved a competent, if expensive, manager in all his affairs he believed in keeping an eye on everything himself. The last few months in London she had proved reliable, of course, but now things were coming to fruition.

Lisabetta understood his need to oversee things. She encouraged him. "You must come down to Brighton. I promise you'll have entertainment. Blue-eyed girls with long legs, a trip to the races and a few games of poker. It's not too bad for the provinces."

And she had been as good as her word. Naturally the old man had a wife and children but he had always frequented prostitutes. One woman was never enough and, besides, his wife was now abroad and he hadn't seen her in over three months. Henrietta was older, as old as he was.

He liked possessing her—some men were squeamish about gray hair and sagging skin, but that didn't matter to him. He loved his wife. Still, it was nice to have a younger woman now and then, if only as a contrast. It made him feel alive. This Delia girl was good—very professional and also beautiful. Even the higher-class prostitutes varied, he found, but he could already tell that he was going to really enjoy himself today. Perhaps he'd order her to stay on a while. He would be in Brighton for ten days, after all—and from what he could see it was a tiny backwater of a town whatever Lisabetta had promised. He might as well make the best of it.

Delia appeared in the doorway of the bathroom wearing her peach satin underclothes, sheer stockings and a pair of very high black heels. Her glossy dark hair cascaded over her shoulders. She leaned against the door frame and posed with one leg against the wood.

"Come here," he told her.

She laughed. "My, aren't you bossy!"

That was the least of it, she knew, but she thought she'd stand up to the old man. Give him a thrill.

"You will come here," he insisted.

Delia sashayed into the room. She was naturally slight, her curves undulating smoothly and her long elegant legs were firm with two tiny moles at her ankle only just visible through the sheer silk. She knelt down in front of him.

"What?" she said with a pouted lip as she looked up.

He pulled her toward him by her shoulders and ran his thick fingers over the creamy skin of her stomach, her breasts, her hips and finally between her thighs. Her skin was as soft as her satin underclothes and when he fondled her, she sighed. She was very convincing. "I will wash you, you beautiful little whore," the old man directed.

"Oh, yes," she breathed and let him pull her toward the bathroom from which there now emanated a steamy cloud of bergamot scent.

After they had bathed together, the sex was dull. It was only to be expected. Delia normally enjoyed sex, she pondered, as he flung her onto the bed. She found she particularly liked having sex with Americans. There were plenty of Americans in London—she had found them to be generous, rich and well informed. Perhaps one day, she thought, she might emigrate to America. Yes, that's what she'd do— she'd live in New York. It would be a fresh start—a splendid idea to put all this behind her and begin a new life. It wouldn't be long now. She moaned encouragingly as the old man turned her over. Lord, old men liked turning her over. At least this would put him into a deep sleep. The Grand Hotel had very nice sheets, she thought. Lovely creamy thick linen.

At last the old man flung himself down on the pillows, mumbling something in another language. Delia spoke most Northern European languages. As well as English she was fluent in Polish, Danish, Dutch, German and Austrian. She even had some patchy French. She had had an open ear at a very young age and at just the right time had come into contact with a wide variety of native speakers. As a result she spoke each language like a native—with no trace of a foreign accent.

"*Liebe, liebe Henrietta,*" the old man was saying.

That, Delia knew, was the old man's wife.

She stroked his head gently. He was falling asleep at last. Perfect. When he began to snore Delia slipped out of the bed and poured a cup of cold coffee. She removed her smudged makeup and got dressed. Then she rifled through the old man's pockets. There was some money and a few identification papers—she left all of that but took a gold coin that he had secreted in his inside pocket. She weighed the coin carefully in her hand. It would be nice to have a souvenir, she thought, as she bit the metal and smiled. It was real. She wondered if perhaps it was a sovereign. She would find out. She had once seen a sovereign pierced and used as a fob for keys. She might do that. It was stylish. Feeling sly, she slipped the coin into her pocket for later.

Delia drew a deep breath. She was ready now. It was time. She picked up her suede handbag and carefully drew a needle and syringe from the magenta velvet interior. She knew he would wake up when she punctured his skin so she'd have to be quick once she started. At first she had considered drugging the old man but had quickly discounted it because drugs would leave traces in his blood. Alcohol was the best thing she could think of to slow him down and cause confusion. He'd had a bucketful and then she'd sat in a hot bath with him—a move designed to enhance his drunkenness. Now, if she injected him, it would look like an embolism. Well, it would be an embolism. But it wouldn't be a natural one. Of course the doctors would assume it was, especially in a man of this age—there was really very little way to tell the difference if you weren't looking out for the signs, and the evidence literally disappeared during the postmortem examination if the coroner wasn't alerted to take steps to preserve it in advance. In a provincial town like this, with the corpse of an old man, Delia knew the coroner would be unlikely to take those steps.

Delia considered her options and decided for the last time to administer the injection between the toes. It was easier to hold him down by the legs. The old man sighed in his sleep and turned. She waited for a moment, standing over him and relishing that she was here at long last. And then Delia plunged like a bird of prey, the hypodermic shooting its deadly load into the old man's bloodstream. He woke immediately, trying to pull back, shouting and confused. Straight away Delia refilled the syringe with air, holding down his calf with her elbow and his foot with the other hand. It would take two syringes to do the job. Just air. Necessary for life but deadly in the bloodstream. God's little joke, or one of them. She plunged the needle in a second time.

"What are you doing?" he shouted. "That hurts."

He pulled back as she let go but it was too late. And then Delia said the words that any old man in his position dreaded hearing most. "You don't remember me, do you?"

But before he could reply or even think which one she might be, before he could reason with her or try to explain, or run out into the hall and get help, the old man found quite suddenly that he couldn't breathe any more.

"Jews," he gasped, his eyes bright with terror.

It took two minutes. Delia watched him struggling, gasping, pissing himself. A lady she met once at a society party in London had remarked that lilies smelled of death: "Makes me quite morbid, my dear, the smell of lilies."

The scent now wafted over from the bright crystal vase on the side table and Delia thought to herself that the lady was wrong—lilies didn't smell like death at all.

At the end she stood for a long while over the old man's still body. A quick end was a luxury he hadn't deserved but it was the best she could do. Death by natural causes was unheard of—something that Delia had never witnessed, in fact, during the brutal course of her life. But this came close. *Bastard.* She wanted to spit on him now, punch him, tear out his balding hair, but she held herself back. If they found marks on the body they would suspect foul play. Instead she let the emotions course through her. She imagined a blue balloon floating off over the ocean outside the window.

Two days before she died Delia's mother had told her that however many bad people there were, she should never lose faith that there were good people, too. In the filth. In the middle of the nightmare. When everyone around had lost hope.

"The good people are everywhere," she promised in a whisper. "And you will find them, I promise. Just survive, my darling. Survive."

Neither her father nor her mother would ever have expected Delia to kill the commandant but from the moment they died Delia knew that was what she would do. She had been ready to dedicate her entire life to his murder. They called him the Candlemaker. Delia shuddered. Men like that should be hunted like animals and executed. Men like that didn't deserve to live.

"I did it, Mama," she whispered. "I did it and I am here."

7

True friendship can afford true knowledge.

Mirabelle Bevan had only just hung up her coat when the secretary from the office down the hall came through the door without knocking. She was a plump black girl in a tight charcoal pencil skirt and a crisp white blouse gathered at the waist with a purple patent belt which matched her shoes. The girl was scarcely twenty but nonetheless had an air of experience and efficiency that made her seem older. She had started work a couple of months before and Mirabelle had seen her on the stairs but they'd never spoken, only smiled and nodded.

"Is your name Mirabelle Bevan?" she asked.

"Yes."

"I'm Vesta Churchill. No relation." She grinned with good humor as she shook Mirabelle's hand firmly. "This letter came for you so I took it in. Had to be signed for, you see. Your boss gone AWOL?"

Mirabelle nodded.

"Mine, too." Vesta plonked herself unbidden on the wooden chair opposite Mirabelle's desk and drew her manicured fingers through her hair. "He's an all right bloke," she confided good-naturedly. "Fond of a drop, but the job is so dull I don't blame him. Now, debt recovery, Miss Mirabelle,

I bet you got a lot of secrets in here! I've been dying to drop by."

Mirabelle smiled. Vesta seemed simultaneously both nice and somehow appalling, but then the day had already been so odd.

"It's insurance down the hall, isn't it?" Mirabelle said.

"Sure is. Car insurance. And I don't even have a license. It's all engine sizes and tire pressure—I can't tell you the sheer boredom of it. Cars!"

Mirabelle slit open the envelope and peeked at the letter. It was from Ralph Peters, the lawyer. It thanked her for the loan documentation, acknowledged receipt by return and said that Romana Laszlo's estate was expected to settle within a month. In his own hand as a postscript, Peters had added that he had checked with Romana's sister, Lisabetta, and the name was Hungarian. He did not comment on how the Dutch passport might have come into being.

"Anything exciting?" asked Vesta.

Mirabelle shook her head. "Paperwork. Thanks for signing for it. Very kind of you. Where are my manners? Could I tempt you to a cup of tea?"

Vesta's expression assumed a serious air. "Got any biscuits?"

"We have some cream crackers, I think."

The girl stared for a second, as if Mirabelle had suggested they have mud pies or grass sandwiches. Then she spoke. "Don't worry. I'll go back to the office and get ours. We've got a whole box of Cadbury's." She darted out of the door without waiting for a response.

Mirabelle put the kettle on to boil. It had been an exciting morning. For months now her life had been lived between her flat and the office, going through the motions, walking on the weekend, sitting in the bath and eating food she scarcely tasted. Today she had somehow put some color back into her drab existence. At the same time she was worried. Whatever had happened to Romana didn't feel right. And now there were rich men and prostitutes in the picture—had Romana been involved? Was it part of the reason she died? Mirabelle reached for the teapot as Vesta burst back through the door and proudly placed a small tin of chocolate biscuits on the desk.

"Present," she said, "from Mr. P. I think he has contacts on the black market, bless him."

"Lucky you!"

"Now, if Mr. P. was chocolate he'd gobble himself right up. He's a cocky guy. But he knows how to get on the right side of me," Vesta volunteered. "I got him bargain coverage on his Morris Oxford 1947 with black paintwork."

Vesta peeked into the box as if she didn't know what was in there and smiled with delight as the biscuits came into view. Her white teeth were dazzling and her dark eyes enormous. She pulled out a chocolate-coated fancy just as Mirabelle popped a cup of tea in front of her.

"Perfect," she breathed, wrinkling her nose.

Mirabelle looked over the rim of the box. As a rule she wasn't fond of sweets, but today was for bending the rules and trying new things. She retrieved a golden brown circle with a smattering of chocolate at the edge. This girl was a strange creature, she thought—at once very young and also motherly. Mirabelle snapped off a piece of biscuit and popped it into her mouth. Then she had an idea.

"Vesta," she said, "do you think you could look after the office for me this afternoon? It's only that I might go up to London."

As anticipated Vesta didn't turn a hair. "Sure thing. You got yourself a fancy man?"

"Oh, no," said Mirabelle, "nothing like that."

"Bit of shopping? Because if you can find me some dark chocolate and marzipan, I'd love you forever. I heard there is this place in Piccadilly and it's pricey but what they've got you wouldn't believe! You going anywhere near Piccadilly?"

Mirabelle nibbled some more biscuit, lifted her cup to her lips and shook her head. She considered how much to tell Vesta—almost like an automaton, running through the security clearance codes in her mind. This girl had a low clearance level, of course. But on balance, odd or not, she was likable enough and if she wanted Vesta's help she had to tell her something.

"Thing is, there's a bit of a mystery with one of our clients."

Vesta's eyes lit up. "I knew it. You lucky duck! Of course I'll look after things here. Don't worry one bit. But you got to let me read all about it. That's the deal. Quid pro quo, like my mama always says. Please. I'm going scatty in that office with the boredom. The clients and the boss—all them men—are going crazy about the new Ford Zephyr and I'm going to die from brain atrophy. Really I am."

"Your mother always says quid pro quo?" Mirabelle repeated.

Vesta shrugged. "Yep. My mama studied to be a legal secretary back home before she had kids. Latin and everything. Course when she met my daddy she gave it all up and decided to come to England. Now she just works in a shop in London. But she's got an education."

Vesta leaned over and surveyed Mirabelle's in-tray.

"It's this one, isn't it?" she said, picking up Romana Laszlo's file.

"How did you know?"

"It says DECEASED right here," Vesta grinned, her childhood Jamaican lilt overtaking her newly acquired Brighton accent through sheer excitement as she flicked open the front cover.

Safe in the knowledge that there was very little detail in Romana's file, the filing cabinets were locked and the keys were in the inside pocket of her handbag—all facts that would heartily dismay Vesta over the course of the afternoon—Mirabelle boarded the London train half an hour later. As the grubby suburbs of Brighton gave way to open fields and then back to the bomb-damaged remnants of the shabby outskirts of London, she stared out of the window and decided on a course of action.

At Victoria she took a long and satisfying breath of thick, city air. It felt good to be in the beating heart, the hustle and bustle again. Mirabelle crossed the station and got onto the tube for Notting Hill, emerging twenty minutes later into the semi-suburban high street near the market. These days Mirabelle only had one lead in London so she made her way straight to the Red Lion pub, asking directions in the street from a succession of drab-looking women wearing patterned scarves, thick coats and comfortable shoes.

The pub was off the main road about five minutes from the tube station. It was a traditional old-fashioned boozer frequented by market traders, hookers, the odd serviceman passing through and, most important, Bert Jennings. Mirabelle was always well turned-out and her entry through the heavy oak door caused some attention. A thin blond girl wearing bright orange lipstick and earrings to match leaned over the bar. "Yeah?"

"I am looking for Bert Jennings,'" Mirabelle said as her eyes adjusted to the dingy interior. "I thought I might find him here."

"You his missus or sumfink?" the girl asked suspiciously with a pronounced nasal twang.

"No, I am a business associate. Do you know where he is?"

The girl shrugged. "I can leave him a message if you like."

Mirabelle looked vexed for a moment. This was her only point of contact with Bert Jennings. Still, she knew the streets of Notting Hill were busy and that news traveled fast.

"I'll wait," she said.

"Can I get you sumfink to drink?"

The whiskey here was unlikely to be good enough without a mixer. Post-wartime supplies were still on the scarce side with downmarket pubs watering down what they had and buying in spirits that were little more than hooch.

"I'll have a gin and tonic," Mirabelle said decisively as she picked up a newspaper that was lying on the bar and settled into a seat.

The jungle drums beat as loudly as expected and it took less than half an hour for Bert to appear, wide-shouldered, through the double doors of the Red Lion. He evidently hadn't been sure whom to expect but he seemed delighted.

"Well, I never. Miss Mirabelle Bevan," he beamed.

"Hello, Mr. Jennings. Could I have a word?"

Bert nodded at the barmaid. "Another, Miss B?"

Mirabelle paddled the remains of her drink around the bottom of the glass. It had been a horrible concoction at best. "No," she said, "I'm fine."

The barmaid laid a very yellow-looking dram on the top of the bar and didn't ask for payment. She moved to the other end of the servery, her jewelery jingling with every step, and hitched one hip onto a bar stool to watch what was going on.

"Is there somewhere we could talk in private?" Mirabelle asked.

"This way." Bert jerked his head to the dingy interior. "Come into my office."

There was a dark wooden table and three mismatched chairs in an alcove at the back of the pub. While a lattice of tiny panes over the double doors let in a modicum of light at the bar, as Mirabelle proceeded toward the rear of the room there were only a couple of dim lamps and it became progressively darker. Bert flung himself into a chair and motioned toward Mirabelle.

"My bad manners," he caught himself up, "not pulling out the chair for you, but my back is giving me gyp something chronic, Miss B. So, how are things down in Brighton? Did Ben find that bird or what?"

"I'm afraid she's dead," Mirabelle told him.

Bert's face betrayed no emotion about either Romana Laszlo or his money.

"I've registered your interest with her executor and the money will come through in due course. There shouldn't be any problems. Mrs. Laszlo had a life insurance policy."

Bert took a sip of his drink and drew in a sharp breath. "Ooof, bites into you, that."

"I notice," said Mirabelle, "that you haven't asked me what she died of."

Bert looked at the ground. "Was it the nipper?"

Mirabelle nodded.

"She was an odd one, that bird. Shame."

"Odd?"

"Well, she was foreign."

"Do you have a London address for her, Mr. Jennings? I'm just tying up some loose ends, you see."

"What loose ends?" Bert asked. "You said I was getting my money."

"I don't really know," Mirabelle squared with him. "Just that there's something wrong. I thought I'd come to town and see what I could find."

Bert paused, hoping for more information. "Seems a bit above and beyond, dunnit?"

Mirabelle raised the glass to her lips. "I'd like to look around, that's all. I'm curious."

"*You're* curious?"

Mirabelle nodded.

"But it ain't your case, is it?"

"Well," Mirabelle didn't want to lie, but there seemed nothing for it, "I said to Big Ben that it seemed fishy. He said I should have a look about, if I liked, so here I am."

Bert regarded Mirabelle. There was a moment of dead calm where he seemed to be considering what to do. Then he decided. "Yeah, all right, then. Look, I got an address. She lived with her sister over in Chelsea. Cadogan Gardens, right off the back of Sloane Square. You might even call it Knightsbridge, I suppose."

"And her sister is Lisabetta?"

"That's right, yeah. I checked the house the day I came down to Brighton to see Big Ben—just in case they was still there. They still got the lease on the place, it turned out, but the flat was closed up. Romana had gone off to have the baby, of course. Where Lisabetta had got to, I dunno. You going to take a look, then?"

Mirabelle nodded.

"Mind if I tag along?"

A flicker of doubt crossed Mirabelle's mind. The cut of Bert's suit would stand out a mile in that neck of the woods. On the other hand it might be good to have a man in tow as long as he behaved appropriately, the odds of which she realized, given Bert's manner and background were probably about fifty-fifty. "You're going to get your money anyway," she said doubtfully.

"Yeah," Bert grinned, finishing the drops at the bottom of his glass, "but I can't help myself—I'm a nosey bastard just like you. Come on, girl, I'll show you where it is. I got a car just parked off Portobello Road."

Traveling on the underground Mirabelle hadn't seen a single glimpse of her former life apart from the familiar rattle of the tube carriage. Now it was like watching a montage of all the places that had been important when she lived here. Rebuilding was well underway to repair the ravages of the Blitz, not that there had been too much damage to the west—unlike the slums close to the river. They passed the little Italian restaurant in Kensington where Jack had loved the spaghetti vongole and then continued through the park where he used to go to think, and where, one evening very early in their romance, they had a picnic on a tartan rug. The sky was a sparkling succession of diamonds on black velvet made crystal clear by the blackout. Jack had pointed out the Plough and they had kissed for a very long time under the half-moon.

When Bert finally turned down Sloane Street he almost collided with a huge olive-green Harrods van coming in the opposite direction. Furious, he hit the horn and Mirabelle jumped as she woke from her daydreams. They missed the curb by an inch at most.

"You fucking idiot!" Bert shouted, and then casting a glance at his passenger he apologized. "Sorry, Miss B. But he was."

At the bottom of Sloane Street they turned into the maze that made up Cadogan Gardens and Bert parked on a stretch with high brick buildings on one side and a locked park on the other. "It's the middle one on that block," Bert indicated. He switched off the ignition. "I reckon the easiest way in is through the gardens at the back. There are French doors. Don't expect there's much in the way of a lock."

"You're going to break in?"

Bert stared. "What? You was planning to come here and just sit on the doorstep?"

Mirabelle took a deep breath. He was right, of course. If the flat was empty she would love to look inside. "And you think we can get in at the back?"

Bert shrugged. "Common sense," he pronounced. "Romana's dead and Lisabetta isn't here, is she? Least she wasn't here a couple of days ago."

"Lisabetta's down in Brighton. She came for the funeral," Mirabelle chipped in.

Bert's eyebrows rose momentarily as if impressed at the amount of information that Mirabelle clearly had to hand. "Well, then, what is it you're looking for anyways?"

Mirabelle surveyed the buildings rising up along the back streets. The Victorian brickwork was intricate with patterns picked out in cream over the upper floors. The paintwork was well maintained. There was a general air of prosperity.

Large planters of geraniums and shiny-leaved rhododen-
drons stood at many of the front doors and Mirabelle
caught glimpses of expensive furniture through the windows. A maid with a shopping basket slipped discreetly
down the stairs to one of the basements. This was not an
area where people had huge financial worries, or at least if
they did, it did not seem the kind of place they would re-
quire Bert Jennings to become involved in order to solve
them.

"Why did Romana Laszlo need to borrow money?"
Mirabelle asked.

Bert snorted. "You don't know much."

"Well, look at it. It's nice round here. They must have
been doing all right. How did she get in touch with you?"

Bert shifted uncomfortably. "Lisabetta. She knew me
through Lisabetta."

Mirabelle nodded.

Bert grabbed the handle of the door. "Come on, then."
His tone was insistent. "Let's have a look while it's good
and quiet."

They crossed the street and eyed the railings. There was
no one around. Bert hauled himself awkwardly over the
top and then turned to help Mirabelle. She took off her
heels and threw them over and then clambered across the
wrought-iron spikes, grabbing his hand to steady her.

"We're a right couple of geriatrics!" Bert laughed.

Mirabelle ignored him. She hadn't dressed that morning
for gymnastics and was not in the habit of scaling fences.

"I saw Lisabetta, you know," she said, starting out
across the lawn. "In Brighton this morning. With a prostitute."

Bert nodded. "She runs 'em. You don't miss much, do
you? Wouldn't have thought a lady like you would have
noticed that kind of thing and the sort of girls Lisabetta
touts don't advertise it too clearly."

Mirabelle did not explain. "She didn't seem very upset about her sister."

A smirk crossed Bert's face. "Them girls don't feel much, if you see what I mean. Tough as old nails, Lisabetta. Looks like a china doll but she'd survive a nuclear blast. Hiroshima-proof, she is!"

"Is that how you knew her? Because she was running a game? It's only that, if you don't mind me saying so, you seemed uncomfortable when you mentioned her."

"Nah," Bert said, "I didn't know her the way you're thinking. You got a dirty mind, Miss B! I knew a couple of girls, posh birds, who got into trouble with money. It's been tough for some of them, after the war and all. I put them Lisabetta's way 'cause she runs them sort of girls up-market. They was ever so grateful. Cleared their tabs in a couple of months, both of them. Suppose you could say Lisabetta and I became friends after that."

Bert loitered beside three iron steps that led up to tall glass doors with white painted frames. Mirabelle noted that despite his long explanation Bert hadn't addressed why he had been uncomfortable and now he was standing in an aggressive position.

"I don't like to pay for it, myself. Takes the fun out," he said.

"Of course."

"Oh," he mimicked her, "*of course*, is it? Don't get all hoity-toity, sweetheart—you're breaking and entering, you know."

"Sorry," she said. He had a point.

"Right, then, do you want me to do the honors? I can tamper the lock no problem."

"Yes, please."

Bert took a flick-knife from his pocket, opened it deftly and drew the blade upward between the doors. When he reached the lock he manipulated it efficiently to one side.

He had obviously jimmied a lock more than once but that was hardly a surprise.

"After you," he said.

Mirabelle stepped inside.

The room was decorated in a soft duck-egg blue with a matching carpet. There were large luxurious peach sofas with hand-painted silk cushions depicting hummingbirds in flight scattered along the length. Beside almost every seat there was a brass-trimmed wooden side table with a glass top. All the furniture was arranged around an ornate white marble fireplace. It was a lovely room and very light because of the aspect onto the lush gardens to the rear.

It suddenly occurred to Mirabelle that she wasn't sure exactly what to look for, other than a general sense of Romana Laszlo, which was so far not apparent. There were no family photographs, only some coffee-table books— one with Victorian photographs of London and another called *The Connoisseur* with pictures of fine porcelain. In all Mirabelle counted four onyx boxes of cigarettes and three lighters dotted around the room, as well as a bowl containing half-used matchbooks from every smart club and bar in the West End. On one wall there was a large gilt-framed mirror and a couple of colorful prints of exotic orange flowers, and in an alcove a well-stocked drinks tray with a variety of shiny crystal glasses arrayed around it, except, Mirabelle noticed, running her eyes over the bottles, there was no gin. That must be the only drinks tray in England without it, she thought.

"Have you been in here before?" she asked Bert.

He nodded. "Yeah, two or three times. I always used to meet Lisabetta at the Kitten in Chelsea, up the road. Bit of a dive but that was her hangout. She likes clubs does Lisabetta—the dark and the smoke, you know? But Romana met me here a couple of times. Not a party girl like her sister and being in the family way and all. She said she needed a hand and that Lisabetta was out of the country. She had some money she was inheriting. I dunno about that—people will tell you anything, but I knew Lisabetta and I thought that was enough."

"You handed over a lot of money though, Bert. What was she like?"

Bert took a cigarette from a box on one of the tables and lit it with a match. "Romana? Pretty girl. Like Lisabetta, attractive. Though Lisabetta is sexier. She wears those low tops and all that. A cracker. Romana, she was more your classical beauty. It's a lot of money, all right! Don't I know it!"

"Do you know where Lisabetta went when she left the country?"

Bert thought for a moment. "Not really," he shrugged. "Got the impression of it being family business, or something. But Romana didn't really say."

"And they got on, the girls?"

"Yeah, I think so," Bert said. "Never saw anything that would make me think otherwise."

Mirabelle crossed the room and peered into the long dark hallway, which led to the rest of the flat. A small kitchen was fitted through a door to one side with a dining room ahead of it.

"You go on." Bert motioned as he lit a cigarette and stood in the bay that led back to the garden, flicking his ash down the steps and onto the pathway. As Mirabelle stalked up the hallway and into the kitchen she could hear him whistling as he smoked. She quickly checked the kitchen cupboards, which were mostly bare, although in one there were several jars of olives and a treasure trove of syrup tins which in one fell swoop was worth weeks of sugar rations. Next she returned to the hall and checked the mail lying on the mat. There were a couple of shop accounts in Romana's name and some letters for Lisabetta—mostly they looked like invitations. After glancing at the dining room—still no photographs—she took the set of stairs that led to the basement.

"Bedrooms down there, I expect," Bert called.

Mirabelle descended. The bathroom contained only some lavender soap and a jar of faded blue bath salts. Not so much as a toothbrush remained. In both bedrooms, however, there were abundant quantities of clothes. Mirabelle checked the drawers and noted that one woman favored black underwear while the other preferred pale pink. There were no clothes, or indeed underclothes, suitable for accommodating a pregnancy bump, though for what must surely be a short time it might be deemed unnecessary to waste money on more than three or four outfits, which probably had gone with Romana to Brighton. Still, something was vexing about the cupboards. The clothes were perfectly lovely, but they niggled. In one of the bedside drawers there was a vicious looking flick-knife with a serrated edge.

Mirabelle sat on the edge of the bed in front of the closet. She turned the knife over in her hand as she considered this but in seconds she was disturbed by a commotion upstairs. There was a man's voice shouting and the sound of a table with a glass top shattering. Then came a sudden roar like thunder and she saw Bert's shoes flash past the sunken window of the larger bedroom as he ran across the lawn, throwing his cigarette to one side as he was pursued by the boots of a uniformed policeman blowing a whistle. Her heart sank as she sprang up and made it back up the stairs in record time. Gingerly she peered into the sitting room, ready to turn herself in and come clean about what they were doing. It had been her idea to come here, after all. It was her responsibility. But as she entered, her heart pounding, there was no one there. Through the open door, across the gardens, Bert was jumping the fence with an extraordinary vigor that Mirabelle felt sure would do his back no good. The policeman was in hot pursuit.

Mirabelle stood away from the window. Weak-fingered, she thought for a moment and then turned back into the flat. There was nothing more she needed to see and there was no point in getting caught as well. Comforting herself that it wasn't the first time Bert would ever have been chased by the Old Bill, Mirabelle picked her way through the broken glass, turned smartly into the hall, sneaked through the front door and slipped down the steps onto the pavement. There was no one around—not even a shadow in the high windows. She turned away from Bert's car and walked casually around the corner to the other side of the park. Ahead of her by two blocks, the policeman was racing toward King's Road, the sound of his whistle intermittent as he ran out of breath. There was no sign of Bert.

Mirabelle turned in the opposite direction and picked up the pace, realizing suddenly that she felt hot in her tan cashmere dress. It was so difficult to dress appropriately when the seasons changed—the British weather was nothing if not erratic. Spring was the worst—freezing in Brighton this morning and then practically tropical in Knightsbridge in the afternoon. And all at once it came to her. The clothes in the wardrobe. Of course. One wardrobe was for the winter season and the other for the summer. But did that mean that the sisters shared everything? Mirabelle had no siblings and she really wasn't sure what was normal. They must have been close, she reasoned; they shared a flat, after all. Or, it came to her, more likely, poor Romana had known there was no point in leaving clothes in the flat because she wasn't coming back. Perhaps she knew she was going to die. Mirabelle shuddered. It felt as if she was looking for a ghost.

8

All knowledge begins with experience.

After some consideration Mirabelle decided to have a look at the Kitten. Bert was long gone and if he had any sense he'd stay away from Cadogan Gardens for a while. He'd said the club was in Chelsea and now it was her only outstanding lead.

Rather than join the main street she followed a warren of backstreets until she came to King's Road, far enough from where Bert must have entered that she was sure no one would connect her with a Notting Hill wide boy on the run. It occurred to her suddenly that he'd been a fool to stand about smoking in that suit in full view of every flat in the vicinity and, come to think of it, whistling loudly, too. No wonder the police had arrived. Bert seemed savvy but there was no denying that he'd as good as advertised the fact he'd broken into the flat. Perhaps he'd meant to. As the lightbulb flashed on in Mirabelle's mind she realized that Bert must have intended it. Her brain began to whir. Was it possible that Bert had already known about Romana's death? He hadn't seemed shocked when she told him. More suspiciously he had only answered what she'd asked, rather than posing any questions of his own. That didn't seem like normal behavior for someone who made their living by lending money. Mirabelle had met plenty of moneylenders. A healthy interest in other people's affairs was a tool of the trade—look how many questions Bert had asked when he first arrived in the Brighton office. In London, this time, he had only volunteered the Cadogan Gardens address when she'd told him that Big Ben sent her—and by implication, if he didn't help, perhaps Big Ben might arrive. And besides that he'd hardly asked a single question.

Also, he'd been keen to accompany her to the apartment—in fact, he'd insisted—and breaking in had been his idea. Why had he been smoking anyway? Mirabelle had never seen him light up before—not in the office or in the pub. He didn't carry cigarettes—he'd taken one from the box on the table. He didn't even carry a lighter. If Bert was involved in some way he might have brought her to the flat hoping it would keep Big Ben away. He knew full well there was nothing much there. Then he'd as good as trumpeted the break-in so that one of the neighbors would call the police. With a sinking feeling she realized how foolish she'd been. Bert Jennings was involved in this up to his neck.

Damn it, she cursed. She'd been duped. It had just felt so nice to have a man around again. Her heart pulsed with sadness as she realized just how much she had missed that feeling. And here she was now, alone in the middle of something that was turning out to be rather complicated. For a start, if Bert was involved, why had he needed Ben to pursue the money in the first place? Surely he could have gone straight to Lisabetta or found Romana Laszlo himself?

It was clearly a lot more difficult in the field than in the office, where you could keep your distance and maintain a calculated composure. Being faced with real people was a far tougher call on one's judgment. The details were a tight knot of information, impossible to draw into easily recognizable strands.

Feeling as if she'd been a fool, Mirabelle tried to think what Jack would do. On the principle that your left hand should never know what your right hand is doing—she could hear his voice now—she stopped at the first callbox and rang the Red Lion. After over a minute the barmaid answered in her familiar nasal twang: "Yeah?"

"When Bert gets back," Mirabelle instructed, "tell him Miss B says thank you and hopes he's all right."

The barmaid sniffed in a way that seemed to imply Bert needed no thanks whatsoever and would be just fine. "Sure, Miss B," she said.

"Tell him I'm a bit rattled and planning to go straight home. We had a close call there."

"Right."

The phone clicked and Mirabelle hung up, heartened that she had at least managed a little disinformation. Then she continued in the direction of Chelsea.

It was warm for April. King's Road was bustling with residents returning at the end of their working day. There was the smell of cooking and an air of domesticity with more than one man carrying flowers and a bottle of wine.

Mirabelle told herself she just had to persevere, and her first problem would be finding that damn nightclub.

"Excuse me," Mirabelle asked a man in a suit carrying a bunch of yellow roses, "do you know where the Kitten is?"

"Sorry, no," he said emphatically.

After asking half a dozen gentlemen, Mirabelle began to wonder how the place survived until at last the aghast expression on one man's face as he denied all knowledge of the club told its own story.

Where angels fear to tread, she thought as she hailed a cab. "The Kitten? Not worth the fare," the driver told her. "It's only a block away. But you're early." He smiled. "It's not even dark yet. I'm not sure a lady like you ought to be going to a place like that, Miss, if you don't mind me saying."

"I have to drop off a letter," Mirabelle reassured him. "A solicitor's letter."

"Well," he said doubtfully, "you can see the turn-off from here."

The lane was downmarket. Despite pretty flowerboxes and well-maintained cobblestones in front of the converted mews houses, it was clear that the dead end contained at least one little casino and two bars as well as the club—none of them currently open for business. The neon signs were switched off—and looked, Mirabelle thought, like strange skeletal winter trees. The Kitten was at the end on the right-hand side. Mirabelle quickly ascertained that the door was locked. She rang the bell. No answer. She rapped on the door for good measure. Nothing.

Finally, she picked her way around the side of the building past the bins beside the back door. There was no bell so, once more, she tried knocking. Still no reply. Then with a shrug she made the decision and crossed the line. Carefully, still wearing heels, she climbed on top of the bins to reach a small window halfway up the wall. Then, with the faintest glimmer of a smile, she withdrew the flick-knife she had found in the bedside table at the flat and following Bert Jennings's example slid the blade along and manipulated it to release the catch. The window opened immediately.

"Not that much of an idiot," she whispered to Jack, and then slipped carefully through the opening.

It was a dressing room. Dancers' costumes hung on a steel rail and feathered headpieces were stacked on two faceless dummies, eerie in the half-light. On the back of the door a riding whip and a feather boa hung on a hook. The place felt grubby, as if it had never been cleaned. Spots of stray makeup dotted the dressing table, which was covered with a light dusting of talc. The contents of an ashtray spilled over onto the floor. Mirabelle looked back at the open window a moment before she decided to continue. Then she tried the door, which opened onto a passageway to one side. It was shipshape out there. There were three locked storerooms, two with iron bars instead of doors. A quick glance confirmed they were full of bottles and kegs. Mirabelle turned in the other direction. She needed to find the office. She might be able to trace Lisabetta and Romana if there was a list of members or guests—even an address book and an accounts log would be wonderful. She pushed a black door and entered the main room of the club. It was cleaner in there though it reeked of stale smoke. The chairs were piled on the tabletops and the floor gleamed—one of many shiny surfaces that glinted in the blackness as the light entered in her wake. The only nonreflective form she could make out was a tiny square stage against the back wall. Mirabelle wedged the door open with a chair to let in the light and crossed the dance floor toward the bar. Perhaps there was something behind there. But as she leaned over, a shape sprang toward her out of the pitch-black. A tray of glasses was knocked from the bar and shattered. Mirabelle screamed as she was wrestled to the floor and a yellow beam of torchlight shone in her face, blinding her.

"Bloody hell," a male voice said in a broad Australian drawl. "Who are you?"

Mirabelle tried to strike out. "Get off me!" she screamed.

The man laughed. "Right," he said, holding her down even more tightly. "I said: who the hell are you?"

Mirabelle stopped squirming. "I'm looking for Lisabetta. I'm a friend of Lisabetta."

The man cast the torch down Mirabelle's body. "Well, you don't look like a burglar or one of Ricky Goodwin's boys. Didn't know Lisabetta had any friends." He loosened his grip. "You gave me a right turn."

He stood up and flicked on a neon light behind the bar. Mirabelle sat up slowly as the light flickered.

"What's a bird like you doing breaking in?" He peered at her.

"You didn't answer the door."

The man laughed. Mirabelle noted he was of middling height and balding but his torso was at least twice the size of any other part of his body. The muscles bulged through his black sweater.

"We don't open till ten," he remarked. His dark eyes were absolutely round. Mirabelle sat, waiting for him to blink. He didn't.

"You hurt me." She got unsteadily to her feet.

"You bloody broke in. What the hell do you expect?"

Mirabelle limped over to a bar stool. "I was hoping for a Glenlivet, actually. It's been a bit of a day. Straight up would be fine."

The man paused for a moment. "You'll pay for it," he said but he put a shot glass on the bar and poured from the bottle. Then he laid a small plate of salted peanuts beside her glass.

"You're lucky it's my night. The other guy would have thumped you first and asked questions later. If you're a friend of Lisabetta's, are you a . . . erm . . . specialist?" He was looking at her now with naked interest.

Mirabelle let out an involuntary giggle. She was, she realized, perhaps a little on the old side for women in Lisabetta's line of business. No doubt upmarket whores of her age stayed in the game through a combination of experience and offering the kind of services that were unavailable elsewhere. She picked up the glass, sniffed the golden liquid and downed the whiskey in one swallow without answering. It tasted good.

"Lisabetta isn't around, then?" Mirabelle asked.

"Nah."

"I need to find her. I heard she was out of town. I wondered about her sister, Romana. Have you seen her lately?"

The man leaned forward. "Don't know anything about a sister. What was your name?"

Mirabelle put out her hand. "Emily," she said. She wasn't going to tell anyone else in London the truth for the time being.

"I'm Frank," the heavyweight replied and shook her hand firmly.

"I heard Lisabetta had taken a couple of the girls down the coast. I wondered if you knew where they'd gone. I've got something for her. It's important."

Frank probably would have shrugged his shoulders but his biceps were so well developed that moving them upward was well nigh impossible. Instead he rolled his dark eyes in a movement that was quite hypnotic. "Brighton. But I ain't got a clue where. It's a small town though. Just try the best hotel, if I know Lisabetta and those bastards. They'll be swilling cocktails there on a regular basis."

Mirabelle toyed with a peanut. "What kind of show you put on here?" she asked, glancing at the stage. "Burlesque?"

"Singer. Girl called Honey," Frank nodded. "That your line?"

Mirabelle nodded.

"We don't need a singer, if that's what you're after."

"No, it's all right. Nothing like that. You heard of a bloke called Bert Jennings?"

Frank's eyes sparkled. "That pansy! You ask a lot of questions, lady. You looking for him, as well? Best bet is the Red Lion in Notting Hill, not in this neck of the woods."

"I heard he was friendly with Lisabetta. Do you think he would know where she might be staying?"

"Those two are thick as thieves, Emily," Frank nodded. "Yeah, I'd try him."

"And he might be able to pass on a message for me?"

"Is this really what you broke in for?"

Mirabelle nodded. "I need to find her, and her sister. It's important."

Frank sighed. "I can't see Lisabetta being out of contact with Bert. She's like a spider that one. Black widow." He looked vaguely surprised at his poetic turn of phrase.

"I'm worried about her. What she's got caught up in."

Frank laughed. The sound was like a bolt banging into a lock. "I wouldn't," he said.

"What do you mean?"

"I wouldn't worry. Now, may I remind you, we're closed."

Mirabelle laid a coin on the bar. "For the whiskey."

"Money makes the world go around." Frank didn't pick it up.

He followed her to the door. The spring sunshine was dazzling after the gloomy interior of the club. The evening smelled fresh.

"You sure you never met Lisabetta's sister?" she asked as a parting shot. "Her name is Laszlo—Romana Laszlo."

"Hop it, Emily," Frank said. "Come back here again and you might not be so lucky."

Mirabelle walked carefully across the cobbles. She was adept in her heels but the uneven surface was tricky and she felt wobbly. She had already decided Romana either hadn't lived in Cadogan Gardens or knew she wasn't ever going back when she left. And now it looked as if Bert Jennings knew a lot more than he'd let on. He hadn't needed any help to find Romana, or Lisabetta for that matter. Even the bartender knew how to track them down, for goodness sake. No, Bert had turned up because he wanted a middleman to collect his money. He didn't want to be too close to the action. Perhaps he'd even known Romana wasn't coming back from Brighton. He was in this up to his neck. He'd meant the police to scare her at Cadogan Gardens. It might, Mirabelle concluded, be time to go home

and call a policeman herself. This whole situation was becoming rather tricky.

When she turned back down the lane Frank was still staring at her from the doorway as she lifted a hand to wave.
Who, if anyone, would he ring as soon as he was sure she had
gone? Probably not Bert, she guessed. Sometimes it was the
little comments, the choice of words that could be the
most revealing.

"Money makes the world go round." She repeated the
phrase to herself. Yes, there was that to figure out as well.

9

He is a hard man who is only just.

Detective Superintendent Alan McGregor teed up the shot. He'd been meaning to fit in a round of golf for months—ever since his move from Edinburgh. It was not only that he'd been too busy but also that he was picky about his course and it had taken him a while to get the measure of Brighton. He'd rather hack round a public fairway, for a start, than cosset himself in the luxury of some swanky clubhouse with all those secret handshakes and trial by who knows whom. McGregor loathed that kind of thing. Some of his fellow officers thought it had held him back, of course, but he was Detective Superintendent McGregor now. It had been a big step and McGregor knew he could prove himself down here—it was worth the boot camp he'd had to go through to convert his knowledge from Scots law to English, and it was worth letting out his family home in Davidson's Mains to move down south. He was going to turn this force around corrupt officer by corrupt officer. That's what he was here for.

McGregor hit the ball smack down the middle of the fairway and an involuntary smile broke out on his face. Perfect. The ball landed right next to the green. He hadn't played for months and he had missed the game. First time

out and a shot like that! He was going to enjoy his eighteen
holes and now he'd found a course he liked, he'd be back. At
home he'd played twice a week. McGregor hauled his clubs
onto his back and set off to find the ball. It was a lovely
evening—the weather had cheered up. He'd bet ten to a
penny it was baltic in Scotland. He was striding energeti-
cally down the fairway toward the green when he heard a
shout from behind. It was a uniformed constable. McGregor couldn't make out who the man was, but he was running.

"Sorry sir," he said, out of breath, "but I thought you'd
want us to catch you before you were too far out."

McGregor looked skeptical. "Government fallen?" he
inquired.

The policeman drew himself up straight. "No, sir. Dead
body. In a suite at the Grand."

"Robinson not able to cover?"

Inspector Robinson was the local boy who hadn't got the
Super's job. There had been so many allegations of corruption that when the senior post came up, the choice had been
made to recruit from outside the local force. The department was still uneasy, settling into the landmark decision
and Robinson had dealt with the slight on his competence
by referring everything to McGregor no matter how small.

The uniformed officer shook his head. "Inspector Robinson said you'd want to see it yourself."

"Look like a murder, does it?"

"No, sir. The duty doctor is on his way though. It was
an older foreign gentleman. Heart attack, if you ask me.
He had a woman in his room, though she's legged it."

"Took his wallet?"

"No, sir."

"Suspicious circumstances?"

"Inspector Robinson thought you'd want to ascertain
that for yourself."

"Of course."

"They're all het up at the Grand, sir. Discretion and all that."

McGregor hauled his clubs onto his shoulder and took one last look at the little white ball on the green in the distance. "All right," he said, "let's go."

By the time they made it to the hotel the police doctor had completed his initial inspection of the body. McGregor had a quick word. There was nothing suspicious, according to the medic. Nonetheless the detective superintendent checked the room and told uniform to take statements from anyone on the hotel staff who had come into contact with the deceased. In his estimation the prostitute had probably left before the old man died—which would explain why the contents of the wallet remained intact. Still, he ordered a description of the girl to be circulated—they might as well pick her up if they could and get a statement. If nothing else it would narrow down the time of death. Perusing the deceased's effects there was little of interest—the man was clearly well-to-do. His papers were in order: a Spanish passport, consistent with the labels inside his expensive clothes and shoes—all from Madrid. By six thirty McGregor was ready to call it a day and release the body for removal to the morgue as soon as the photographer was finished. He was just beginning to think about what to have for supper, when a terrible wailing sound came from the hallway. A pretty girl in a red cocktail dress with mascara running down her face appeared at the door. One of the hotel's senior staff hovered uncomfortably behind her mumbling condolences and behind him there was a bored-looking chap in a tweed jacket.

McGregor stepped forward and offered the girl a handkerchief. "Did you know this gentleman, Miss?"

The girl sniffed, took the handkerchief and nodded. "Yes," she whispered and a large tear dripped down her face. "Señor Velazquez. We came at once."

"We knew that Mr. Velazquez had friends in Brighton,"

the hotel manager explained apologetically. "The desk clerk phoned Dr. Crichton here. The doctor made the booking on Mr. Velazquez's behalf two days ago."

"What happened?" the girl interrupted and McGregor noticed the whisper of an accent in her voice. It was difficult to identify with all the crying.

"Well, Miss, he appears to have suffered an embolism."

The man in the tweed jacket perked up. His eyes caught the girl's in a moment of what McGregor recognized as relief.

"There," Crichton said. "Happens all the time. Very sad but he was quite elderly, Lisabetta. He didn't suffer. It would have been very quick."

The girl sniffed. She sat down.

"Did he have family? Do you know how to get in touch with them, Miss?" McGregor asked.

"I will do it." She waved a dismissive hand.

"Did Mr. Velazquez have business here?"

Lisabetta shrugged. "I suppose so," she said. "He was a family friend. My own father is dead, but I've known Señor Velazquez since I was a little girl. His wife and children are out of the country. I will send a telegram. I will arrange everything."

Her eyes fell to a pocket watch, which sat on the side table by the bed. It seemed to provoke a memory and more tears filled her eyes. She crossed the room and stroked it. McGregor thought it strange, but then, bereaved people behaved oddly sometimes.

"I'll get in touch with the undertaker," Dr. Crichton said, and he laid a hand on Lisabetta's shoulder as if to pull her back. The look she shot him was steely. "When will the body be released?"

"A day or two," McGregor replied. "It would be very helpful if you could make a formal identification."

Lisabetta waved her hand once more. "Of course. And we can take his effects? His wife will want them."

McGregor nodded. This was a local doctor and a respectable lady with a longstanding connection to the dead man. The regulations were hazy but it would be easier for them to manage the affair if they had a direct connection with the family and probably kinder that way, too.

"We will need the details but I don't see why not," he replied. "Though you will need to appoint a solicitor to execute his estate in this country—he'll be subject to British law, you see."

Dr. Crichton nodded. "That's no problem. I have a solicitor who can do everything for him. Ralph Peters, here in Brighton. He's the man."

Lisabetta sank back in her chair.

"Please allow me to have a maid see to everything in the room," the manager offered. Velazquez had been an excellent tipper—and from what he'd heard when this young lady had met him earlier in the day the waiter who served them had pocketed a half sovereign. These people were the kind of exalted customers the Grand wanted to attract now that the war was over. It was too bad this had happened—too bad. A death in the hotel was terribly disquieting for the other guests. "We can pack up all poor Mr. Velazquez's things for shipping. With the utmost discretion, of course. I'll have it done straight away."

"You really should have let us send an officer to inform this poor lady rather than breaking that kind of news over the phone," McGregor said in annoyance.

The girl buried her face in a handkerchief.

McGregor took the opportunity to draw Dr. Crichton aside into the hallway outside the suite. "Dr. Crichton," he said, "I feel I ought to inform you that there was a woman in the room with the Spanish gentleman. A lady of the night."

The doctor's face betrayed nothing at all. Not even surprise. He merely peered back into the room to check on Lisabetta. "I see. Where is this girl?"

"She left. The hotel staff didn't notice the time, but it was probably before he died. The . . . erm . . . activity might have brought on . . . well, you know."

"Did she take anything?"

"Not that we can tell—there is money in his wallet and in the room's safe."

Crichton felt himself relax. "In that case, Detective Superintendent, can we perhaps count on your discretion? The young lady is upset enough as it is and we'll have his wife to deal with, too. How Mr. Velazquez decided to spend his time here, is neither here nor there now."

"Of course, but we will pull the woman in if we can find her. For a statement. It's only procedure. I thought it best that you know. I don't expect to have to bother the ladies."

Dr. Crichton glanced past the detective superintendent into the room again. Lisabetta dabbed her eyes with the handkerchief. Then she picked up the old man's jacket and laid it over her arm. She stared pointedly at him.

"I think I better look after her," he said with a sigh. "Another death."

Detective Superintendent McGregor's eyes opened wider. "What do you mean another death?"

The doctor coughed, cursing himself. "Oh, nothing. Her sister died in childbirth. She's had a run of it."

If Lisabetta hadn't looked so pretty McGregor might have asked another question. If there had been any evidence of foul play he would have picked up on the comment and been up half the night looking into the matter. As it was, he was only looking forward to a half and a half in the pub on the way home and perhaps fish and chips. Robinson should have been dealing with this—it was a bloody public relations exercise. Very sad, but hardly a criminal matter.

"I'll see if we can speed up the autopsy," he said, "to make it quicker for the lady. Give your contact details to the constable and if you want to appoint the solicitor first thing, that would help, too."

McGregor shook Dr. Crichton's hand.

"Of course," said the doctor. It was a hell of a relief—their first assumption had been that Velazquez had been murdered. It had been a hellish week. But so far they seemed to have got away with it all. He looked McGregor straight in the eye, shook him firmly by the hand and said, "Thanks for all your help."

Ten minutes later, alone in the lift, Lisabetta turned to the doctor. "Where the hell is Delia?" she snapped. "We have to find her."

Crichton sighed. When she had been based in London, Lisabetta had been demanding but manageable. Now she was living in his house and so many things seemed to be going wrong. She was permanently in a foul temper and, in his opinion, not a little neurotic. He'd hardly had a moment to himself since she got here.

"Delia will have gone back to London. It looks like he died after she left. Brought on by the exertion." He couldn't help smirking. "She hasn't stolen anything."

"*Schrecklich*," Lisabetta snarled.

"You'll still make your money," Crichton bumbled, trying to reason with her.

Before she spoke Lisabetta shot him a poisonous glance that sent a cold blue chill down his spine. "Money! Pah! Of course! I'll make more money this way. But I want to know exactly what happened. I can smell it. Something is wrong here, Eric, and I will get it out of her."

As the lift reached the hotel lobby Lisabetta raised her handkerchief and clutched the doctor's arm, as if she needed him for strength. Crichton couldn't help but admire her for that. Lisabetta was very good at putting on a show.

10

There is no such thing as accident; it is fate misnamed.

When Mirabelle woke it was early. The events of the day before filtered into her mind bit by bit. Under the covers she hugged her knees to her chest. This Romana Laszlo business had opened her eyes to what she had been missing. She realized that she had been sleepwalking for a long time—it felt good to wake up again and she was, for the first time in several months, looking forward to going into the office. She wondered what Big Ben would make of the dead woman's story and the intriguing mystery about her sister. She was sure he'd have an insight or two about Bert Jennings. Only one day till he's back, she thought, as she got up and pulled open the thick curtains onto the sunrise. Perhaps today she'd solve it.

She washed and changed into a freshly laundered white shirt with a green tweed pencil skirt. Then she slipped on her high-heeled court shoes and combed her hair while applying some lipstick. Mirabelle checked her watch—it was barely seven o'clock. As the rays of orange faded out of the sky and a bright morning emerged, it was still too early to open the office. There were loose ends, of course—an array of intriguing possibilities.

Mirabelle slammed the front door with more vigor than

she'd had, well, since Jack died. She walked to the main road and caught a bus. Brighton was busy. As the bus hurtled along the street on the way into town, she watched two shabbily dressed schoolgirls scrubbing the steps of the fine stucco terraces for a penny, left out beside the milk bottles. Brighton suddenly seemed full of interesting people. Perhaps, she thought, I could ask Ben to let me be a little more hands on. It might be nice to get out and about more.

At the pier Mirabelle got off. She walked past the newspaper stand. Then she stopped and walked back. The headline read BODY OF FOREIGN GUEST FOUND AT THE GRAND. She bought a copy from the vendor and sat on a bench to read the story. There was no photograph but the description was enough—Señor Velazquez was an older Spanish gentleman. He had arrived to visit friends in Brighton the day before. The people around Lisabetta seemed to be dropping like flies—of natural causes, but still. Mirabelle wondered if the household would mourn this second death more than Romana's. She considered for a moment and then stood up with a determined look. She wasn't just going to leave it. There were far too many suspicious circumstances mounting up and with Ben away she had plenty of time on her hands. Decisively she walked back to the stop and took another bus from Old Steine up Preston Road as far as Patcham. She wondered if Cobb's Funeral Directors started early, or worked late, deciding the odds were on there being more bodies to pick up in the mornings. Yesterday Michael Smith had made it to the office after his delivery at Second Avenue right across town and it was still before ten in the morning. Yes, she decided, the undertakers would be at work already.

In Patcham Mirabelle got off on the main road. The street was busy with workers at the window-blind factory heading to clock on for the day. There was a queue outside the bakery where a sign proclaimed "Best Pies in Patcham" and a man passed her cramming a beano into his mouth, as if to illustrate the point. A quick inquiry at the newsagents on the corner sent her down a side street toward a well-kept old house, which bore a black sign with COBB'S FUNERAL DIRECTORS CO-OP APPROVED written in gold script. There was a lane down the side, leading to a yard where, when Mirabelle strained, she could just see the rump of a black horse, its tail swishing from side to side. She bypassed the front door and strode down the muddy cobblestones. The horse was tethered to an iron loop worked into the wall and Mirabelle petted him. In the corner of the yard there were two shiny black hearses.

Mirabelle approached the back door, which lay ajar and peered in. The room was large. There were two tables for laying out the dead and a few empty coffins propped up against the wall. In the harrowing nightmares following Jack's passing she had dreamed of his corpse over and over, begging for help, waving good-bye or just lying unresponsive as she screamed. Now the back room of Cobb's Funeral Directors seemed too quiet. If she went in would she be faced with a waxen-faced Señor Velazquez laid out in his box? Or perhaps Romana Laszlo's body was here— the welcome normality of which would be a relief, in a way, but still. With sweating palms she knocked on the door jamb and waited. There must be someone working here— a living soul somewhere among the coffins and bales of black satin. Where was Michael Smith?

"Excuse me," she hazarded and cleared her throat. "Mr. Smith? Anybody there?"

"Put it on the side there, love," a cheery voice emanated from beneath the floor.

Mirabelle looked around nervously. "Excuse me," she repeated, pulling herself together.

"Just leave it on the side," the voice boomed.

Mirabelle hesitated. She wanted to run. "I'm looking

for Michael Smith," she said bravely to the disembodied voice as her hands trembled. "Is he here?"

There was an ominous stomping and then from a trap door at the back of the room a red face appeared through the floorboards. "Oh, apologies, Ma'am. I thought you were from the florist. With the wreaths."

As he emerged into the room the man blinked, as if unaccustomed to the daylight. He was a Dickensian creature. At first glance he seemed to be dressed entirely in rough lengths of cloth. A cream burlap scarf was wound around his neck and his hands were swathed in purple home-knitted mittens. "I'm Cobb," he offered. "You're looking for Michael, you say?"

"Yes, please." Despite the man's eccentric appearance, Mirabelle was relieved that he was, in fact, alive and hopefully able to help her. "And you are?"

"Mirabelle Bevan. It is a private matter."

The man considered this. He seemed dubious about the possibility of the likes of Michael Smith having private business with the smartly turned-out woman before him. "Well, he's not here this morning. Michael went out on a call very early, I'm afraid. He won't be back for at least a couple of hours. Can I help you?"

"Mr. Smith came to see me yesterday and we discussed a delivery he made for someone known to me. Romana Laszlo."

"Yes, yes."

"And now, well, there is someone else. A body at the Grand Hotel. A gentleman, also known to me."

"Mr. Velazquez."

"Indeed. I wondered if he had had the same kind of coffin as Romana? And I wondered if he was here."

The man leaned against the table. He was used to strange questions. He dealt with upset people all the time. Clarity, he believed, was always the key. "The bereaved often find it difficult," he said with a somber expression, "to accept the departure of their loved ones. To lose two people, Miss Bevan, is a difficult thing. I don't wish to distress you, but Mr. Velazquez's body is in the hands of the police. He died away from his home and family. It's what the police call an Indigent Death, though, of course, your friend was very far from indigent in the real sense. Once there's been a postmortem, we'll prepare his body for burial."

"Ah, they've arranged it?" Mirabelle did not correct the man's assumption.

"Yes. I would offer you the opportunity to augment the package, Miss Bevan, but his family and friends have been very generous. He has the best already."

"And Romana?"

"That's out of my hands. Standard casket only," he said, with disapproval in his voice.

"Same casket as Señor Velazquez?"

The man shook his head sadly. "It's too late, I'm afraid. The body is already at the Sacred Heart Church. We didn't even lay her out, poor soul. It's most unlike Dr. Crichton."

"I beg your pardon?"

"It's not like him, I said. Hove addresses. We often get Dr. Crichton's patients when they pass away and normally they take our more extravagant packages. Full service. It seems a shame for the poor lady."

"Mr. Cobb," Mirabelle fished, "what I am wondering really is whether you saw either of the deceased? My ones? It's such a worry not to have seen them, you see. Poor things."

"No, Miss, I haven't. The doctor laid out Romana Laszlo himself—some families prefer that. We'll have the Spanish gentleman here tomorrow sometime, though, if you'd like to come back."

"I see." Mirabelle turned to go. At least they weren't

keeping both bodies hidden from view. "And you have no idea why they bought such a poor coffin for Romana?"

"No, no idea at all, I'm afraid."

"Thank you, Mr. Cobb," Mirabelle turned. It was time to be getting back to the office. She could try to piece it together there. "I simply wanted to know. Good morning."

1 1

Let wisdom make you a good gamester.

It was nine fifteen by the time Mirabelle made it back into town. She unlocked the door and leafed through the mail. With Big Ben sick there was a dearth of payments coming through. It would be a quiet day but there might be more details about Señor Velazquez in the early edition of the *Argus*. Vesta, she noticed, had left her mark—a greasy stain in the shape of a slice of cake on the blotting paper covering the desktop. Still, the geranium was in pride of place, back on the desk and looking distinctly perkier, the soil now moist and the leaves wiped down and glossy. A note was propped up by the sink: *I have news*, it read.

Mirabelle set off down the hall toward Halley Insurance. She was, she realized, looking forward to seeing Vesta. It was remarkable. Mirabelle hadn't looked forward to seeing anyone for quite some time. She knocked on the door and peered into the office. Vesta had clearly been expecting her. She was perched beside the fireplace with a long brass fork in her hand.

"Toast?" she asked as Mirabelle came inside. "No butter. I got cinnamon or jam, or both."

"A cup of tea will be fine," Mirabelle assured her.

Vesta looked shocked, as if Mirabelle had declined elevation to the peerage. Mirabelle was clearly lonely, and in Vesta's opinion she'd never bag a fellow looking like a half-starved foal, no matter how captivating her long legs and huge hazel eyes. "You sure you don't want something to eat?" she asked quizzically.

"Absolutely."

The girl sighed loudly and propped the toasting fork against the wooden mantelpiece. "Well," she said, rallying, "I can't wait to hear all your news. And I have to tell you what I found! You'll die!"

Mirabelle smiled as it became apparent that Vesta could wait long enough to exchange her news to fuss over the kettle, fill a teapot, open a box of biscuits and light a cigarette with a slim gold lighter.

"How did you get on?" She pushed the biscuit box across the desktop and inhaled deeply as she finally settled down.

Mirabelle sank into a chair. "Well, it's a mystery, all right."

Vesta leaned forward. "Do tell," she breathed.

Mirabelle sighed. It was nice to have someone to share things with. She lifted the teacup to her lips and sipped. "Firstly, I think when Romana left London she knew she wasn't coming back. Her sister is vile. Completely unaffected by the death—absolutely stone cold. I don't mean to shock you but she runs a prostitution ring up in London and God knows what else. Wealthy clients. That kind of thing." Vesta looked not the least bit taken aback by this information so Mirabelle continued. "And the doctor she was staying with is involved. I don't know why. Drugs? Abortions? I have no idea. Except that there's an astonishing amount of money floating around—he tips five-pound notes. And now there's another body. A client. And he tips generously, too. These people have money to spare and plenty of it."

Vesta took a draw on her cigarette. "Another body? That's two in two days. Shit. That's a lot of dead bodies all at once."

"He died yesterday. At the Grand Hotel. The papers say it was natural causes. I'm interested because they picked a cheap coffin for her and an expensive one for him—despite all the money. I can't work that out. I mean, if your sister and her child died . . . well, it seems very odd. Perhaps they hated her. Also, so far no one has seen the girl's body. Not even the undertaker."

Vesta considered this. "Oh, I'd say she's dead all right. I did a little digging myself yesterday."

"Vesta! You were supposed to stay in the office!"

"Oh, I stayed! I was here until after six! When I read that file I got to thinking about the life policy. I know a girl at the Prudential. She used to work at this agent who wrote cover for us on upmarket cars—Bentleys and Rolls-Royces. Anyway, she moved. She works in life insurance now. I wanted to ask her about how that would work—you know, the policy your client had. She checked for me. The Prudential are the biggest underwriters in the country. Turns out, they issued the policy on Romana. Not just Romana, but her sister, Lisabetta, too—they both took out cover and named each other as the beneficiary. The policy is just over a year old—so this is before Romana got pregnant. Before she moved to the country even. So why did she name her sister and not her husband? There could be reasons, of course, but how many wives would do that? Anyway, then the Pru charged an excess because Romana was abroad, and abroad is more risky so covering her life was more expensive than covering Lisabetta's. Romana objected—said she was definitely moving to London, but the husband was Russian and the British wouldn't let him in. Six months later and, bingo, she gets back to the Prudential. Would they forgo the excess now, please, because she's pregnant, the husband's dead and she's moving to London after all."

Vesta sighed. "You know I have a lot of experience with people filling in forms. Everyone thinks they're unique, but, really, anything that doesn't fit in the form, that isn't standard, well, my experience is it's either a lie or a problem. When I heard that little story there were too many questions and it was all too damn convenient. Romana Laszlo, lied, I reckon. Through her teeth. And that husband of hers is another dead body, now I come to think of it. I'm surprised the Prudential haven't sent an investigator. Probably the only thing stopping them is that Lisabetta has a policy, too. Let's say they killed her—for the money. And that old guy in the hotel—they killed him as well—either for more money or because he knew something—too much. Is that crazy?"

Mirabelle considered the information. The girl hadn't done a bad job. "It's about money, then," she mused.

"I think, you know, I could do with something savory." Vesta paused to stub out her cigarette. She rummaged in the desk drawer beside her and drew out a Cadbury's tin with the legend MILK CHOCOLATE FANCIES on the top. Inside there was a square of Cheddar cheese wrapped in a slip of greaseproof paper and some biscuits in a bag from Sainsbury's on St. James Street. Rationing didn't seem to impinge at all upon Vesta's diet.

"Mr. Cadbury wouldn't approve," Mirabelle pointed out.

"What Mr. Cadbury doesn't know about what goes on in his boxes won't hurt him," Vesta roared.

Mirabelle stared at her. "That's it, Vesta," she said. "That's bloody it. We have to look inside the casket. I mean, that's the only way to really find out. She could have died in childbirth or she could have been killed for this insurance policy. No one's seen her body except them. If she was killed there will be marks or wounds or something and we'll know. We'll have evidence we can go to the police with. I thought perhaps Cobb had seen her, but he hadn't. No one has. But it's the key to the whole thing. We've got to examine her."

"Ugh," Vesta pushed the tin away, "that's put me right off."

Mirabelle ignored the comment, continuing. "*I* can't go to the funeral. They saw me yesterday at the surgery. Oh, God, it starts in half an hour." Mirabelle checked her watch. "They haven't seen *you*, though. You've got to do it, Vesta."

Vesta eyed Mirabelle with suspicion. "That sounds dangerous. People are dropping like flies round this Lisabetta character. Shouldn't we just call the police? I mean, that's their job."

"There's no time for that—the body will be under the ground by lunchtime and then the police won't take it on without something concrete. All we have is a lot of suspicion—circumstantial details. Nothing definite that's criminal. They won't dig her up on a whim! *You've got to go*, Vesta. If they've killed her and you see the body we can go to the police with something real—something we know for sure. No one will trouble you at the funeral. You can say you're from the Prudential."

"They might be murderers!"

Mirabelle was already pulling Vesta's midnight-blue coat from its hook on the back of the door. "Don't be silly. If you hurry you can find out what's what before they even get there. Look, it's broad daylight and you're in Brighton. Besides, I know the priest. Father Sandor. No one will hurt you with him there. He's a war hero. Any problems, you can count on him. Get to the funeral. The Sacred Heart. Norton Road. Somehow or other, you have to check. It's our last chance to get any reliable information on how she died."

Vesta heaved a sigh. "How am I supposed to look inside a dead woman's casket? Oh, and a little dead baby in there, too. It's horrible."

"I don't know. Just try. It's your duty. Something bad is happening, Vesta, and there's no one else to find out what it is. And if she did die in childbirth, which I doubt, at least we'll know and we can let it go."

Vesta looked sadly at the abandoned tin of cheese and biscuits but she pulled on her blue coat. "My boss might keep irregular hours but he isn't going to stand for this if he finds out, you know," she said, half sadly and half to make it clear that the coffin breaking was not going to be a regular occupation.

"I know. Mine, too," Mirabelle replied. "And Mr. Mc-Guigan will be back tomorrow. He'll take over. Big Ben will work it all out and he knows lots of policemen. Unless you know a reliable policeman we could go to now? Someone on the straight?"

Vesta rolled her eyes. "Snowball's chance in hell."

"Well," said Mirabelle, "if we can only find out enough of what happened, Ben will deal with it for us. It'll be far easier. And we'll have real evidence. I'll cover here, and if your boss shows up I'll tell him you weren't well and nipped out to the chemist. How long does he normally disappear?"

Vesta shrugged. "Depends on how much money he's got."

"Well, leave it to me," Mirabelle promised.

As Vesta reached the door she halted in her tracks and spun round. "You know anything about cars? I got a guy coming at half ten to cover his new Ford. It's one of those rotten Zephyrs—brand-new and due on order any minute. 1951 registration and custom white paintwork—flashy! He's all excited and we get good commission on those fancy vehicles. Look after him for me, will you? Just get the license details and write down his insurance history. I'll ring him back with the quotation when I get in."

"Sure thing," said Mirabelle and wondered how Vesta's lazy idiom had managed to get inside her head.

12

Never was anything great achieved without danger.

Father Sandor entered the vestry to change into the appropriate garb for the funeral. This set him thinking about his encounter with Mirabelle. The poor woman had been troubled, clearly, and he had wanted to comfort her. Now he realized that his need was personal—selfish even. Mirabelle Bevan was the only connection with his former life that had surfaced in the six years since he'd come to Brighton. The horror of what he had witnessed, the bodies piled in the woods, the starving Roma children, the sunken-eyed Jews, the decimation of the countryside held no romantic attraction for Sandor. He was glad the war was over. The SS men he'd ministered to in Paris had been at once the most evil and most tortured souls he'd ever encountered. These days Father Sandor was glad to live in uninteresting times, though he followed the War Crimes Tribunals in the newspapers as they tailed off and the war seemed to recede. England suited him. Still, now that Jack was dead, aside from dusty notes in a file, it was likely that only Mirabelle knew exactly what he'd done for the Allies. There was something about that which was still important to him. He wondered if he was succumbing to the sin of pride. He must pray.

Sandor slipped into his vestments and checked his watch. The doctor had said it would be a small funeral. They only wanted something simple. "Poor Romana, she didn't know a soul here apart from Lisabetta and me. We'll see her off," he'd instructed with a boyish expression.

The sealed coffin had arrived the night before and the gravediggers had prepared its stand. Father Sandor turned the iron handle on the vestry door to enter the church. As he did every day, he swore to buy some oil and see to the creaking catch. Every day he forgot by the time he reached the altar. Today he stopped on the way and scooped up a prayer book from the shelf beside the front pew. Sandor knew the funeral service by heart but he usually held a book anyway. It gave him something to do with his hands. The gravediggers were coming at ten sharp. They'd carry the coffin outside then.

As he approached the altar Father Sandor stopped. There was a plump black woman in a long dark coat with her back to him. She seemed frozen as she bent over the coffin so he hadn't noticed her immediately. As Vesta turned and smiled, her teeth shone in the gloom of the church.

"Father," she said, "this coffin is closed. I had hoped to pay my last respects properly."

"Did you know Romana?" Father Sandor asked gently

"No, not really. I'm from the life insurance company,' Vesta replied. "The Prudential. We sometimes attend."

"I see. The coffin arrived closed."

"Is that normal?" Vesta inquired.

"Sometimes. Look, this isn't a good time, Miss. The poor woman's sister will be arriving any minute. She has lost n only a sister but a nephew as well. Please show some respect

Vesta cast her eyes to the ground. This encounter w not going well. "You're Father Sandor, right?"

"Yes."

Vesta leaned toward him conspiratorially. "Well, I'n friend of Mirabelle," she whispered.

Sandor felt himself standing up straighter. "Mirabelle sent you?"

"She's kind of my boss," Vesta replied, "if you see what I mean."

"You need to see inside this casket?"

Vesta crinkled her nose. "Uh-huh, that's what she wants me to do."

At that moment there was the echo of high heels and Lisabetta appeared on Dr. Crichton's arm in the doorway of the church. She was wearing a tight-fitting black suit with slingbacks and a tiny black hat made entirely of feathers. Vesta took a step back and hung her head. Lisabetta was carrying a white handkerchief that stood out against her mourning garb and she sniffed repeatedly as she walked toward the front of the church.

"Father Sandor," she said, staring at Vesta with naked interest. "Who is this?"

Vesta stepped forward with her hand held out. "Vesta Churchill. Prudential Insurance. Our condolences on the death of your sister."

Lisabetta nodded gracefully but did not touch Vesta's outstretched fingers. "Thank you," she said, her eyes lingering, taking in every detail. "Romana had only recently arrived here. She knew few people in England and none in Brighton save myself and Dr. Crichton. I'm afraid the funeral is only for us."

"I understand," Vesta said. "You'd like me to leave?"

Lisabetta brought the handkerchief to her nose. Vesta noticed that Dr. Crichton touched her arm very slightly and stepped in. "I think what Lisabetta means is that this will be a very humble funeral. Please don't feel you have to stay out of a sense of duty."

"I'll stay," Vesta said firmly. No one looked at her like that. It had been an inspection and an insult all at once. "I'd like to."

The coffin bearers arrived and the little party proceeded

outside to the churchyard. There was no sign of rain as they walked between the gravestones to a newly dug plot. Sandor nodded at Vesta and opened the book at a random page. He began the funeral service while Lisabetta sniffed quietly and Dr. Crichton hovered protectively over her tiny frame.

"Our sister, Romana, came from a tiny village. A village I knew well. She traveled a long way and was poised on the verge of taking on the new role of motherhood with all that has to offer a young woman. It was an exciting time and tragically the Lord took her in her prime. We commend Romana and her dear child now to the earth."

Here he began to talk in what Vesta at first thought was Latin but quickly realized was Hungarian. Lisabetta held the handkerchief to her face and kept crying. Dr. Crichton's face froze. After a minute or two the Hungarian gave way to what sounded like a prayer. Vesta bowed her head. The coffin was lowered into the ground and Lisabetta threw in a clod of earth.

"I will organize a nice headstone," she sniffed, "perhaps black with gold lettering."

"Not now." Dr. Crichton put his arm around her. "Don't worry about that now, my dear."

Sandor led the party to the church. The gravediggers hung back. They would fill the plot when the grieving relations were out of sight. Despite the fact that mourners often threw in a handful or two of earth or even some flowers, there was something about actually watching the top of the wooden box disappear that made mourning women inconsolable. It was the custom to wait for everyone to leave before the men with the spades finished the job.

"We will go home," Lisabetta announced and reached out regally to shake Vesta's hand. Dr. Crichton discreetly disappeared to fetch the car.

"A tragic loss," Vesta said. "We lose fewer women in childbirth nowadays. I'm so sorry your sister had to be one of them."

"She had a little boy, you know," Lisabetta volunteered. "He was dead when he came out. She always said she'd name a little boy Dominic."

"Awful."

Lisabetta touched Sandor's arm lightly. "Thank you, Father. Such a comfort."

The car pulled up at the curb and Crichton leapt out to open the door.

"Do you always come to the funerals of your clients?" Dr. Crichton asked as Lisabetta ducked into the front seat.

Vesta shook her head. "One in four," she replied in a matter-of-fact tone, before adding, "and she was so young and it seemed such a shame. We pick out anything unusual. Did you know her well, Doctor?"

"Not as well as I know Lisabetta. Romana had only just arrived." He closed the door. "She lived in Paris until her husband died recently. Poor Lisabetta is alone now. Utterly alone."

Vesta noticed that Lisabetta did not appear to be the kind of woman who ever had to be alone if she didn't want to be. She couldn't work out if it was only jealousy of the other woman's beauty but she didn't like her one bit. That was unusual—Vesta was in the habit of giving everybody a chance and the poor woman was bereaved after all. She and Sandor waved as the Jaguar drove away from the front of the church.

"Come along," Sandor said without taking his eyes from the road as the receding car turned the corner. "We will stop them filling in the earth."

Back in the graveyard the diggers were smoking a shared cigarette before they started.

"Please, gentlemen," Sandor asked them, "could you give us some privacy?"

"You want us to leave it open, Father?"

"I will shovel in some earth myself when Miss Churchill is finished. Come back after lunch and you can do the rest."

The men sloped off between the graves.

"Have you known Mirabelle long?" Sandor asked.

Vesta shook her head. "Two days. You?"

"About ten years," Sandor admitted. "I knew her during the war."

Vesta had been a schoolgirl when Sandor was sneaking details of Nazi campaigns through the Vatican's channels.

"Mirabelle is a very brave woman," Sandor said. "An intelligent woman. The man she worked for is buried here. She loved him, I think."

He nodded at a grave set beside a cypress bush. Vesta, her interest piqued, walked over and read the carved sandstone: JACK DUGGAN 1900–1949. MISSED GREATLY BY HIS DEVOTED WIFE MARY AND DAUGHTERS LILIAN AND ISLA.

Mirabelle was turning out to be more and more interesting. She didn't seem the type to get involved with a married man.

"Did he love her back?" Vesta wondered out loud.

Sandor shrugged his shoulders. "I don't know," he said, "but bravery does not always necessarily mean battle." He drew out a Swiss Army knife from the folds of his vestments. "Keep a look out," he said and dropped silently into the open grave.

Vesta looked around. The church was silent and the graveyard empty. There was nothing to look out for—the churchyard was quieter than a rainy Monday in Margate. Her stomach was churning but Sandor was so matter-of-fact that it was far easier than if she was alone. In fact she wasn't sure she'd have been able to manage this without his help. She stared at the priest taking the screws out of the coffin lid. The cheap wood was easy to work and it wasn't long before the top was loose.

"Help me out," he directed.

Vesta leaned over and heaved Sandor back to the surface. His robes were streaked with yellow mud. She was very glad she hadn't had to get hands-on with the coffin—

the idea of jumping into a grave gave her the creeps. Inspecting the corpse would be bad enough. These older people who had gone through the war seemed to be made of sterner stuff and Vesta wondered what Mirabelle had actually done to bring her into contact with this stolid Hungarian pastor. It was interesting. Sandor picked up the spade the diggers had left and leaned back into the hole to lever the coffin lid open.

"You've done this kind of thing before, haven't you?"

Sandor blushed. He felt proud of himself for the first time in years. The adrenaline was surging through his bloodstream and he liked the feeling, pride or not. Reaching down as far as he could he got the spade in place and swung the lid of the box upward as Vesta peered down beside him.

"Shit," she said, as the interior became visible. Looking at a corpse wasn't as terrifying as Vesta imagined. But this was, without question, the wrong corpse.

"Who in heaven's name is that?" Sandor said as he flipped the lid closed again.

Vesta remained silent. She was trying to remember. She'd seen him before somewhere.

"We need to ring Mirabelle from the phone in the vestry. Really, I ought to call the police. It's illegal to bury . . ." Sandor stopped. He could feel cold metal on his neck, right at his jugular.

"Oh, shit," said Vesta.

There was a shock of searing pain for no more than a second and they both blacked out.

13

There is no sinner like a young saint.

Mirabelle checked the clock. It was quarter past eleven. The funeral must be over by now, she reckoned. Vesta would be back soon. The mail was done and the plates and cups washed up. Back at her own desk Mirabelle stared out of the window as a line of sunshine worked its way slowly up the street in the approach to midday. It was the perfect weather to have lunch on the beach, but somehow she didn't feel like it today.

Mirabelle sat up in her chair. There was the sound of the door to the street opening in the hallway below, though the footfall that Mirabelle heard coming up the stairs was definitely not Vesta. Only a man with nothing to hide could make that much racket, she smiled. Behind the frosted glass a tall shape approached and the door opened.

"Is this Ben McGuigan's office?"

Mirabelle looked up. "Mr. McGuigan is out. Can I take a message?"

Detective Superintendent Alan McGregor scowled, his blue eyes intense. "Where would I find him?"

Mirabelle sighed. "I don't know. He's out. Working. What was it regarding?"

"I'd like a word, that's all. Is he out most of the time?"

"Yes."

"Well, I suppose that's the mark of a good man in his line of work."

Mirabelle nodded.

"When do you expect to see him?"

"Tomorrow."

"When did you see him last?"

Mirabelle hesitated and McGregor felt in his pocket for his warrant card. She carefully read the details, which, McGregor noted, was unusual. Most people only gave a cursory glance to police identification.

"Yesterday morning, Detective Superintendent," Mirabelle said. "He had a bad cold and went home to nurse it."

"I thought I might catch him at home before work, but he wasn't there," McGregor admitted.

"That's odd. What time?"

"Half past eight. On my way to Bartholomew Square."

"I can take a message, if you like."

McGregor paced a little, his policeman's mackintosh open except for one straining button at the waist. "This was found," he said, reaching into his pocket and laying a black leather wallet on Mirabelle's desk. She reached to open it but before she did she already knew it belonged to Ben McGuigan and her fingers were tingling with anxious anticipation.

"Where did you find it?" she said.

"The racecourse. Near the men's toilets."

The wallet contained very little. Some money and a couple of betting slips for races that took place, she noticed, yesterday afternoon after Ben became ill. Mirabelle took a mental note of the bookmaker. M. Williams. How peculiar. She had never known Ben to gamble.

"I see," she said.

"I wondered if he might have someone who owed him money? Someone dangerous?"

Mirabelle turned the ledger toward the policeman. "Every-

one and his wife owes Ben money," she said. "Or rather they owe his clients money, though generally people consider it the same thing. If something has happened to Mr. McGuigan I'm very glad that there is a detective superintendent on the case, but that isn't normal, is it, sir? For lost property."

McGregor didn't explain Robinson's habit of referring everything to his superior, but in this case he was rather glad that Ben McGuigan's wallet had come his way. He'd only met McGuigan twice, both times at the bar in Sussex, but he'd liked him.

"I know Ben," McGregor said. "I've met him a few times. And this isn't like him, is it? He's an army man—everything ship-shape and accounted for."

The policeman flipped through the pages of the ledger. His eyes lit on Romana Laszlo's entry but he didn't say anything.

"That job came in after he'd left," Mirabelle explained. "He didn't know anything about it."

"And you haven't seen him for two days. What time was he last in the office?"

"Lunchtime. About one."

"And would he have owed anyone money, himself, do you think?"

"I doubt it."

McGregor paused. He doubted it, too, but he had to ask. "Do you have a recent photograph of Ben?"

Mirabelle shook her head. "I can give you a detailed description," she offered.

"No, that's all right. I have his army records—height, weight and so on. I can use that and I can submit a description myself. Nothing works as well as a photograph though. If he turns up, have him ring me at the station. May I ask your name?"

"I'm Mirabelle Bevan. But, isn't it unusual for the money still to be there? In the wallet, I mean?"

McGregor turned in the doorway. She was a smart cookie, this one. "Yes, it is, Miss Bevan."

As the sound of McGregor's feet on the stairs receded Mirabelle had a sinking feeling in the pit of her stomach. Something was very wrong. She was tempted to run up East Street after the detective superintendent and beg him to keep her informed but instead she reached for her coat and hat, scribbled Vesta a hurried note and left the building.

Big Ben McGuigan had a small house on Kensington Place. He'd lived there, in a two-up, two-down on the terrace, since he left the army. The house was painted white— the only neutral color on the row, which was a faded pastel selection reminiscent of a child's drawing. Perhaps Ben had some pretensions to family life, because the house was really too large for a man on his own, but whatever his reasons any plans he'd made had never come to fruition. Mirabelle had never been there before. Her arrangements with her employer were strictly business, but she had all his details in the office file. She passed the Pedestrian Arms, noting that this was the closest pub to her employer's home, and made straight for Big Ben's front door where she knocked twice and waited. No answer.

"Mr. McGuigan!" she called out. "Ben!"

Two doors up, a woman in a floral housecoat looked out onto the street but when Mirabelle noticed her she moved back behind the curtain. Mirabelle walked round to the rear of the terrace, along the lane at Trafalgar Place. Each house on the right-hand side of the street had a small yard that opened onto the rough cobbled lane. There were no lights on in Ben McGuigan's property and no sign of life. The high back gate was locked from the inside. Mirabelle jumped up to reach over the top, pulling the catch out of its holster. The gate swung open easily and she walked into the paved backyard. As she turned she noticed two little boys in short trousers staring at her through the gateway. One was holding a football covered in mud.

"Do you know the man who lives in this house?" Mirabelle asked.

The boys nodded simultaneously.

"Have you seen him in the last day or two?"

The boys shook their heads.

"Shoo! Shoo!" She waved them off and they disappeared up the laneway like little birds.

First, Mirabelle tried the back door but, like the front door, it was locked and bolted. There was no chance of jimmying that. She peered through the kitchen window. Ben McGuigan liked everything in order and the place was immaculate. The bread on the wooden board on the table had a light dusting of mold, though, and that was enough for Mirabelle. Ben would never have put up with that—he was very particular about cleanliness. Something was wrong. The window was fixed, so she smashed the glass with her elbow, knocking it through, and climbed inside carefully, avoiding the sharp shards scattered in the way.

"Ben!" she called. "Are you here?"

There was no point in shouting out. She already knew the sound of the glass shattering would have brought Ben McGuigan to the kitchen no matter how ill he was. If he was in here, he was unable to move. Like a cat burglar Mirabelle took in the surroundings. There was a comfortable chair by the fire in the front room, a few letters at the front door, postmarked in the last couple of days. There were no Beecham's powders and no eucalyptus oil anywhere and she immediately decided that it was unlikely Big Ben McGuigan had come home after he left the office, which meant he had been missing for almost exactly forty-eight hours.

Carefully Mirabelle climbed the stairs to the first floor.

The bedroom to the front contained only an empty brown leather suitcase and a rolled-up length of carpet. In the larger rear bedroom there was a bed made up with military precision. It was strange, she thought, for someone who spent his whole life chasing other people's money to live in such austere surroundings. She knew that if he wanted to he could afford a more sumptuous home. Here the only items she could really call a luxury were a few Ballantine's beer bottles lined up in a row beside the hearth. Imported beer was expensive. It crept into her mind that there was a sharp contrast between this little house and Lisabetta's flat on Cadogan Gardens where the furnishings were luxurious and the cupboards bulged with black market items.

Mirabelle realized that this was her third break-in in two days. She took a deep breath and reconciled herself to the fact that she had gone well off the rails.

Forging ahead she opened the cupboard in the bedroom and perused the two suits suspended on wooden hangers. She checked in the pockets. Nothing. Next she tried the little bedside table, which yielded a pristine copy of the Bible, a box of tissues and two pairs of socks. Mirabelle closed the drawer. She hadn't known Ben was religious. In fact, come to think of it, she was positive Ben wasn't religious. She opened the drawer again and flicked through the pages of the Bible. Cut into the Old Testament there was a small notebook. She retrieved it. Mirabelle knew the shorthand Ben used in his notes—it was the same notation in his ledgers. This looked like a double entry system for loans though these weren't the loans she worked with in the office. There wasn't a single sum of money less than fifty pounds and they seemed to go up into four figures— an absolute fortune by any standards. She slipped the notebook into her purse. Next she turned her attention to the wastepaper bin by the bed. Contained inside there were some tickets and a pink *Racing Post*. She read the ticket stubs—one entry for Brighton racecourse on Fairfield Road and two more betting slips—one horse called Blue Diamond and the other called Casey's Girl—dating from the previous weekend. Mirabelle scooped the papers out of the receptacle and examined them. The bookmaker was M. Williams again. Neither of the slips could have been winners, she reasoned, or they would never have ended up in the bin. But it didn't make sense. The whole thing was completely out of character. Ben McGuigan didn't take chances. He wasn't a betting man and in no regard could he be called speculative or a risk taker. The best investment he said was bricks and mortar, and the main thing was never to take chances with your security. What was he up to at the track on Fairfield Road?

Mirabelle was startled by a rapid knock on the front door. She got up and smoothed her skirt as she checked the room. Then she came down the stairs smartly, her steps echoing on the bare wooden staircase. At the bottom she lifted the latch and pulled aside the chain. The lady in the floral housecoat was standing outside with one of the little boys from the lane behind her.

"Hello," she said. "We heard glass breaking and I can see that window at the back has gone for a Burton. What's going on?"

"Oh, yes," Mirabelle replied. "Do you know Mr. McGuigan?"

The woman nodded. "He's a neighbor. Of course I know him. I almost called the police with you crashing around like that. If you was a fella I would have."

"Yes, yes, of course. Thank you. I work for Mr. McGuigan," she explained. "Have you seen him the last couple of days?"

The woman shrugged her shoulders. "I dunno," she said. "I don't think so."

"He hasn't been into the office and I got worried. I thought he was ill—he had a cold, you see—but he isn't here."

"Man on his own," the woman observed. "You want me to send the boys to fetch the constable?"

"No, I'm sure I'll find him," said Mirabelle. "I spoke to the police myself this morning and they know he's missing. Don't worry. I just wanted to have a look around. I was worried about him."

"What about that window? You can't leave that out the back. It's not safe."

Mirabelle reached into her purse and pulled out a handful of change. "Would you mind awfully getting it fixed for Mr. McGuigan? I'd be very grateful. Someone round here will have a spare piece of glass, I'm sure."

The house had no more to offer and Mirabelle didn't want to risk further confrontation with Ben's neighbor. She stepped into the street and slammed the door as the woman counted the coins.

"My George might fix the window," she observed. "He's handy. Leave it to me."

"Thanks," Mirabelle smiled. "If he doesn't mind that would be terrific. And if you see Mr. McGuigan can you say that Mirabelle came to look for him and that Detective Superintendent McGregor would like him to call."

"Mirabelle. Yes. Detective Superintendent McGregor. Gosh, I hope he's all right. Man in his line of business—well, there's all sorts in that trade."

Mirabelle didn't want to think about that, far less discuss it. "Well," she said, to reassure herself as much as the other woman, "he wasn't well the last time I saw him. Perhaps he went to a friend's to recuperate. I'm sure I'll find him. Thanks for your help."

Mirabelle strode more confidently than she felt back down Kensington Place toward the Pedestrian Arms. Big Ben's house was located only a couple of miles from the racetrack—had he been living some kind of double life? It didn't seem like him but then what else could she think?

She pushed open the door and took a seat on a pew-style bench next to the beer taps.

The landlord leaned over the bar. "You all right, Miss? Can I get you something?"

"A whiskey, please. Glenlivet if you have some."

The man turned to fill the glass. "You're not local," he said with a smile. "Visiting?"

"I'm thinking of going to the races." Mirabelle raised the whiskey to her lips.

"Nothing on today, love. The big meeting is tomorrow. Friday. And they'll all be down from London. A cup winners' race weekend can be busy. Like the horse racing, do you?"

"Actually a friend gave me a tip. Ben McGuigan. Do you know him?"

"Yeah, course I do. Lives up the road, doesn't he? Old school. Drinks light beer. Always asking when we'll get in those fancy foreign bottles, but me, I'm a keg man. Won't catch on, I always tell him. Light ale! People want it off the tap, most of them, these days."

"I didn't know Ben liked the races." Mirabelle shrugged.

"Never heard him mention them, right enough. Most fellas like the races, though, Miss. It's only human nature."

"I thought I might lay a bet with a bookie he mentioned—called Williams?"

"What's the form?"

"Horse called Blue Diamond. And one called Casey's Girl. Have you heard of this Williams? Do you think he's all right?"

"Don't know the name. What with the new covered stand, I hear there are more bookmakers than ever over there. A right collection! I usually lay my bets with Houghton. Sam Houghton. You look out for him, if you like. He's reliable."

"Thanks," she said and finished the whiskey. "I'll pop along tomorrow."

Mirabelle walked smartly back to the office. She wondered fleetingly what Vesta might make of Big Ben's disappearance as she pushed open the door but the offices of both McGuigan & McGuigan and Halley Insurance were empty. With a sigh she took a sandwich from her lunchbox, laid Ben's notebook on her desk and grabbed some paper. As she ate she transcribed the figures in the notebook from Ben's bedside table. They were payments that ranged over a fortnight and totaled almost twenty thousand pounds. What was he up to at the racecourse? She checked her watch. It was getting late and Vesta should be back by now. Mirabelle missed her a little. The feeling sat, a pang on her stomach. Sandor must have enticed the poor girl into tea and brandy.

Without thinking Mirabelle picked up the phone and dialed the number of the vestry at the Sacred Heart. There was no reply. She looked out of the window down onto the street.

"Damn it," she said, glancing at the list she'd made. There was nothing more to do until she found out how Romana Laszlo died and, really, if she had that piece of the puzzle Mirabelle had decided to go to Detective Superintendent McGregor. He seemed trustworthy enough. She could drop off Ben's notebook at the same time—perhaps it might help him to make sense of where Ben had got to. Mirabelle checked her watch again and then fixed her hat as she muttered under her breath, "I'll just have to go down there and get her."

Ever efficient she scooped the papers off the desk and locked them in the filing cabinet then made her way down onto the street and hailed a taxi to the church.

14

He who would search for pearls must dive below.

When Vesta woke it was dark. It took her a moment or two to remember what had happened. Her head ached and her mouth was dry—an uncomfortable combination which she hadn't experienced before. When she tried to get up she found she was bound to a chair and couldn't move her arms or legs. She struggled but it was no use.

Stay calm, she thought. Just wait until your eyes get used to the lack of light and try to figure out where the hell you are, Vesta Churchill.

As she became accustomed to the silence she heard the sound of shallow breathing and she remembered that when she'd blacked out, she hadn't been alone. "Sandor," she whispered. "Sandor, is that you?"

There was a moan.

"Sandor, Sandor, wake up."

The priest said something in Hungarian and then began to cough. Vesta waited. She heard him struggling and then there was a crash as he fell on his side.

Vesta squealed. "God, Sandor. God."

"I'm all right," he said. "Do you know where we are?"

"No."

"Do you know who brought us here?"

"No."

"Do you know how long we've been here?"

"No."

"Are you tied up?"

"Yes."

"Me, too. My eyes aren't so good these days. Can you see anything?"

Vesta squinted. "Not really."

"But you are all right?"

"I guess. My head feels pretty bad and my mouth is dry. I could do with some water."

"All right. We have to try to work these ropes. Just keep moving. Tiny movements, Vesta. It could take a long time, but they will ease."

"Sandor, I'm afraid. Really afraid," Vesta admitted.

"I know. I've been in worse situations, though. Honestly. Can you move at all?"

"Sure."

"Good. We have to make little movements. It'll ease the knots."

There were a few moments' silence, which Vesta broke. "Did you see how that guy died? The guy in the coffin?"

"Yes, there were marks around his neck. I think he was strangled. Which is unusual for such a big man. He was strong. It takes a lot of strength to strangle such a man even if you get behind him. I wonder who he was?"

"I've seen him before," said Vesta. "At first I didn't recognize him because he was dead and they'd put him in that funny position. But I know who he is, or was. Ben McGuigan."

The sound of Sandor struggling became louder. "Who's that?" he asked.

"Ben McGuigan? He's the guy Mirabelle works for. He's her boss," Vesta replied. "McGuigan & McGuigan. Though I only ever heard of one McGuigan. I don't know if there ever were two of them. I've only seen him going in and out of the office."

"That means Mirabelle is in a lot of danger," Sandor said. "We have to get out of here."

"No shit, Sandor. Mirabelle's in danger? I think we're in a whole load of danger of our own."

Then from one side they heard footsteps and a door opened. Outside it was sunny and the sudden light hurt Vesta's eyes. A man walked into what they could now see was some kind of outhouse with rough stone walls and a squint roof. The man was of medium height with gray hair and was wearing a suit. He was smartly turned out for a kidnapping murderer, Vesta thought. And he was cool in his manner. She decided that she would try to match him.

"Well," he said with a downmarket English accent that gave her a start, "it seems to me that you've uncovered something rather unfortunate in your investigations, Miss Churchill."

Vesta tried to stop herself but she couldn't. She was furious. "You think you can get away with this! Kidnapping people—a priest as well!"

"Oh, yes," he cut her off. "We will definitely get away with it. No question about that." The man walked around until he was standing directly in front of her. "The question is whether you'll end up in the wrong grave while we're getting away with it. The question is do you want to stay alive, Miss Churchill? Or are you prepared to die for the sake of the Prudential Insurance Company? Just how much do you think you owe your employer?"

Vesta spluttered. Luckily she didn't say what came into her mind that moment—that she didn't work at the Prudential at all.

"I'm serious. I'm asking you a serious question, Miss Churchill. I have no qualms about killing you but it will be easier if you cooperate. Now if I were to let you go, would you report back that everything was in order and make sure the money was released? That's all I want. That policy."

Vesta stared at him in disbelief as it dawned on her that her cover was working to her advantage—it was keeping her alive. "And the man in the grave?"

"Oh, don't worry about him. He was dead all along anyway."

"What happened to him? What happened to Romana Laszlo?"

The man kept stock still. "You don't really expect me to give you details of that, do you? It's none of your business. Now, here's what we will do. You trot back to the Prudential—naturally I'll be keeping an eye on you—and you tell them everything is fine and you see to it the money is paid out. Take it from me, Romana Laszlo is no longer with us, whatever you saw in that coffin. Just because she wasn't in it, doesn't mean she isn't dead. So, you make sure that they pay out the money. And the day the money is paid out you receive fifty pounds. Straight into your bank account. Or at least, a bank account that we'll open for you. A little bonus, shall we say?"

"You think I'd do that for fifty quid? I wouldn't do that for any money! Are you mad? It's fraud. And there are two dead people involved."

"I'm not mad, Miss Churchill. Not in the slightest. The cash is just another little insurance policy. It implicates you. Really, I think you'll do what I want you to do to save your own life and, of course, the life of the good pastor here. We'll keep him, you see, until after the money is released. Think of it as a policy with a bonus. Of course, if you go to the police I'll kill him. If you tell your insurance colleagues, I'll kill him. In fact, anything you do that I don't approve of, I'll kill him. You do care about the pastor, don't you?"

"It's all right, Vesta. You don't have to worry about me," Sandor said. "They'll kill me anyway. They'll have to."

The man hit Sandor hard and he slumped a little in his chair. Vesta screamed but he ignored it. When he continued his voice was completely calm—devoid of emotion—just as it had been before. "Shortly after the money is paid out everyone involved in this will be long gone." Vesta could just make out his face in the shadows as he licked his lips in a way that made her feel uncomfortable—as if he were hungry. "We don't really want to kill anyone we don't have to. Dead bodies are always difficult to clear up. So as long as the money is paid out . . ."

"This is about some lousy insurance policy for a thousand pounds?" she blurted. "You have to be kidding me."

"I can see you're a practical lady," the man continued without turning a hair. "I can see that. So there's no point in saying anything more. Now, do you agree to the arrangement or do I shoot you both today and simply let the Prudential wonder why you never came back to the office? A lot of things can happen on the way back to the office, you know. All kinds of things completely unrelated to insurance policies. Violent place, England these days. Especially for darkies. I do like to help you people, you know, when I can. Gave money to Africa to help the black babies, and all that. Now, why don't you let me help you, too, love? Eh?"

Vesta felt her knees weaken. She looked at Sandor whose eyes were burning with fury and for the life of her she couldn't see that she had a lot of options. After all, if they knew she wasn't from the Prudential they'd probably kill both of them straight away. Suddenly Vesta felt at a dreadful disadvantage not having been through the war. She was sure there was a clever way out of this. She was sure that Mirabelle would know what to do but as far as she could see she was caught in a rat trap and there was really only one option available to her. "All right," she said. "I'll do it. But I need to know Sandor is safe. I need to be able to check."

The man smiled very slightly. "Good, very good. Well, you'd better give me a telephone number, then. A discreet one. We can certainly arrange that."

"Untie me," Vesta directed. "There's a little office here in Brighton where I can use the phone—a regional office called Halley Insurance. I'll give you the number."

15

Friendship: *a state of mutual trust and support.*

Mirabelle strode down Norton Road and turned smartly into the Church of the Sacred Heart, heading straight down the aisle. Father Grogan was sitting in the front pew. He looked up as soon as he heard the sound of her heels on the stone floor.

"My daughter," he said, recognizing her. "I'm afraid Father Sandor is out."

"Where has he gone?"

Father Grogan shrugged his shoulders. "I'm not sure. He had a funeral to conduct this morning and then he seems to have been called away suddenly. It happens sometimes—we are a busy parish. Are you sure I can't help you?"

"No, thank you." Mirabelle looked through the side door of the church, which opened onto the graveyard. She desperately didn't want to enter the churchyard, but she knew that she probably had to. "Is it all right if I go into the graveyard?" she gestured along the transept.

"Oh, surely."

Tentatively she walked through the door. It was clear where the new grave was. A fresh mound of earth was marked at the head with a wooden stick. Mirabelle walked cautiously toward it. She could make out where the mourners had stood, two men and two women. On one side there were shoeprints clearly visible in the mud—two sets of high-heeled shoes and two sets of flat wide men's prints. From the other direction there were the gravediggers' footprints, the jagged patterns on the sole of their work boots etched into the mud. At the other end, at the foot of the grave there were some smears as if something had been dragged—the coffin perhaps? She turned toward the gate to the street, avoiding looking at the plot where she knew Jack had been laid. There are spring daffodils on his grave, she thought, without fully registering the flash of yellow. Then she turned to leave quickly with her eyes firmly on her own feet. It was then she saw it. A half-eaten biscuit with a smattering of chocolate lay in the grass. It was only as she bent down to pick it up that it dawned on her what it might mean. It wasn't like Vesta to toss food aside. If she needed to get rid of it she'd put it in her pocket or, she thought with a smile, just as likely, in her mouth. Then Mirabelle suddenly felt sick. She stared at the smeared mud. "Oh, my goodness," she said, turning back toward the church.

"Father Grogan," she called, "when did you arrive here? Do you know when they left?"

Father Grogan looked up. "I can leave a message," he offered.

"What time did you get here? You didn't see them?"

"Who?"

"Father Sandor. And he was with a woman. Vesta. My friend, Vesta. I'm worried something has happened to them."

Father Grogan had the engaging presence of an unexploded mine. He hardly reacted to her concern and he certainly didn't hurry. "Now, now," he said without sounding the least bit comforting, "no need to panic. I'm sure something just came up. We have a lot of parishioners here at the Sacred Heart, you know."

Mirabelle could have screamed with frustration. "Of course. Only, what time did you get here? Were you here early this morning?"

"No, I wasn't."

"So what time did you arrive?"

"About half past eleven, I suppose."

"And the church was open?"

"This is God's house. We don't lock the doors. Not during the day, in any case."

"And he wasn't here? The funeral was over?"

"Yes, yes. Calm down, my child."

"That's three or four hours they've been gone. Where is your phone? We have to phone the police!"

"Now look here," Father Grogan started, "you need to calm down!"

There was no point in having an argument. Father Grogan had an immovable quality. Trying to make him understand would take too much time. Instead Mirabelle ran back up the aisle. She burst onto the street and looked left and right. There was no sign of anything. She strode into the traffic and flagged down a taxi, jumping into the backseat.

"East Street and please hurry," she snapped at the driver, making the decision not to go to the police station—cases got caught up at the front desk of police stations. If you phoned, you could get straight through. The office was closer in any case. As the cab pulled away, she swiveled in her seat to check she wasn't being followed. Who knew if the people who took Vesta were still nearby? She cursed her stupidity as the car sped along, flinging some change at the driver when he stopped at the curb on East Street. Then she burst out of the cab and hurtled up the stairs. But what she saw there made her stop in her tracks and take a very deep breath.

Vesta was sitting at the desk—she was disheveled and her face was wet with tears but she was safe and sound.

"Oh, thank God!" Mirabelle started in a rush. "I was terrified. I thought . . ."

Vesta put up a hand. There was still mud on it from Romana Laszlo's grave. She was shaking. "Whatever you thought had happened, you were probably right. And they still have Sandor."

"We have to go to the police." Mirabelle picked up the telephone directory and started leafing through it. "There was a chap here today. Detective Superintendent McGregor. Looking for Ben . . ."

"No," said Vesta decisively, "we can't go to the police. That's certain. If we go to the police and they get a sniff of it they'll kill Sandor. And, Mirabelle, I'm sorry, I'm not quite sure how to tell you this, but Mr. McGuigan is dead."

16

Ratissage: a counter-espionage manhunt

During the course of three cups of hot sweet tea, Vesta told Mirabelle everything that had happened. As they sipped, Mirabelle was glad to see the girl's hands stop shaking. It was hardly surprising that the shock had made her sick and tearful. Mirabelle laid her hand on Vesta's shoulder and tried to comfort her. As the news sunk in, Mirabelle forced herself not to think of what had happened to poor Ben and focus instead on the fact that Sandor's life was at stake now—that was the most important thing. This wasn't the time to grieve and she knew it was important to focus on the living, not the dead.

"So," Mirabelle said, "they think they're being investigated by the Prudential and they've bought you off so their policy will be safe?"

"Yes."

"And they don't know where you really came from? They've no idea?"

Vesta shook her head. "I told them Halley Insurance is a regional office. I told them I'd be here. They're going to ring every lunchtime and I can check on him." She put down her cup.

"And you don't have any idea who he was, this man?" Mirabelle tried.

Vesta hung her head. "No," she said. "He was English. White. Middle-aged. He was wearing a suit but he wasn't posh. I couldn't see him properly—he blindfolded me before we went outside and in there it was all shadow."

"But you think he's watching?"

Vesta shrugged. "Can we take that chance? If we get it wrong and we go to the police, then he'll kill Sandor. Even if he's not watching, who knows who they have on the inside at Bartholomew Square. Policemen! They'd sell their own mothers, wouldn't they? It's too risky."

Mirabelle weighed it up. Vesta was right. Even if McGregor was straight, there was no saying who else might be on the team. The main thing was to do what was best for Sandor—whatever was safest. "Well, we can't just sit here," she said. "We should try to find out more. See what we can come up with."

"That's what got us into this situation, Mirabelle!" Vesta spat. She was angry. "If you hadn't sent me to that stupid funeral none of this would have happened. Do you really want to continue with this—just the two of us? Are you crazy? These people are dangerous. We should just do whatever they say."

Mirabelle noticed out of the corner of her eye the cup that Ben always used sitting beside the sink. She tried to ignore it. "If we don't do anything then we're just leaving Sandor's life to chance. Can you sit here and say that's all right? We should at least try to find out where they held you. We need to do something. Perhaps he's still there and we can get him out."

Vesta slumped. She had had a difficult day—unarguably her most difficult day—and now it struck her that Mirabelle sounded like her mother. The reason Vesta had come to Brighton in the first place was because she had had enough of being told what she had to do and how to do it. This was too much. And even if Sandor was in danger, who knew if digging around would do him any good?

"It's all right for you," she said petulantly. "You weren't there. I thought you knew about this kind of thing!"

Mirabelle glared. "You were supposed to be the lookout, Vesta!" she snapped back. "All I'm talking about is doing some surveillance."

Vesta made a dismissive motion with her hands. Did Mirabelle really expect her to become some kind of undercover Mata Hari? "Yeah, that's easy for you to say. You're a white woman. I can't do surveillance! Do you know how many people turn round and stare when I walk down the street? You've got to be kidding!"

Mirabelle paused. She felt sorry for Vesta. Black people were stared at here in Brighton more than London. They shouldn't be stared at, at all, of course. But it was still no reason not to help Sandor. "That's fair enough," she said. "We can work around that."

Vesta banged her cup onto the desk. "No. I'm not doing anything else. I'm going to sit here and hope Sandor rings when they said he would. I'm going to hope they keep their word and let him go when the insurance money clears. All this cloak and dagger stuff—it's crazy."

Mirabelle took a deep breath. "If we stop now it will endanger him more. These things don't come off well, Vesta. And there's no one else to bother with it. It's only you and me. Think what it felt like to be held, to be in danger and completely vulnerable. Think about what Sandor would be doing right now if it were the other way around. If you were there, would you rather no one was looking for you? Would you really think that was safer? We owe Ben now he's gone and we owe Sandor. And perhaps we owe Romana Laszlo, wherever she is. And Mr. Velazquez. Something happened to all these people—something bad—and it's landed in our laps. Sometimes life isn't what we want, it's what we get."

Vesta held her head in her hands. The picture that came back into her mind again and again was of Sandor, tied to a chair in that dank outhouse God knows where.

"Shit," she said, as it dawned on her that Mirabelle was absolutely right. If she'd been stuck in that chair she'd be praying that Mirabelle and Sandor were doing whatever they had to. She let out a deep breath, shrugged her shoulders and glanced at the open biscuit box lying on the desk to one side. The shock had confused her, she thought. Still, despite what her mother believed, perhaps she was a responsible adult after all. It might be easier to just sit there but it wasn't right. She picked up a biscuit and with a heavy heart made her choice. Not much of a choice, really, but she made it.

"So what exactly are we going to do?"

Mirabelle turned to the map of Brighton on the wall and pried out the pins that held it in place. "You said they took fifteen minutes in a car to bring you back here?"

Vesta nodded. "About that."

Mirabelle drew a circle around the city center—locations all within a quarter of an hour's drive. Then she marked in the house at Second Avenue, the Grand Hotel, the racecourse, Big Ben's house, Cobb's of Patcham and Sandor's church—all known and potential locations connected to Lisabetta in one way or another.

Vesta eyed Mirabelle, waiting for her to speak.

"Right, so we're looking for an outhouse in that area. We have to try to find out where they held you. And you have to think, Vesta. Did you hear anything? Smell anything? Was there anything that would give us a clue?"

Vesta shook her head sadly. "I was so scared. I don't remember."

"You need to try," Mirabelle insisted. "Do you think it could be the house on Second Avenue? They might have outbuildings in the garden."

"No, that's not far enough away," Vesta said decisively,

placing her finger on the spot. "Anyway, there's nothing like the place in that part of town. I mean outside. I only caught a glimpse but I think it was pretty open—not too many buildings. And the fact I don't remember any noise indicates it's probably pretty quiet. Second Avenue is near the front and it's busy. I'm sure I'd have at least remembered hearing some car engines. I was there for a while and there's traffic on that road during the day. And there was something else. I felt warm. I remember it being quite hot. But I was panicking. Perhaps I just got flushed."

The girl was doing all right. "Warm . . . and quite quiet." Mirabelle cast her eyes over the map. "Open scrubland. Well, that's a start. And meantime I'm going to find out what Ben was up to. If he was buried in Romana Laszlo's grave then there's a connection between what happened to her and whatever he was doing at the racecourse. It's not only some thousand-pound insurance policy, let's face it. He was tracking some kind of payment system for far more than that. He's written down figures for more than twenty grand. So what are they really up to?"

"Whatever you got up to during the war, it was important, wasn't it?" Vesta asked.

Mirabelle looked up. "Everyone was important during the war. Everyone. We worked together and we won. And that's what we've got to do now. Shake hands on it, Vesta."

Vesta gripped her hand firmly over the top of the desk.

"I thought I'd lost you there," Mirabelle admitted.

Vesta shook her head. "I was just scared," she shrugged. "Sorry, Mirabelle."

Mirabelle glanced at the clock on the wall. "We better leave now. It has to look like the office is working normally. Just in case we are being watched. We usually lock up about this time." She folded the map. "Come on, let's get out of here."

17

The only thing to do with good advice is pass it on.

Lisabetta's voice could be heard from the hallway of Dr. Crichton's house. She was speaking in German on the telephone. The housemaid lingered by the kitchen stairs, openmouthed, and only managed to get out of the way just in time as the doctor came downstairs two steps at once and burst into his study.

"Jawohl, aber es ist nicht so leicht."

She sounded calmer than she had when he first heard her voice. He motioned to attract attention. "Lisabetta," he hissed, "everyone can hear you!" and he gestured toward the door behind him.

Lisabetta swiveled his chair, turning away, but she conceded by lowering her voice as she spoke into the receiver.

The doctor felt uncomfortable hearing German spoken, and not only because it might be overheard by others. He had been attached to The King's Own Scottish Borderers during the war—an officer like all medical staff—though he quickly discovered there was money to be made if he turned a blind eye to some of the body bags being sent out by air. He told himself that his negligence benefited refugees as well as ex-Nazis and that it was simply a matter of who had enough money. Money was the key to everything—for right or wrong. The great decider. Before he had managed to secure a scholarship to study medicine Dr. Crichton had come from nothing and from nowhere. He had no intention of going back there.

He glanced nervously at his desk. What had Lisabetta been up to? She had been in his house for three days and it felt as if he had been invaded. His safe respectable existence meant nothing to her. In the general run of things she'd left him alone—asking for a prescription now and then, an occasional consultation for a client or, once, medical care for a thug who had been shot. And, of course, he also saw to the coordination of some of her activities outside London. In essence she'd wanted him for his respectability and now she was compromising it by shouting at some Hun down the wire. Thank heavens she'd be going soon.

"*Vielleicht. Guten Tag.*" Lisabetta finished the call and set the heavy black receiver back on the rest, pausing a moment before she turned.

"Who was it?" he asked gingerly.

"His wife," she said blankly. "Not happy."

"No widow is happy."

Lisabetta shrugged slightly. She'd known a few. "Well, there's nothing she can do. And, of course, I will have to handle everything as usual."

The doctor took a cigarette from a silver-plated box beside the fire. "How many have there been? Your clients? I don't always get to meet them. Quite a menagerie. You can't have the staff hearing you speak German, you know. It's not on!"

Lisabetta got up and crossed the room prettily. She stood over him. "Who the hell do you think you are? It's all gone haywire down here, Crichton, and I hold you responsible. Three bodies in less than a week!"

"Hardly!" The doctor stifled a laugh. "Come on!"

"And there'll be more," she said ominously. "Getting rid of bodies is so . . . troublesome. You do realize what's at stake?"

The doctor nodded.

Lisabetta turned with a swish. She crossed to the drinks cabinet and poured herself a brandy with a dash of soda and a shot of whiskey for the doctor, which she handed over solemnly.

They clinked glasses.

"Just don't forget how easy it would be to poison you," she said, once he'd swallowed.

18

As a man is, so you must humour him.

"This flat suits you, Mirabelle," Vesta announced the following morning. She had never slept anywhere so swanky—it was a far cry from the sparse bedsit she rented on the top floor of a shop along from the People's Picture Palace on Lewes Road. She'd known, of course, that Mirabelle had some money—you could tell by her clothes—but she hadn't expected the high-ceilinged apartment, the brand-new kitchen and the expensive furnishings including an ornate pair of solid silver candlesticks perched on the alabaster fireplace. That said, the flat was a mess—there were newspapers everywhere for a start.

Neither of the women had slept well, and now Vesta was concerned she wasn't going to eat well either. Having skipped dinner she found herself, unsurprisingly, searching in vain through Mirabelle's kitchen cupboards for something worth the effort of breakfast. It appeared that Mirabelle subsisted on tinned soup and sandwich paste. There was nothing else in the pantry. Vesta, however, did come across an abundance of ration slips in one of the drawers—Mirabelle never used much in the way of her weekly allowance—so she set out early for the nearest shop, bringing home butter, eggs, sugar, milk, coffee and some very nice bacon which she had bought under the counter.

"I'm making pancakes," she called out.

Mirabelle sat in the armchair by the high window with the map spread out before her. She rarely ate before lunchtime but whatever Vesta was doing certainly smelled nice. It was strange to have someone in the flat again—another human being.

Vesta strolled through with a large plate piled high and two delicate china cups full of steaming strong black coffee. She fell cross-legged to the floor next to Mirabelle.

"I know you don't eat anything, but you got to try this, Mirabelle. Mmm."

Mirabelle reached over, tore the corner from a pancake and slipped it into her mouth. It was heavenly.

"You're a really good cook," she said to Vesta.

"I'll make some man a great wife some day," Vesta chimed. "Just got to find me some lucky black man who's worth the trouble. Oh, and not get murdered."

Mirabelle smiled. "So, today," she picked up her cup, "I'm going to the racecourse. It's the last place we can actually place Ben McGuigan."

"OK," Vesta agreed, her mouth still full. "And I'll stay in the office. At one they'll ring me and let me speak to Sandor. Do you think they'll kill him?" she asked, not for the first time.

"Not until they're sure they don't need him. He's a bargaining chip," Mirabelle said. "We have to keep him that way. Do you suppose people dress up for the races?"

Vesta shrugged. "What—like they do at Ascot? Shouldn't think it's quite so swish." She pondered the question with tremendous seriousness. "Have you got a nice hat, though? That's what ladies wear to the races, isn't it? A hat?"

Mirabelle disappeared into the bedroom and emerged wearing a glamorous pink silk confection on her head. She had bought it to wear at a wedding—it seemed like a hundred years ago.

The peach shade brought out the hazel of her eyes, which were quite startling when you noticed them, thought Vesta. It was the first time she had seen Mirabelle wear anything frivolous. The splash of color sparked her dark understated brown dress into life and easily knocked five years off her age. "That's lovely!" Vesta giggled.

"I have to look like I belong there but I don't want to attract attention," Mirabelle said.

Vesta nodded. Her first thought was that with those eyes you would notice Mirabelle anywhere—she was simply too striking. Then, as her mind flew forward, she ran through what she'd be doing later in the day while Mirabelle lived it up at Fairfield Road. She felt a flicker of emotion. "Mirabelle, what should I say to Sandor? They're going to ring in four hours." She checked her watch. "What should I tell him?"

"He's a priest. Just say you're praying for him—something like that. Don't mention anyone or anywhere specific and talk about yourself as 'I' not 'we.' They'll be listening. Say you're sticking to the plan and that your thoughts are with him. And take a note of whatever he says—he might try to tell us something. The details are important."

Vesta frowned. "If anything happens . . ."

Mirabelle laid her hand on Vesta's arm reassuringly. "We have time. We'll find him. We're going to do our best." Her tone was more confident than she felt. Mirabelle knew all too well that kidnap attempts rarely went to plan. It simply wasn't a linear process. Sandor's odds were poor, especially given what Vesta had told her about his attitude—he was fighting his captors openly rather than trying to befriend them. She buttoned her chocolate-colored taffeta coat and tried not to think about it—Sandor had survived the aerial bombing of Berlin in the last few months of the war, he'd made it through SS screening procedures and, after VE Day, he had got himself to London, to the department, without any official help. He was tough and experienced, and that would count in his favor. After everything Sandor had survived he deserved to die safe and sound, at a good age, in his bed. Mirabelle dismissed the thought from her mind. Worrying would only distract her from helping, and it was helping that was important. "Come on," she grabbed the younger girl's arm, "we'd better get you into the office. We've got work to do."

Forty minutes later Mirabelle entered the turnstile at Fairfield Road. It was still early, but the racecourse was buzzing and she was surprised to see how many women were already there. Racing was not something she associated with women—it was certainly not a pursuit in which she had ever taken an interest but, she noted, it couldn't be much less than 50/50 at Brighton today. Many of the ladies were attired far more glamorously than she was, even in her fancy hat with smart high heels. The site was enormous—the crowd ran to a few thousand people already and in the next hour or two that number would double or triple easily. The morning trains from London were set to empty their load almost exclusively for the racecourse and the traffic in the center of Brighton that morning attested to another large contingent arriving by car.

The sun was shining and the snippets of conversation wafting by sounded knowledgeable. Mirabelle knew little about livestock and less about horses. She had no interest in riding and as a child she had been brought up in the city by parents who were both wealthy and modern in their outlook. They had, as far as she could remember, always traveled by car. As a result, apart from a rudimentary and mathematical knowledge of the odds given on the horses in each race, Mirabelle had no understanding of how the whole thing worked.

This was, she cursed, somewhere Sandor would have been able to help. She knew he had grown up on a farm in Csikós, homeland of the Magyar cowboys. He had told her once that when he had announced he was going into the priesthood, his mother had cried. If Sandor left, the family's animals would go, in due course, to a cousin. He had been quite old when he got his calling—most priests knew from their choirboy days that the church was their vocation. However, he said when the revelation arrived he was adamant. His mother had been devastated. Perhaps, Mirabelle mused, Lisabetta's interest in horses came from the same source. Hungarian society lived close to its animals but then, she recalled, Lisabetta probably wasn't Hungarian. Almost certainly not. And Lisabetta's interest, it would seem, was taken not by sport but by money.

With this in mind, drawing her coat around her and checking her pretty pink corsage was in place, Mirabelle made her way down to the touts that ran along the border of the track. Business was already brisk—a lot of money was set to change hands today, the majority of it in one direction. Ready to receive it, the bookmakers were smartly turned out, making notes in their black-bound books and calculating every second while they took the bets placed by the more organized punters, well ahead of the first race. The crowd milling nearby smoked an endless stream of cigarettes, men leaning over smiling women to help light them up, serious-looking older gents smoking cigars or Camels with a contemplative air as they read the *Racing Post*, and jumpy bookmakers taking a couple of puffs of a Regal or Senior Service and then throwing away the stub with their eyes darting.

It was a clear day and the vista of the suburbs stretched out into the distance from the racecourse's vantage point on the hillside. Two little boys sat on the steps to the stand sharing a pie out of a brown paper bag, transfixed at the site of an old black man in an exotic outfit who was shouting, "I'm Prince Monolulu and I gotta horse." A crowd was gathering around him, waiting to hear his tips. Farther off it looked as if people were attending a cocktail party— dressed to the nines and clutching champagne glasses as they chatted in the sunshine ignoring the show. There was a sense of excitement, even away from the track. Close to it Mirabelle caught the odd glimpse of a horse going through its paces or simply being checked over in the paddock by a trainer or a brightly colored satin-clad jockey. Right, she thought, I had best be methodical.

She pushed her way through the crowd to inspect the touts one by one, heading for M. Williams where Ben had chosen to place his bets. Already there were small queues of people in front of each stand, jostling to get their bets in early. After ten minutes and some fine fresh bruises on her arms, she finally came to the stall marked M. Williams in green paint. There were figures written in chalk on the board—odds on horses in the first race—but the stall itself was empty. With determination Mirabelle pushed her way toward the bookmaker next door—a clean-shaven young man with sparkling green eyes and a crumpled brown suit standing next to a man of similar appearance—could it be his brother?—who was signaling with his hands and face at another bookmaker farther up the field. Mirabelle didn't focus too much on what he was doing.

"Excuse me." She pointed at the neighboring stall. "I'm looking for Mr. Williams."

"What do you want, darling? I'll give you any odds he's offering you. Just tell me what you fancy."

"I'm afraid it's Mr. Williams I'm looking for." Mirabelle tried to think of a reason she'd need to see Mr. Williams in person. "I'm collecting," she came up with, "from the other day."

"Oh, right." The young man completely lost interest. "Well, he's round here somewhere, love. Seen him this morning early. Takes a lot of bets from private clients these days, does Manni. Might be off seeing one of those."

Mirabelle's heart jumped. Manni. Manni Williams. Of course, the man who had taken Lisabetta to the Grand. "Does he wear a gray suit the same color as his hair?"

"Thought you laid a bet with him?" he said suspiciously.

"Yes, yes. I mean, is he wearing that suit today? So I can spot him."

"Love, he always wears that suit. Some posh bird bought it for him and Manni won't take it off until he's in his box, I reckon. Maybe not even then."

"Thanks."

Mirabelle retreated into the crowd with her mind running through the possibilities. Here was the link between Lisabetta and the racecourse. The next task was to find out if Manni was simply an upmarket client of Lisabetta's who paid well for her company or the company of women Lisabetta procured for him, or if he was more than just a punter. Was there money being made illicitly here—and was that what Ben had been onto?

Mirabelle wasn't sure how bookmakers worked but if there was a system then there was a way of bucking it. She and Vesta had pored over the figures in Ben's notebook the night before, but beyond the fact that the dates tied in with the days there were races, they hadn't got very far. Had Big Ben been onto some scam? The sums he'd written down ran into thousands but betting wasn't a safe way to make money and you surely couldn't fix more than the odd race. Whatever he'd been up to, someone had caught him. In fact, in all probability, Lisabetta or Manni *had* caught him because he'd ended up in Romana Laszlo's grave. Yes, the man in the gray suit was definitely involved. There was no other way she could see it working. Though if Ben had taken Romana's place, where was the girl and, for that matter, her baby?

Mirabelle started as she saw Manni Williams arrive at his stall, joking with a few punters who were waiting. He cheerily bantered with the bookies nearby and looked in his element as he drew a chalk from his pocket and altered the odds on his board. In between, he laconically ate a bacon roll he'd picked up from one of the catering stalls. Between bites he leaned down to take on a couple of bets from the crowd—a drunk woman in lemon yellow ostrich feathers handed over a sheaf of notes, laughing like a drain as she pointed, picking her horse. Then Mirabelle saw Detective Superintendent McGregor emerging from the throng with two uniformed policemen. What was he doing here? Was the bookmaker about to be arrested?

"Good morning, Manni." McGregor smiled unpleasantly as the policemen blocked the front of the stall.

Manni balanced the remains of his roll on the edge of the blackboard. "Morning, sir."

"Don't let me stop you eating. Please."

The bookies on the stalls to either side froze so they could listen. One of them held off a fellow trying to hand over some money by motioning him to back off. Manni eyed his roll dubiously and instead rubbed out a set of odds and replaced them.

McGregor stared. "Late breakfast, is it? Had mine before I left the house. Got to be up early to catch the worms, Manni."

"You got nothing on me," Manni said.

"No, I haven't, Manni. Not a sausage. Not a bean. Not a bacon roll."

Manni smirked.

"All I've got is a funny feeling. So I thought I'd come down here today. I'm looking for a friend who appears to have taken up horse racing all of a sudden. No one's seen him for a few days. Ben McGuigan. Know him?"

Manni nodded. "Yeah, one of my punters. Big bloke, isn't he? Can't imagine much can have happened to him."

McGregor pulled two tickets from his pocket. "I wondered if either of these were winners?"

Manni peered over to inspect the tickets. "Nah. Richy Rich placed but you only got on the nose there. Sorry, sir, I don't remember taking your bet."

"These are McGuigan's slips, Manni. As well you know."

"Oh, I think I might recall him putting down some money. He was hanging around earlier in the week—and last week, too. Thing is, I love my job, me. I got to concentrate on what I'm doing so I don't always remember names and faces, see? Just numbers. That's all. Don't worry, nothing wrong with cashing in your mate's chit, if you get your hands on it. Legally that's a bearer bond, that is."

"Thank you very much, Manni," McGregor said sarcastically.

"If you want to lay a bet I can give you a tip," Manni offered. He was getting carried away. "The Twelve Thirty!" he called out. "Little Boy Blue! I'll give you three to one."

"I'm just a spectator today, Manni. I'm watching. I'm going to be watching all day."

"No fun in that, sir." Manni picked up his roll.

"You tell him, Manni, my old son! Three to one on Little Boy Blue is good odds. Might take a shilling or three on that myself," the bookie on the next stall shouted.

McGregor turned. "I'm watching," he said.

Mirabelle moved back. She was only one layer of the thickening crowd away from Williams, right behind McGregor. She followed him farther into the melee but his mackintosh disappeared in the crush. Casting an eye over her shoulder she turned to see Manni taking bets again. His tone had reminded her of some of the war crimes cases—soldiers who had insisted they had only been doing their duty when they had been on the take or cocky deserters engaged in black market activity. His attitude was too bluff—too defiant. He was definitely up to something— she knew it as well as McGregor. In fact she knew more. But, it would seem, there was nothing stopping him taking bets—that part of what Ben had been looking at was above board and so far there was no sign of the kind of high rollers that Ben had been noting down. So what was Manni doing with these bets that wasn't legal? Suddenly Mirabelle felt a heavy hand on her shoulder.

"Miss Bevan, isn't it?" said a deep voice. "I wonder if you're heading for Mr. Williams's stall. I think it might be best if you come with me."

The detective superintendent manhandled her through the crowd and up to the stands where he stopped to light a cigarette, keeping his eyes firmly on Mirabelle. "What are you doing here?"

Mirabelle clutched her bag very tightly. "Is it illegal to go to the races now?"

McGregor stared at her and waited.

She knew that by acting this way she appeared guilty. "All right," she said. "I wanted to come and have a look. This is where Ben made his bet before . . .."

McGregor eyed her suspiciously. "Before what?"

"Before his wallet went missing." She composed herself. "And I still can't find him, Detective Superintendent. Not anywhere."

"Were you going to or coming from Manni Williams's stall?"

"I was going to ask Mr. Williams if he remembered see- ing Ben. He placed at least two bets with M. Williams the day he disappeared, didn't he? I saw the slips in the wallet you showed me. Then I found some more from a few days before that. In the wastepaper bin."

McGregor eyed her once more. What was she so het up about? There was a flash of passion in Mirabelle's eyes beyond what you'd expect from someone idly investigating the disappearance of a work colleague. Was she romantically involved or did she know something?

"This is where Mr. McGuigan was last seen, isn't it?" Mirabelle explained. "Unless you have another lead I don't know about. That's what you were asking Mr. Williams, wasn't it?"

The policeman stubbed out his smoke. Manni Williams was dangerous—he'd probably knocked off McGuigan for a start—and this woman, a complete amateur, was blundering around. Either she was incredibly brave or she simply didn't realize how murderous the criminal element could be when their backs were up against the wall. "You're unusually observant," he said. "Don't worry, I'm looking for McGuigan. I'll keep going till I find him. This is a matter for the professionals. You've been reading too much detective fiction if you think this is something you can handle, Miss Bevan. Ben didn't want you involved. That's why he told you he was ill. To keep you out of it."

Mirabelle didn't lose a beat. "He was investigating something here, wasn't he, Detective Superintendent? A betting scam?"

McGregor nodded slowly. "Yes, he was working for a member of the racing board. They hadn't called us in because they didn't have any evidence. Ben had been charged with using the utmost discretion in his investigation. He had been doing so for two or three weeks before he disappeared. I am extremely concerned for Mr. McGuigan's welfare."

"I think he's dead too," Mirabelle admitted sadly.

McGregor's eyes lifted and he became distracted by something in the distance. He scrambled in his pockets for a small pair of binoculars and Mirabelle followed his line of sight. There was Dr. Crichton and another man with a military bearing, a jolly expression and a huge camel-colored jacket. Manni bent down and shook the man's hand with fervor as a grin spread over his face. McGregor and Mirabelle both leaned forward on the rail to watch.

"He's got a lot of legitimate high rollers all of a sudden, that guy," McGregor said. "Turns out we've had him on our books for one thing or another for years but Manni Williams has always been strictly small-time. Then, over the last eighteen months, the little toe rag has made a fortune and paid out a fortune, all at once."

Dr. Crichton's companion handed over some money and Manni gave him a chit.

"But I can't see what he's doing that's wrong," Mirabelle said. "He's licensed to take bets, isn't he? You can't fix every race. It's just not possible."

"Yes, I can't work it out either. The books tally, too. Bets are scrutinized by the authorities but one of the board here at the racecourse had a funny feeling about what Williams was up to. Seems odd to say in these surroundings but the man had been too lucky and this board member was sure there was something going on. Thing is, most of the people betting with Williams had been coming to the races for years, knew their stuff and were all above board. Thing is, he's paying out more or less as much as he's taking in—he's just hauling a fairly small and strangely regular profit. It doesn't make sense as a scam. But the profits—well, let's say, it's practically a steady wage and a good one. That's unusual. He's on the fiddle somehow. I can't yet see how many people are involved—he has a lot of legitimate clients—but his books don't look like any other bookie's set of accounts. The detail is way too steady."

"So that man betting now could be legitimate?"

"Oh, yes," McGregor replied. "Well, I hope so. In fact, they're probably both legitimate. One of those men is Brigadier General Spence and the other, if I'm not mistaken, is Dr. Eric Crichton—I didn't expect to see him here. And that's part of the bloody trouble, pardon my French. The damned Chief of Police bets with Manni Williams these days. He's got every respectable punter going. That's why the board called in Big Ben McGuigan. They needed someone who could be discreet."

"So Ben was gathering as much information as possible to see if the bets Williams was actually taking tallied up with what he presented for inspection in his books?"

"But now both he and the information have disappeared. Whatever he was up to, he rattled Manni's cage good and proper. But I don't know why."

For an instant Mirabelle considered telling McGregor about Ben's coded notebook but decided against it. There was no doubt in her mind that whatever was inside the ledger would illuminate the scam but the police making progress on what happened to Ben could be dangerous for Sandor—as fatal even as if she'd told McGregor that she knew Ben's body was in Romana Laszlo's grave. This was all tied up somehow and until she could work it out or at least get Sandor to safety she had to keep it to herself.

Dr. Crichton and the Brigadier disappeared into the crowd and McGregor put his binoculars back in his pocket. It was then that he noticed for the first time that Mirabelle Bevan had extraordinary hazel eyes. The observation worried him. His mother always said he had terrible instincts about women. So far she had been proved right several times. McGregor had never married—never even got close. He lived for his work. There was nothing like getting your teeth into a really good case. This was moving from a missing person's investigation into something more complicated and dangerous and there was no point in involving this beautiful woman—she was only a secretary, after all. To uncover what was going on with a nest of thieves like this one, you needed a lot of tenacity and the will to upset people. She couldn't be any help.

"It's back to the office for you, Miss Bevan, I'm afraid. You leave this to me."

McGregor motioned to a uniformed constable and gave

some instructions. Mirabelle was escorted off the premises, into the backseat of a police car and, after fighting through the traffic all the way down the steep hill back into town, she was dropped, unceremoniously but safely, on the corner of East Street and Brill Lane. It was humiliating. The constable even sat there with the engine running to make sure that she went inside.

19

Common sense is not so common.

When the office telephone rang Vesta jumped to answer it immediately, almost knocking over the thin wooden desk. "Sandor, is that you?" she said, tears already welling up.

"Yes." His voice was calm but it still sent shivers right through her. She tried to sound even and clear, as if this wasn't shaking her up. She pictured Mirabelle, with her seemingly glacial nerves, and tried to imagine what that must feel like. Still, Vesta felt herself wavering. "Are you all right?" she managed.

"Yes."

"Have they fed you? Did you drink something?"

"I'm fine, Vesta."

"I'm sticking to the plan. Don't worry. They will let you go."

A heavy sigh crackled down the wire and, just as it did, Vesta heard a metallic hammering noise in the background. It sounded, somehow, dangerous. Where was he? What were they doing to him? Vesta panicked. "Are you all right? You'll ring tomorrow, won't you? I'll worry myself to death otherwise."

There was a hesitation while, she supposed, Sandor caught

the eye of whoever had let him use the phone. In the interim there was more hammering. It was a curious sound—almost industrial. Definitely a hammer hitting metal—something along the lines of a blacksmith shoeing a horse.

"What's that noise?" she asked.

Sandor ignored her, replying in a measured tone, "It's fine. I'm all right. They'll let me call again at one o'clock tomorrow but now I have to go."

When the receiver clicked, Vesta dissolved into tears. What was happening was huge and she couldn't quite reconcile Sandor's down-to-earth tone with the vastness of the events. They were holding the priest against his will. She had been held for a few hours at most but he'd been captive for more than a day now. It already felt like forever and insurance payouts could be a lengthy business. Vesta stared at the map, fiddled with her papers and didn't stop crying until Mirabelle came through the office door. The older woman slipped off her racing hat and hung it up. Vesta's eyes were red and her cheeks were damp. There were soggy tissues scattered across the desk and all over the map upon which she had been trying to work.

"He called then?" Mirabelle said.

"One o'clock. Exactly." Vesta sniffed. "It's more difficult than I thought . . ."

Her mother's words echoed through her mind. "Real life, young lady, is tough," she had said. "Consequences, mademoiselle. Con-se-quences." Well, Vesta understood about consequences now. Sandor was trapped. He might die. And yet he'd sounded so calm. How did he manage that? The normality of it was the strangest thing. Vesta felt suddenly terribly glad that Mirabelle was back. If nothing else it would distract her from dwelling on the conversation and the vision she had of Sandor tied up in that hut in the dark.

"Did you find anything at the racecourse?" she asked.

"Oh, yes." Mirabelle sank into the chair opposite. "Lots

of interesting things. M. Williams is Manni, Lisabetta's sidekick at the hotel. The place is crawling with police looking for Ben. He was investigating whatever betting scam it is that Manni is running—something that ties in with those figures in Ben's notebook. The police haven't worked it out yet and, to be honest, it might take them a while—Ben was onto it for a fortnight and he hadn't cracked the case. I can't see how Detective Superintendent McGregor will be able to work any faster. I saw Dr. Crichton there, too. They're thick as thieves. Actually, they are thieves some-how—all this money is coming from somewhere and it's definitely not legitimate. Perhaps they're part of this betting scam. Though McGregor says it's a small but regular profit which doesn't sound like five-pound tips and gold sovereigns to me. Anyway, after that I came back." She hesitated. She didn't want to admit that McGregor had dismissed her like some stupid schoolgirl. "So," she changed the subject, "what did Sandor say?"

Vesta blew her nose. "He's fine, I think. I did exactly as you said. It's just difficult. We have to get him out of there."

Mirabelle moved closer and applied herself to the impor-tant task of extracting detailed information. "Did he mention anything about the temperature?" She drew the map toward her across the top of the desk and flicked the crumpled tis-sues to one side.

"What?"

"Did he say if he was hot or cold?"

"No, should I have asked him?"

"No. No prompts."

"How do you mean?"

"No prompts. You let him volunteer the information. Would he have been able to say something if he'd wanted to, do you think?"

"Yes, I suppose so. He just kept saying that he was all right and he'd ring again tomorrow. Are you worried he's going to catch a chill or something? Because, really, I think that's the least of our worries, Mirabelle."

"No. It means they haven't moved him. If he says he's hot he's closer to home base. If he complains he's cold then he's farther away. Or thinks he is. If he didn't mention it and you think he could have, he's at the same location."

Vesta's jaw dropped. "You people," she started, "don't you know someone who could help us? Someone at the department? Sandor used to work there and . . ."

Mirabelle looked paler than usual. "I could ring," she said, her voice very flat. "Things change in two years but I'm sure I could ring. The thing is that it's a police matter. No one at the department owes me anything—never did. It doesn't work like that. So, most likely, they'd simply refer it on to the police. I don't want to endanger Sandor. Or Romana come to that—we haven't had a trace, not a scrap of the poor girl. I'm scared she's locked up some-where, with or without her baby. She might be dead, of course, but you never know. Sandor did an amazing job during the war, but the department," she hesitated a mo-ment, unsure quite how to put it, "is very focused on catching the criminals they are after now. They have a job to do."

It was one of the toughest things. Jack had been de-lighted when Sandor turned up in London. He'd thought the priest was dead. The truth was that he'd left him for dead. Afterward he'd felt guilty about it but in the same position he'd have made the same choices with any field agent. He'd made those choices many times before. It was all about the bigger picture. Whoever had taken over at the department that wouldn't have changed. One Hungar-ian priest in his fifties, ex-informant or not, was expend-able. Sandor was only caught up in an insurance scam—it wasn't a matter of national importance, no matter how vital he'd been to operations during the war.

"I don't think they'd be interested, Vesta. It's just not their area."

Vesta cast her eyes up to the corniced ceiling. "So Manni is laundering money?"

Mirabelle shrugged. "Yes, I think that's what's going on. Part of it, in any case. These people have a lot of paper money and I've seen a few tips in gold coins. They can't put sovereigns through at the racecourse, of course. I think that Ben would have copped it if they tried! But Manni can certainly launder paper money—fivers and so forth. And what McGregor said about his regular profit—well, that's his fee. Probably quite a good one."

"And Ben was monitoring it."

"Yes, that makes sense. It fits. And it explains why they killed him. There's been a lot at stake here. More than we thought. The figures are high stakes."

"So what do we do now?"

"Well, the same thing, really. We don't care about the money, do we? We have to try to find Sandor and Romana, too, if she's still alive—wherever they're held. We're the ones who care about them the most. It's down to us."

Vesta nodded slowly. Then she drew her finger across the map as she realized she hadn't told Mirabelle about the hammering she'd heard during the call. "Thing is, I might have something. There was a noise in the background when Sandor was speaking."

Mirabelle smiled. Vesta was noticing things now—she was picking it up. "Good. So what kind of noise? What did you hear?"

Vesta sat up straight. "I think it was a blacksmith. That's what it sounded like. Metal being hammered. A high tone. Not in the same room or anything, but nearby. But there's nothing on the map. I've checked it over already. I'm not a complete idiot, you know! There are only two blacksmiths in practically the whole of Sussex—I got out the telephone directory and everything. They're miles away—at least half an hour's drive from Brighton. So then I checked through factories. Anyone manufacturing, but that doesn't happen down here much. We're by the seaside and it isn't industrial—not fifteen minutes from the office, anyway. By the time you get that, it's inland and miles away."

Mirabelle's face broke into a grin. "You're doing really well." She reached out and touched her hand. "You're doing amazingly. Now, what about garages? Ships' chandlers?"

Vesta's eyes lit up and she picked up the directory, which she'd let drop to the floor by the desk. "Garages. Garages with workshops. Boat yards. Of course."

They set to it and the afternoon passed quickly. Shortly after five o'clock it occurred to Vesta that she had been working on the phones, checking different locations for almost four hours and not so much as a sip of tea had passed her lips. Their investigations uncovered that there were three working garages that fell into the zone. One was closed over the race weekend but the other two were open. Vesta had called and made inquiries. All the ship's chandlers were too close to town to have been the starting point of her journey.

"Mind you," she pointed out to Mirabelle, "the noise might just be some bloke working on his own car or boat or whatever in a private garage. The place we were held could be somewhere completely residential. Just because there's a noise doesn't mean that we'll find the right outhouse because of it."

"I know," Mirabelle replied, "but we have to try." She had seen too many cases of people coming through against the odds to give up. Vesta had no such experience to inspire her.

"And you're going to check out any place we find?"

"Oh, not just me. It'll take two," Mirabelle said emphatically. "We need each other, Vesta. You're coming with me. And there's something else. More important, I think. We've got to go back to Second Avenue. It's the hub of everything and our best chance of finding out where they're keeping him. Romana died there. Lisabetta and Dr. Crichton are living there. And Manni has at least visited. Tonight, first we'll try to find Sandor anywhere that has a good chance of a hammering noise nearby. But if we don't strike it lucky, we'll wait till really late, break into Second Avenue and search the doctor's study. It's the best tactic I can think of. There's got to be something that will give us a lead—an address book perhaps or a key. If they have a different property somewhere else, there must be a record of it—a lease perhaps or a letter."

"But . . ." Vesta started to object.

"Don't," said Mirabelle, raising her finger. "We're house-breaking and that's it."

A ghost of a smile passed across Vesta's face as the plan sunk in. *Breaking in?* she mouthed. Mirabelle was turning out to be increasingly surprising the more she got to know her.

At the end of the day the women locked the office and walked down to the front. Crowds of day-trippers were congregated near the pier and those who weren't going into or out of the pubs—mostly engaged in flirting—were queuing for fish and chips. The air smelled salty and delicious, the aroma of batter in hot oil wafting across the pavements on the spring breeze that came off the ocean. There was a holiday atmosphere on the front for the first time that year—a precursor to the long hot summer of visitors when the beach became crowded and there was mayhem on the pier.

"Hungry?" Mirabelle inquired.

"You bet," Vesta nodded. They decided to pick up fish and chips.

"You mind eating with your fingers?" Vesta asked.

Mirabelle shook her head.

"Ha! You ain't such a lady after all!" Vesta teased. "Come on, I know a place."

She cut uptown, arm in arm with Mirabelle. Most of the shops had closed for the night though by contrast the pubs were busy with customers pouring out onto the narrow cobbled streets.

"It's just up here," Vesta promised.

The queue was already snaking toward them. Several women turned as Vesta passed. Mirabelle heard one whisper, "look at that darkie!" and her friend, all bobby pins and red glossy lipstick, peered over the top of her sunglasses. Vesta didn't turn a hair, just joined the end of the queue as sly eyes took in the color of her skin and there was giggling up ahead. Between the barely subdued "look at hers" Mirabelle heard the girls discussing the relative merits of two dances on that evening—one at the Palais and one at the Regal. Then from beyond the queue an older woman in a wide gingham skirt touched Vesta surreptitiously, looked at her palm and wiped her hand, running off towards the pub to be reunited with her friends.

"Well, really!" Mirabelle snorted but Vesta hardly blinked. She had become accustomed to it.

The queue moved on, though when they finally made it inside, the man serving behind the counter ignored Vesta completely.

"For two, is it?" he asked Mirabelle.

"Fish and chips for me," Mirabelle said gently, "and what would you like, Vesta? Do tell the gentleman."

Later, as they walked toward the flat at the Lawns, the last salty remnants licked from their fingers, Mirabelle asked, "Doesn't it make you angry when people stare at you like that? If people in shops don't serve you?"

Vesta shrugged. "That's just the way it is, isn't it? If you're different. Mostly I don't take it. I say 'Excuse me' very loudly and make them sell me what I want. When I was a kid my mother used to stamp her feet and cough, but I don't—I just shout my order. I'm in there once a week or so—they never know what to say. And the girls in the queue—well, it's everywhere, but it's still rude."

Mirabelle nodded. "It is," she said quietly. "And it's wrong, Vesta. Really wrong."

"Can't do much about it, though, can you? You'd spend your whole life scrapping. Fighting all the way. I just insist on manners when I can, that's all. The rest is their choice."

Mirabelle hesitated. "Are your parents in London?"

"Yeah, my daddy works on the docks. At Limehouse. It ain't swanky but it's home."

"Do you see them much?"

Vesta frowned. "I went to secretarial college. Did some temping up in London. After that I got the job at Halley's. I'll see them at Christmas."

Mirabelle turned off the main road toward the apartment deep in thought. Poor kid, she must be scared out of her wits. She needs to learn to stand up for herself, she thought, and right then she decided to help Vesta as much as she could.

20

Blowback: the unintended consequences of covert operations.

They had to wait for a while. As the sun set through the Georgian windows of Mirabelle's drawing room, the two women sat watching the view. Neither of them said anything, though periodically Vesta sighed. Once it was dark, Mirabelle fetched some clothes from her wardrobe and they got changed.

Dressed in black and with low heels they sat side by side on the lower deck of the bus all the way through town and beyond. The pier was lit up, the focus of the evening's frantic activity with crowds thronging, the men jockeying for position, the women red-lipped and exuberant. The suburbs by contrast were dull, the streetlights sparse along the dark streets. Gradually the bus emptied until they were almost the last onboard. When they alighted toward Rottingdean they were deep on the east side of the city—the first possible location for the kidnap scene—near one of the workshops Vesta had identified. Outside the town center the streets were deserted. Still close to the shore the sound of the waves was clearly audible. The women disappeared from the main road and made their way uphill toward the first garage.

"You've done this before, right?" Vesta checked.

Mirabelle made a face.

"In the war. You did this in the war. All the time."

Mirabelle shook her head. "I worked in an office during the war, Vesta. This is my first outing in the field."

"No," Vesta replied, "you were a spy or something. You had to be."

"I've never been in operations. I dealt with spies and informants later in my career but mostly I worked in the office. I was a researcher. And a coordinator. I managed information and passed it on."

Vesta looked crestfallen. "But you know what you're doing," she ventured.

"Well, I've read the manuals," Mirabelle replied. "Actually, I wrote one or two of the manuals."

"Shit," said Vesta.

"Look, we just need to check out each of these businesses and see if the area rings a bell or we can find any suitable outbuildings. We might find Sandor. I hope so. If there were more of us we'd cut the whole city into a grid and search everywhere, but it's only you and me, so we're doing it this way. Finding someone is only a matter of time. We have some time. That's good. We just have to try. And keep trying. And later we'll be intelligence gathering at Second Avenue and we'll have a good chance there, I reckon, of finding out where they've got him if we haven't hit on it by chance."

"Shit," groaned Vesta.

Mirabelle ignored her. She clicked on her torch, checked the map and pointed in the right direction.

The first garage was in what was now a field. The building had miraculously survived what had clearly been a prolonged aerial bombing during the war and the area around it had been cleared but not redeveloped. The land probably wasn't worth enough to build on and instead the small warehouse stood alone in a sea of parked cars, some intact and others stripped for parts. Rotting tires and dis-connected axles littered the dark ground like waves creep-ing up a beach. There was no building near enough to be able to hear hammering on metal over a phone and the place was empty. This established, they gave up quickly and walked to the north, heading for the second address.

This looked more promising but half an hour scouting the district within acoustic range provided no buildings of the size and construction Vesta remembered. At the third location there was an alleyway of lock-ups, which they checked carefully, knocking on walls and climbing up to peer into the small square windows set at the top of the peeling painted doors. Sandor wasn't there. They brushed themselves down and headed westward, toward two more possibilities. Neither was fruitful. It was well after mid-night, even after two, perhaps, by the time they made it back across town to Hove, the smell of the sea suddenly coming toward them on the incoming tide as they walked down the hill toward Second Avenue. Mirabelle's hands were shaking but she hid them behind her back. This was the lion's den and Vesta was reticent enough as it was.

"This way." Mirabelle led Vesta to the rear of number 22 where, warmed up by the succession of commercial premises, they easily scaled the low garden wall and tip-toed across the lawn, hearts pounding. The lights in the sleeping house were out and the dark building lay silent.

"The doctor and Lisabetta probably sleep on the first floor," Mirabelle whispered, "and the staff will be right up at the top, I expect."

"Or maybe in the basement," Vesta pointed.

There was a window with closed curtains, which opened straight onto the lawn. That made sense if there was a live-in cook. In any case, both the basement and pantry win-dows were barred and the kitchen door had a stout lock, but the sitting room to the rear had sash windows and when Vesta clambered up she found one of the sashes had not been locked. She rolled up the window silently and pulled Mirabelle into the house behind her. Inside they scanned the dark room and then, so nervous they could hear blood rushing in their ears, they opened the door, which led to the hall. The click of the catch seemed to echo up the stairs and Mirabelle felt her heart in her mouth but there was nothing else for it—they had to get on with the job.

She peered round the doorpost and waited for a second. Nothing stirred. The hallway remained absolutely silent. The house smelled of stale cigar smoke and abandoned port glasses, as if, somewhere, dinner had not been cleared away. Mirabelle sneaked across the rug on tiptoes, followed by Vesta, and then she gestured toward the doctor's study. The door was locked but the key was in place. Getting used to the tension now Mirabelle turned it and eased the door open. Inside the women made for the doctor's desk—a heavy mahogany Victorian piece with four drawers down both sides and a green leather top. Sharing the torch they took one side each—Vesta started from the bottom, Mirabelle from the top. Vesta turned the key in the lock and pulled the drawer open. She immediately gave an excited squeak as Mirabelle abandoned her side—stethoscope, torch, prescription pad and some wooden spatulas.

"Jesus!" Vesta whispered.

The drawer was deep, very heavy, and half-packed with gold coins. Mirabelle selected one and examined it in the torchlight. It was a sovereign. There must have been over a hundred coins in the drawer—easily worth a couple of thousand pounds. Mirabelle slipped the coin into her pocket with Vesta staring on wide-eyed.

"You can't do that!"

"It's evidence—we might need it," she whispered. "Come on. These won't tell us where Sandor is being kept. We need to find some keys or a lease or something."

Grudgingly Vesta pushed the heavy drawer back into

place and they turned their attention to the job in hand. There was nothing else of particular interest in the desk and they moved onto the chiffonier that clearly held some of the doctor's medical equipment. Vesta peered at a speculum quizzically while Mirabelle disappeared into a small walk-in cupboard that appeared to be full of bandages and splints. None of this was any help. She tried to think where, if she were Crichton, she might keep a key or even, come to think of it, an address book, if not in the desk. Cautiously she pulled back from the cupboard, wondering about a hiding place in easy reach of the desk, along the book-shelves. Just as she was pushing the cupboard door closed, she happened to cast her eyes downward. On the bottom shelf she spotted a strange padded bandage. Trusting her instinct she picked it up.

"Oh, my goodness!" she whispered as she realized what it was. She held it away from her body.

"Is that . . ." Vesta started, but her eyes widened and she stopped speaking as Mirabelle fitted the foam padding to her own stomach in the quivering torchlight, giving her the outline of a heavily pregnant woman.

"Do you think . . ." Vesta put two and two together.

"Romana Laszlo," Mirabelle confirmed. "She wasn't having a baby at all."

"They made it all up? But why?"

"For a thousand pounds, maybe? It's a lot of money . . ." Mirabelle whispered.

"There's more than that in the drawer," Vesta hissed back. "Never mind whatever they're up to at the racecourse."

And then they heard the sound.

Upstairs a door creaked and the muffled click of slipper-clad footsteps pattered across the hallway on the first floor.

"Go!" Mirabelle whispered.

Vesta moved like a cat over to the window. She un-locked the catch and pulled it open in one movement, slip-ping over the windowsill and down into a flowerbed at the front of the house. Then she took off toward the nearest cover, behind a privet hedge across the road. Mirabelle stuffed the prosthetic belly back into the cupboard. She panicked. If she got caught hauling herself over the windowsill they'd have her just like they had Sandor. The footsteps were now approaching fast down the stairs. There was no time. Just as the study door flew open she drew back into the cupboard. Her breathing, she realized, sounded incredibly loud. She tried to slow it as she crouched in the cramped space, peering through the keyhole.

Accustomed to the dark she saw Lisabetta run straight to the open window and look out over Second Avenue. Lisabetta drew a gun from the pocket of her dressing gown. She raised the weapon smoothly and fired without hesitation. The muffled sound of the silenced barrel made less noise than a book toppling from a bedside table. Hardly able to breathe Mirabelle watched as Lisabetta swore quietly. Good, she hadn't found her target. The woman hovered a moment in the bay, clearly contemplating facing the chilly spring night in a thin nightgown and a pair of slippers with a gun. It wasn't feasible. Instead she snapped on the light and closed the doctor's curtains to inspect in private what the intruders had been doing.

The drawer of the desk was slightly open and she fell to examining that. Now with proper light Mirabelle could see, as Lisabetta emptied the coins, that there were several different kinds. Two-pound coins, five-pound coins, guineas and half-sovereigns as well as the standard sovereign she had in her pocket. Lisabetta sat in the doctor's leather chair and poked the nozzle of her gun into the stash, making—as Mirabelle and Vesta had done earlier—a calculation as to how much was in there. With the additional currencies it was worth even more. Lisabetta raised an eyebrow. It was clearly in excess of what she thought he was creaming off. "That greedy son of a bitch," she muttered.

Lisabetta began to look around, wondering what else

the doctor had been up to. She pulled open the other drawers of the desk. Then she sat back letting the chair swing at an angle. What was in easy reach from here? With her beautifully manicured fingers she picked out a black notebook on the shelf closest to the desk. It was at just the right height for Crichton to bring easily back and forth and was filed between medical books that no one else would find the least bit interesting. She opened it and flicked through pages of handwritten notes. Her eyes were ablaze with anger.

"Middlemass!" she hissed.

The name was familiar. Mirabelle thought a moment. Ah yes, that was the name of a man who had been murdered in London a couple of months ago in Kensington Park Gardens. She had read about it in the *Times*. The murder had been shelved by the police due to a complete lack of evidence. She had thought it was an interesting case—Middlemass had apparently been a forgettable man. On the evening of his death he had given a woman a light with his gold Dunhill on the corner of the street. It was the last time anyone had seen him. The police had said that locals with whom the victim had done business found him difficult to describe as there was simply nothing distinctive about him. This notebook obviously contained details of Lisabetta's operation—other clients, perhaps. Maybe even murders. What occurred to Mirabelle at the same time as it occurred to Lisabetta on the other side of the cupboard door was that Crichton could only be keeping the information for two reasons. It was either to inform on Lisabetta and curry favor with the authorities or it could be used to blackmail her.

Lisabetta began to search through the book once more, calling out names in German under her breath until she stopped on a recent page where he had made a few notes in pale blue ink. Here she almost spat with rage as she read the sentence out loud, her accent stronger than Mirabelle had heard before: *Lisabetta shows sociopathic tendencies—a complete inability to feel emotion. I wonder if she is psychopathic?* For a moment the woman seemed stunned and then, suddenly, it hit her. She was utterly incensed. This was treason!

It was interesting, Mirabelle thought, that the doctor had misjudged her. Lisabetta appeared to have plenty of emotions. Perhaps he had meant empathy. She certainly lacked that.

Furious, Lisabetta snapped off the light and crossed to the window. She flicked the curtains aside to check the street but there was no one there. Then she turned and dialed a number on the telephone. There was a long pause as the phone rang out. It took a while before anyone answered. Her voice, when she spoke, was cold as ice, replying to the sleepy and no doubt grumpy mumbling of whomever she had woken.

"I have no idea what time it is," she dismissed the complaint. "That's by the by. I want you to go round to Cadogan Gardens, Bert. I want you to pick up my things. Pack it all. Send it to Brighton. No, no. Not my name." She stopped for a moment. "Send it with the usual name to the usual place. You know what to do."

Mirabelle heard Bert Jennings's voice as a distant echo. He was arguing with her.

"Don't be ridiculous! I can't be French! I will have married a Frenchman, I'm sure." He was objecting. "But you have your cut. It's on the way and it's guaranteed, isn't it? I have something to deal with here. But I won't be long. It's all winding up very nicely. I will be in touch soon. Send my things. The first train, remember. The early one."

The phone clicked. Lisabetta crossed the room.

Mirabelle could just make out her dark figure crouching in front of the fireplace. She dropped Dr. Crichton's notebook onto the grate and lit it. The dry paper cover set alight easily and she stood back to watch it burn, turning over the

ashes to make sure that not one single word of the journal remained. Then she stooped to light a cigarette on the flames,
the warm light playing on her skin. Her face looked almost
diabolical.

"Sociopathic," she muttered under her breath, trying
the word out for size.

As the flames died she poked them with a brass fork to
make sure nothing remained. Then she closed the window
and crossed the room to Crichton's locked medicine cabinet. She picked out a small bottle of chloroform and a
patch of gauze. Mirabelle prayed Lisabetta wasn't going to
come into the bandage cupboard but the woman merely
checked her face in the mirror, blew herself a sinister kiss
and disappeared back out of the door.

Mirabelle exhaled. Hearing footsteps overhead she opened
the cupboard door, crept into the room and checked the
grate. The journal was completely destroyed. She wondered
what Lisabetta was up to but decided this was the moment
to leave. She checked the desk one more time, slipped a
couple of different coins into her pocket and then slid behind the curtains. Across the road Vesta had been watching. She came out from her hiding place behind the hedge
and motioned Mirabelle over. The catch clicked softly, the
window slid open and Mirabelle Bevan disappeared into
the darkness of Second Avenue.

21

It takes two to speak the truth.

Waclaw Gorski couldn't sleep. He hadn't slept properly in weeks but usually he managed at least a couple of hours a night. Tonight he had resigned himself to forgoing even that. He had suffered from insomnia for years but it had got far worse of late. He couldn't stop worrying, that was the problem. It was all taking longer than he had expected.

That evening Manni had turned up later than usual and he'd come in with a self-satisfied air that had set Waclaw's nerves on edge. He brought food, though, and four bottles of beer. Waclaw would have preferred some vodka. It sometimes helped get him off to sleep when all else failed. But they'd cracked open the beers together and Manni had stayed for a while and played cards. Waclaw knew Manni counted cards, so he avoided pontoon. Instead, they played gin rummy for over an hour, betting with the little slabs of gold that were piled up on one side of the workshop. Just for fun, of course. The gold was always returned at the end of the session.

"I'll play you for a night outside," he offered. "I could go on the town, you know. A fancy restaurant and a cabaret. You could take me."

Manni laughed. "You know she won't 'ave it, Waclaw. You can't leave until it's all done, you poor sod."

Waclaw shrugged and lit a cigarette. "No one must know I am here," he said blankly. "No one must know what I am doing. Or there will be no passports."

Waclaw hadn't left the place for over six months. The cabin was built of pale stone on three sides with a tin roof fanning out from the huge chimney and a sheet of wooden facing on the front. The furnace kept the place permanently hot, often unbearably so, and when he was working he opened the door wide even though Lisabetta had warned him about it several times. It was too hot not to. He never thought he would but lately Waclaw had begun to miss the Polish winter—he fantasized about the biting chill of the air in Warsaw in January. He longed to see his breath appear before him and rub his pink fingers to keep them warm on the Nowogrodzka as he came out of the little café where he used to have a strong black coffee and a shot of vodka. Ah, Warsaw! It had been a long time. How much of the city was still standing, of course, he couldn't be sure. But whether it was bomb damaged or not, Waclaw missed its ice and snow. It made him feel alive as he walked home along the river. When all this was over he was going somewhere that had snow all winter. Not, he thought with a tinge of sadness, back to Warsaw, of course. He had long realized that he couldn't go back to his native country now the Soviets were in power, but perhaps Canada, Scotland or, if they'd have him, Sweden. There were several possibilities, he was sure of it. Waclaw had stayed alive this long because he was useful and his skills extended beyond wartime. Somewhere would have him. Somewhere that was nice and cold.

The weather and the temperature of his surroundings were the least of the poor man's worries but they were easier for him to focus on than the difficulties that were really on his mind. He missed Marianne and their sons Udi and Mikhail, but he didn't dwell on them these days if he could help it, otherwise he'd never sleep at all. Lisabetta had got him out, and she'd get them out, too, when the job was done.

The job, naturally, had grown. Waclaw didn't wonder about where all the gold with the Nazi insignia came from, or whom he was really working for. Instead he concentrated on the minutiae—the practicalities of getting everything absolutely right.

"I can just recast these as unmarked gold bars," he'd offered when she'd shown him what he'd be working with. He knew full well that wasn't quite what Lisabetta had in mind but he'd hoped the speed at which he could work for that kind of turnaround might make the proposition attractive. She had listened to what he had to say and then dismissed the idea quickly. Coins might take longer to make but they were, in effect, worth more than the gold they were made of and prompted far fewer questions about the vendor. Gentlemen collected coins. Fleeing Nazi war criminals, tinpot dictators and criminals of various persuasions had gold bars.

So they had started, and from the outset she had been determined to make the very most of the gold. At the beginning she'd had him gilding five-shilling pieces—that old game. He'd set up a tank of acid laced with granules of gold and sent a current through it. The silver coins had gilded easily and the results had looked exactly like five-pound gold pieces. But the weight had been wrong. He'd told Lisabetta that upfront but she hadn't understood the significance of the scale. She was going to be left with thousands upon thousands of five-pound pieces that no professional would ever convert to cash. There were only so many gullible punters to sell them to. Lisabetta had taken the whole of the first consignment—a gross of them—up to

London and had Bert Jennings flog them in Notting Hill, Ladbroke Grove and Kilburn, door to door, one by one. It had taken over a month.

It had quickly become apparent that as the gold was hardly in short supply it would be far more effective simply to mint solid gold coins. It meant less profit but there would be no problem in selling the coins later. With Waclaw's undeniable talents in play, the fake currency was indistinguishable from the real thing.

He had flung himself into the job. The first load of sovereigns had been a huge success but then Lisabetta had decided that she didn't want to flood the market and insisted he branch out. Waclaw researched the exact measurements of individual coins and painstakingly made stamps to use on the blanks he cast in batches of twenty-four. He never minted the very rare years, or the most prolific. The first forty-eight attempts, Lisabetta and Eric Crichton had sold to antique dealers around Brighton. Not one of them had noticed a thing. Why should they? The coins were solid gold and Waclaw was a master goldsmith making exact copies. They might not be produced by the Royal Mint but that was the only difference from the genuine article. Lisabetta had tested and tried—she had sold one of Waclaw's fakes and a genuine coin, together, in half a dozen batches. Even side by side not one dealer had questioned the authenticity of what they were presented with. That was that—the coins were indistinguishable from the real McCoy.

Larger-scale production had started immediately. The little blocks with the Nazi markings on them had disappeared from the stack against the wall of the foundry. He had worked very hard but the supplies of gold were replenished several times. It was coming to the end now—Lisabetta had assured him it wouldn't be much longer. This was the very last batch.

Last week Lisabetta had come to the foundry. She had perhaps realized that his patience was wearing thin and turning into a kind of vicious desperation. She'd told him that Marianne and the boys were in Berlin.

"I almost have the papers organized," she said. "Your family is safe and we can get them out in a month or two. We'll bring them here, Waclaw. All you have to do is finish the job."

"The job we agreed on was finished over three months ago," he murmured.

Lisabetta crossed her legs daintily and held out an envelope. A letter. He tore it open with shaking fingers. It was Marianne's writing—the familiar tiny circle over the "i" and the way she crossed her "t." She was in Berlin, all right, in a flat just off Unter den Linden. They were fine. Thank God, they were fine. "We are very hopeful," she had written. "I can't wait to be together again. The boys have picked up some German and we are being well cared for. We miss you though."

"Now," said Lisabetta, "we are almost there, I think."

He hadn't wanted to break down in front of her. But he had. "Can't you bring them now?" he sobbed. "Please."

Lisabetta looked sad for a moment. "The papers aren't ready yet. It's not easy. But we'll get them here. Probably through Amsterdam. It's dangerous. Berlin. Difficult. It's not like bringing people out of cities in the west of the country. Berlin is so far in, well, it's surrounded. I'm working on it, Waclaw, really I am, but there's only one shot at these things. If they come up on the Russians' radar . . ." She let the sentence linger in the hot air. "I like these five-pound gold pieces. They aren't so obvious somehow as the guineas."

Waclaw wanted to scream. The coins were perfect. They all were. He even aged them slightly. Victorian guineas hadn't been freshly minted for over fifty years, after all. He was doing a very exacting job. Each coin, though he said it himself, was a masterpiece. The two-pound coins were especially good. "I'm doing my very best."

"And it's wonderful, your best," Lisabetta assured him. "Now, don't worry, Waclaw. You're a master goldsmith and a good one. That's your talent. My talent, well, I'm good at getting people out of Europe. It's a fair swap—one set of skills for another."

Waclaw knew she'd already had her money's worth but he didn't say so.

"Just bring them to me as soon as you can." He smeared his tears across his face. He didn't want to let himself think that he couldn't trust Lisabetta. He didn't want to dwell on the kind of woman she clearly was. She was his only hope. Why wouldn't she do what she said? He'd been damn useful to her after all. When he worried too much, when it became unbearable, he just told himself that it would be easier for her to simply do what she'd agreed. That she might need him again. That it was nothing to her and he'd done so much. Marianne would be here later in the summer. His boys were on their way, perhaps, even now.

The night of the Brighton races, when Manni left the foundry, it was after one. He was tired, he said. It had been a long day and after the day's business he had paperwork to do—bets to write up. Now he just wanted to sleep. Waclaw lit a cigarette and stood in the doorway as Manni's figure disappeared into the still black night. The moon was tiny and the sky was very dark. Waclaw wasn't sure exactly where he was in England but he suspected he was close to the sea. There were gulls most mornings, perched on the roof. It must be warm up there. Now, in the silence, he could swear he heard a rush of waves but perhaps it was only his imagination. He threw the cigarette onto the waste ground and sighed. He'd work if he could but the foundry was noisy to operate so he kept to respectable office hours. There were houses not very far away and they'd complained before—it had been touch and go at the beginning.

Pushing the boundaries of what had become a very

small world, Waclaw took two steps away from the building and lay down on the dry earth, looking up at the sky. As his eyes became accustomed to the light he thought he could pick out some of the stars. The distinctive slant of Orion's belt. He sighed and followed the line of sight to the Pole Star. It was so dark and so quiet, Waclaw wondered if perhaps he should sleep outside tonight. The air was crisp and that was a relief. It had been a mild winter and now spring had arrived. Marianne and the boys were under the same sky. In Berlin the stars would look slightly different, of course, but they'd still be visible. He liked Berlin—he'd been there often before the war when he'd worked for Deutsche Bank and once or twice when he'd done specific jobs for wealthy clients. He remembered being in the Tiergarten and having champagne with an old Jewish man who was delighted to have an ancient Egyptian gold ring conserved. "Such talent. Such wonderful craftsmanship," the man had congratulated him. That old man was probably dead now, he thought sadly. I wonder what happened to his ring?

Then, suddenly, as he daydreamed Waclaw heard a curious sound in the darkness off to his right. He sat up. There it was again. Almost like an animal but he knew there were only a couple of pet dogs nearby—sheepdogs, which sometimes barked. This sounded too deep. It repeated again. It was heavy breathing. Damn it, it was snoring! He sat listening for another moment or two. Whatever it was, it was very close. He squinted into the darkness, made the decision and set off toward one of the old stone outhouses. He hadn't been out of the foundry for weeks. It had affected him, he realized. He was nervous—nervous even walking a few yards! What was this doing to him? He had been a soldier, for heaven's sake, and here he was, heart fluttering at the thought of a walk across a bit of wasteland toward some strange sleeping creature.

The door was locked from the outside with a long rusting bolt. Waclaw drew it back and peered inside the dark shed. The snoring stopped suddenly.

"Hello," he ventured. He made a clicking sound that he hoped seemed friendly, in case it was an animal inside. "Are you in there?"

There was a muffled sound—someone trying to speak.

Waclaw went inside. It was so dark that he lurched straight into the man, who was tied to a chair.

"Oh, I'm sorry." He bent down and felt his way. The man was gagged. He pulled away the dirty strip of cloth. "Are you all right? What has happened?"

"My name is Father Sandor," said a deep voice.

"You're a priest?"

"Yes. Please, will you untie me?"

The man had soiled himself. It was clear he must have been there for a while. As Waclaw struggled with the rope, he questioned what he was doing. But he wasn't prepared to walk away. Leaving someone tied up like this would be wrong. Waclaw had seen a lot of suffering—enough to last a lifetime. The hut stank and it was a smell he had sworn he'd never have to live with again—the stench of piss and crap and unwashed fear.

"Come with me," he said gently. "It's not far and I can help you clean up."

The priest couldn't walk on his own.

"Did they feed you?"

"No."

"Put your arm around me."

They stumbled across the waste ground toward the foundry. As they neared the yellow light of the fire and the gas lamps, Waclaw saw that the man was middle-aged. His lips were flaking and dry, and when he reached out his hands to warm them by the fire, his pink fingers shook. He was wearing priest's robes all right, smeared in mud and worse.

"How long were you in there?" Waclaw asked.

Sandor sank to the ground. "Two days."

Waclaw handed him a tin cup of water and went to fetch some clothes as the priest gulped it down gratefully. The outhouse had been used for a while to store supplies but as the job progressed they needed less storage space. Now, it seemed, Manni was using it as a prison. What had this man done? A priest!

"Do you know why they're holding you?" Waclaw asked.

Sandor studied his rescuer. He licked his lips. "Yes, I know that they murdered a man. I know where the body is. Why are you here?"

Waclaw gestured toward the tools of his trade. "I work here."

Sandor's blue eyes softened in understanding. "They have you? My son," he said in sympathy.

The words stung. Instead of finding a tin of soup for the priest and warming it on the fire, as he had intended, the goldsmith's eyes narrowed in anger. Kindness was too painful. It had been a long time since he had had to endure it. Waclaw picked up one of the pokers he used to stoke the flames and drew it like a sword. What business was it of this old man? The tone of Sandor's voice physically hurt. Waclaw couldn't bear it.

"I'll burn your clothes," he said, "and let you go free. But don't start with all that." No one really cared. No one.

"How long since you slept?" Sandor reached out his hands, palms upward.

Damn him, was it that obvious? Waclaw brought down the poker hard and left a dent in the dirt floor. It did not deter the priest.

"I can pray for you, my son," Sandor said, "but if you like, I'll take you with me."

"Get changed, old man."

The priest did as he was asked, struggling to his feet, loosening his dog collar and throwing it on the fire. Then he unbuttoned his shirt and Waclaw drew in his breath.

On the man's chest there were horrible scars, a tangle of thin white lines criss-crossing the skin above deeper mauve slashes where he had been badly cut and the skin hadn't healed cleanly. Sandor met his eyes but didn't say anything about the injuries. He just kept trying to reach out to Waclaw. The man looked like a burnt-out shell. There might be no apparent scars on his body but Sandor could see that he was wrecked, cut to pieces inside.

"You know they probably intend to kill you. How can they let you live with whatever it is you know? The woman has no emotions, no morals, no decency that I can detect, and I have some skill at finding the good in people. What is your name, my son?"

Waclaw hesitated. "Did they do that to you here?"

Sandor shook his head. "No. That was a long time ago. Another lifetime. And I didn't tell them anything. I shall tell you, though, if you like . . . if you tell me your name."

"Waclaw," he relented.

"Waclaw. Polish?"

The goldsmith nodded.

"Fine work the Polish army did for the Allies. You should be proud. I am Hungarian, of course, but I worked for the British Secret Service in the war. And they are here now, in Brighton. They will help you, Waclaw."

The goldsmith laid down the poker. "She has my wife, Marianne, and our boys. In Berlin. She is finding them passports and papers. She is bringing them here."

"You believe that?" Sandor asked.

The question hung in the hot air and Waclaw did not answer.

Sandor continued. "The Allies are strong in Berlin. Help us and I am sure they will help you. The British are honorable. How long has that woman had you here? Has she given you anything for all your hard work and loyalty?"

Waclaw hesitated. He was so close to completing what he'd started. So close to the passports and the escape

route. And yet he knew what the priest said about Lisabetta was absolutely true. It was far easier for her just to
kill him once the last coin was minted. Of course it was.
He had no leverage—no way to make her do what she had
promised. And then what would happen to his family?

Sandor pulled on a sweater and eased himself out of his
filthy underwear. It smoked when it hit the hot embers.
"I'm sorry," he said. "It isn't pleasant to see a grown man
in his own filth. So, tell me, what exactly is it that you're
doing for them here? I heard hammering. Are you making
something?"

The Pole watched the priest pull on the rough trousers
he'd given him. He thought over everything the man had
said and took a deep breath. He held Marianne's fragile
heart in his hands and pictured the eyes of his children as
he made his decision. The British Secret Service could do
whatever they wanted these days in Europe. The British
Secret Service had won the Allies the war. Lisabetta had
made him wait far too long and she couldn't be trusted.

"I'm making Nazi gold into British coins," he said. "I'm
a goldsmith." He walked over to the corner of the room
and dramatically pulled off the tarpaulin to reveal a small
stack of gold bars sitting against the wall. "We can take
this with us, if you like. To prove it."

22

Where there is a mystery, it is generally suspected there must also be evil.

Vesta ran silently into the middle of the road at Second Avenue and flung her arms around Mirabelle as she made her escape.

"Quick!" Mirabelle instructed, glancing back at the curtained windows on the first floor. "We have to get away!"

"What happened?" Vesta insisted as Mirabelle pulled her onto the pavement. "What did she do?"

"She has a pistol. We have to get off the street. Come on, let's go through the back gardens on the other side of the road. That way the houses will hide us. We can get down to the front and walk along the beach. There's almost no moon and dressed in black no one will be able to see us."

The gardens were bounded by high walls. A dog barked inside one house. In another the lights were still on in the kitchen. The women moved smoothly along the bottom wall. Halfway along, a terrier loose in the garden yapped and jumped up to see them off but couldn't reach.

"Shit!" Vesta swore. "Down, boy, down!"

Mirabelle had her mind on what she'd seen. "Lisabetta is going to get away!" she said. "I think she's leaving the country. Bert is packing up the flat at Cadogan Gardens and sending her things down from London. Lisabetta went into the cupboard and took some chloroform. I have no idea how she intends to use it. We have to find Sandor now."

"And Romana . . ." Vesta said.

"Perhaps she never existed. I think it was Lisabetta who wore that thing. That and a wig perhaps and some different clothes."

"For a thousand pounds? They're making a lot more than that. It doesn't make sense."

"A thousand pounds is still a lot of money." Mirabelle was thinking on her feet. "And, oh, it's being used to pay off Bert, or at least part of it. I saw to that for them. That's quite tidy really. No one has to trust each other. They set it up and then Bert gets his money no matter what happens. I wouldn't trust Lisabetta if I knew she was leaving, would you? This bypasses that. He can trust the Prudential, don't you see? They'll pay out. There never was any debt—it was just a secure way to pay off Bert Jennings for whatever he'd done, whatever he's still doing."

Mirabelle flipped one of the coins from hand to hand while she thought, leaning elegantly against the high wall. "If she's leaving she'll go to Sandor. She'll need to tidy everything up . . . Vesta, we have to follow her."

"We don't have a car!" said Vesta.

Mirabelle raised her shoulders very slightly. "We have to try. I could hide behind that hedge over the road and just see if she does anything, goes anywhere. If it gets light, I can follow in a taxi but it's too quiet now to follow anyone anywhere without being seen."

Vesta nodded. "OK, we can try. But nothing dangerous. You scared the life out of me when you didn't make it to the window."

Mirabelle stopped her with a steady hand on the shoulder. "I should go back on my own. We need an insurance policy, Vesta. It's our turn. You go back to the flat," she said, handing over the key. "Take these," she scooped the coins out of her pocket. "Get a big envelope and put everything inside—the coins, Big Ben's notebook, the betting stubs and our map. The lot. Then write everything down. Every detail you can think of. Address the envelope to Detective Superintendent McGregor. It'll take you a while. Leave it propped up on the mantelpiece. Then come back and find me—I'll be over the road, watching the doctor's house. I'll meet you behind the hedge."

"And if you're not there?"

"Then just wait. Stake out the house. If it's getting light and I've not come back, get dressed and go to the office. If they don't let Sandor ring at the usual time and I still haven't showed up, then pass on the envelope to McGregor. Tell him everything. Only McGregor. You can't trust anyone else. And if I get caught or we both do . . ."

"Then we're betting McGregor will have the wit to find the envelope."

"OK." Vesta hugged Mirabelle. "Be careful," she urged.

"Go! We'll be fine. We might even find him! Walk along the beach, Vesta. That way no one can see you from the road."

Vesta carefully scaled the wall. From the top she saw Mirabelle's shadowy head at the other side of the garden moving back toward the top of the road. The dogs started barking again. With a smile Vesta dropped onto the pavement. The front was deserted and inky black. She checked the gold coins in her pocket and took out one. It gleamed in the lamplight and she flipped it in the air, copying Mirabelle. To the sound of waves on the pebble beach opposite, she crossed the road toward the darkness. She didn't even look at the indistinct outline of the black box on the other side. When the man's voice rang out, her heart lurched and she took a second to be sure where it had come from.

"Well, well, I wonder what someone like you is doing climbing over the back wall of a house on Grand Avenue."

The shadowy figure of a middle-aged constable came into view. He scrutinized Vesta as well as he could in the orange streetlight. Then he stepped out where she could see him properly. In his hand he held a tin cup of steaming tea. He squinted. Through the open door of the police box Vesta could see a broken-down but comfortable-looking chair. The constable had been on a break when she had fallen out of the sky, or rather, over the wall in the distance. He'd dimmed his gaslight and let her walk toward him.

"My, rather exotic, aren't we?"

Vesta looked at the ground.

"Do you live in that house, Miss? Number 2 it would be, I think."

Vesta shook her head.

"I see. Are you in service there?"

"No."

"Well, I think that perhaps it would be best if I took some details and called the station. A bit irregular, this. Name?" The constable put down his tea, reached under his cape and pulled out a notebook.

"It's not illegal to be out at night, is it?" Vesta spluttered.

"Well, Miss, it isn't, but I have my suspicions. There is the unorthodox manner of your appearance on the street. Any explanation for that?"

Vesta glared.

"Right. And I'm guessing you don't live in the area."

"No, but I'm staying with a friend. Farther along." Vesta gestured in the direction of the Lawns. "I don't know the address. It's along there."

"Yes, that's the thing. The system works on names and addresses. And so far you've avoided giving me either. I'll just ring in and see what crimes have been reported. If not we can nip round the local houses—check everyone is all right. Door to door. Identify the thief on the spot as it were.

It's easiest if there has been any disturbance to take you to the premises straight off and see if anyone might recognize you. That's how we like to do these things—on the spot."

"No!" Vesta burst out. Mirabelle would be furious! If the police went door to door and Lisabetta saw Vesta—the woman from the Prudential—Sandor was as good as dead. "Please."

"I beg your pardon?"

"You're treating me like a criminal."

"Well, yes," the constable said. He took a slurp of his tea. "At a little after three fifteen you climbed over the back wall of a property where it would seem you do not reside, and if I'm not mistaken you have a gold item of some kind in your hand. Let me see, Miss." Vesta slowly opened her hand to reveal the gold coin. "We treat that kind of thing as suspicious. It's part of being a policeman, Miss, I imagine, that makes me suspicious about it, but well, we're highly trained to spot these kinds of incidents. I just wonder if the residents of any house reporting missing property this evening might recognize that coin in your possession. Not legal tender, I imagine. Is it yours?"

Vesta stared at the seashore. She calculated her chances and without hesitation took off along the shingle. I only have to make it as far as Mirabelle's, she thought. The constable, however, was quick off the mark. He dropped his cup with a clatter on the pavement and pursued. It was difficult to run on the pebbles but back up on the promenade the lights were brighter and of the two options, Vesta chose darkness. She dodged, trying to disappear, but it didn't take long before he caught her, tackling from behind and wrestling her to the ground. For an old bloke he could move and if it came to a fight he had the advantage of weight.

Vesta hit out but he only caught her fist and forced her down further. He pushed the side of her face onto the rough stones until her skin stung. He was out of breath as he hauled her to her feet. Twisting her arm he led Vesta back to the police box where he handcuffed her to a small rail just inside the door.

"Now, about this coin of yours."

Vesta let out an audible sigh of defeat. She drew the other coins from her pocket. "All right," she said as she handed them over. "I can't explain to you why I have these but you'd better call Detective Superintendent McGregor of the Brighton force, rather than your local station in Hove. They come from a house on Second Avenue. But I don't think he'll want you disturbing the residents. My name is Vesta Churchill, by the way."

The constable looked bemused. "Detective Superintendent McGregor?" he repeated. "For petty theft? I can't imagine he'll be too pleased at this time in the morning."

Vesta checked her watch. It was almost twenty past three. "He wasn't supposed to find out until tomorrow. The coins are headed for him in any case."

"Thing is, you have been apprehended in Hove, Miss. The arresting officer, being myself, is of the Hove force."

Vesta rolled her eyes in exasperation.

"Tell you what, I'll ring for a car," he volunteered. "They'll deal with you at the station and you can call him from there."

"Thank you," Vesta said. At least she wasn't being frog-marched back to number 22. Cursing her luck, she waited in silence for the constable to make the call. She thought of Mirabelle waiting for her. She had so nearly been useful. Still, McGregor would have got the information the following day anyway—this way she'd just tell him the story in person.

The car arrived promptly.

"They'll deal with you at the nick," the man muttered as he bundled the girl into the back. "The sarge can sort it out and send you onto Brighton if he wants. I don't expect anyone will be disturbing Detective Superintendent Mc-Gregor in the middle of the night, to tell you the truth."

There was no time for Vesta to object. The constable passed the coins to the driver who drawled, "Gawd, Fred, you don't reckon there are more of these darkies about, do you?"

"Appears to be just this one," the constable said. "I'll keep an eye out." He duly returned to his beat, or at least, a fresh cup of tea, thankful that he'd controlled the situation. He didn't like having something so untoward on his watch. It felt untidy.

23

Death is not the worst that can happen.

Mirabelle crouched behind the hedge and peered across at the house on Second Avenue. Upstairs a light had come on, first in one of the upstairs bedrooms and then in a second. Lisabetta and the doctor were up and about. The street was absolutely silent now. Mirabelle waited patiently, wondering if perhaps she should sneak over and look through the windows. If only she had a pair of binoculars . . . After about fifteen minutes she resolved to make a circuit of the gardens. She slipped across the road and down the side of the house. The lights were still out at the rear so it looked as if none of the staff had been roused by whatever Lisabetta and the doctor were up to. As she came round the other side of the building, the front door opened and light from the hallway flooded down the path.

Mirabelle flattened herself behind a camellia bush and peeked between the leaves. She saw Lisabetta stride briskly down the front steps and turn up the road. She had changed out of her nightwear into forest-green woolen slacks and saddle shoes with a pale peach cashmere sweater. Her hair had been combed and pinned with an ivory clip to keep it in place. Mirabelle considered what course of action to adopt from her vantage point and decided to let Lisabetta almost reach the top of the road before she followed, but Lisabetta did not get that far. She turned into a lane at the end of the block. Mirabelle knew it was a dead end: just a row of garages and old stable buildings. Sure enough, less than a minute later, she heard a car engine start. Lisabetta drove the doctor's Jaguar back down the road and parked it in front of the house. It was difficult to see in the street—one or two of the lamplights were out—but darker was probably better in the circumstances.

As she switched off the engine Lisabetta inspected herself in the mirror. She tossed her head and gave an open grin. It was the kind of display she seemed able to switch on and off at will—a show of a carefree girl having light-hearted fun. Then, as the expression dropped away, a cold determination returned. Leaving the keys in the ignition she disappeared back into the house. A minute later she returned and stowed two bags in the boot before mounting the steps again and closing the front door behind her.

I wonder why the doctor didn't bring out the cases. It's hardly very gentlemanly, Mirabelle thought. Her heart raced. Lisabetta was getting away! If she let her go, they might never find her again. Bert would send down her things on the first train and after that it was anyone's guess where she'd end up. A sense of tingling outrage spread through Mirabelle's body. What about Sandor? If she lost track of Lisabetta how would she ever find him? Carefully she got up and ran across the pavement, before ducking behind the body of the car to shield herself from sight of the house. If Lisabetta had to wait for the first train why was she leaving so early? There were still at least a couple of hours before dawn broke. Surely those two bags—both quite small—couldn't contain everything she wanted to take with her. No, Mirabelle realized, Lisabetta was on her way somewhere else. To see Manni perhaps? Or even Sandor.

Mirabelle peered into the interior of the car. It was up-holstered with dark leather—two seats at the front and three behind with a deep carpeted indent. Without thinking too clearly, on impulse, she opened the door and slipped into the back, curling up behind the driver's seat. It was, she thought, just as well she'd worn black. A minute passed. Mirabelle shifted—it was hardly a comfortable position. Then she worried. What could be seen from outside? Was her initial reckoning right? Her heart stopped. She squirmed around so that only her dark clothes could be seen from the outside, hiding her pale face and hands. Then she heard the front door of the house creak and slow, heavy steps approach the car.

The passenger seat swung open sharply and Mirabelle caught a glimpse of Lisabetta maneuvering something bulky into the front seat. She was carrying it over her shoulder. As she positioned it into place Mirabelle realized it was the doctor's body. His hand, in a smart driving glove, dropped onto the handbrake. Lisabetta had clearly administered the chloroform.

"There, there," Lisabetta whispered as she pushed the doctor's limbs into a sitting position. He was dressed in the same buff trousers and tweed jacket he'd worn when Mirabelle had had her consultation. Lisabetta was crooning, as if he were a child. "There you go. Into your car. Such a lovely car."

There was an ominous pause.

"Eric, have you left this car to someone?" Lisabetta slapped the doctor and a sharp crack rang out. She bent over him now like some dark angel bent on her purpose. "Eric! Do you have a will?"

The doctor stirred and sat up blearily, looking around in complete incomprehension.

"Do you have a will, Eric?" she repeated.

"No," he slurred. "Never got married, you see. No family."

"Pity."

He squirmed, trying to get up, but it was no use. Chloroform left you woozy for a while and Lisabetta was already administering another dose. He tried to push her off as she held the handkerchief over his mouth but he didn't have the strength. As he fell back heavily into the seat Lisabetta clicked his door closed.

Mirabelle twisted, trying to get as comfortable as possible. Once Lisabetta was in the driving seat she mustn't move an inch. Her face contorted with fear as the door on the driver's side opened and Lisabetta took her place.

"So," she said, switching on the engine, "where shall we go, Eric?"

The doctor was out cold but Lisabetta chatted as if they were off for a holiday in the country. "If I can't have your car, I might as well wreck it. Drive it into the sea. Or at least you can!"

Mirabelle's heart somersaulted.

"A little bit psychopathic? Perhaps sociopathic? Ah, such diagnoses! Have you been laughing at me, Eric? I do hope not."

The car pulled away from the curb. Stripes of light and shade flickered over Mirabelle as the Jag moved in and out of the amber pools cast by the streetlights. Then Lisabetta turned left onto the front.

"I'll tell that horrible little maid of yours that you had to go up to London unexpectedly," Lisabetta explained. "I packed everything you would have taken for a couple of days. They won't suspect a thing until it's far too late. There are a couple of dangerous corners along the coast. Not on the direct route to London but not so far away. I'll be back before they even get up. I'll say I'm going up to town myself. 'Dr. Crichton went up to London in the middle of the night,' I'll say. 'An emergency. He took the car.'" Lisabetta laughed. "London is such a dreary city. It smells. I swear! It's time for somewhere completely new, Eric. And I have so many grateful clients in Buenos Aires and Santiago—and sunshine. I'd like some sunshine!"

The Jag purred as she speeded up. The car glided past the Grand Hotel and then the pier. Mirabelle was terrified that she wouldn't be able to get out before Lisabetta wrecked it. There was nothing she could do but hope. Once the town was passed it was impossible to tell in which direction they were moving until at last Lisabetta stopped. She pulled on the hand brake, switched off the engine and slipped outside. Mirabelle waited a moment and then decided to raise her head. It was a risk but she couldn't simply stay hidden. The car might go over a cliff any moment. Hardly able to breathe she rose slowly and peered out of the back window. It wasn't a cliff top at all. Lisabetta's figure was receding over a waste ground, past a row of derelict houses. Mirabelle sighed with relief and nudged the doctor sharply. "Come on!" she said, giving his shoulder a shake. "She's going to kill you! You have to wake up!"

The doctor didn't move. Mirabelle looked around frantically. There was nothing here. No one to help. She opened the car door and slipped outside. Across the wasteland Lisabetta let out a stifled scream of what sounded like frustration. Mirabelle took in the details. It was open scrub. About fifteen minutes from town, she calculated. This was the place they had been looking for! This must be where Sandor was being held!

"I'll come back," she whispered to the doctor's comatose figure as she crept away, low across the landscape.

Sure enough there was an outhouse—in fact, there were three or four dotted across the scrubland, two stone-built and another couple, more like small wooden sheds. And, she thought, it's warm here. Vesta had mentioned that. Then she heard Lisabetta's gun fire. Mirabelle panicked and rolled the last few yards in a scramble toward the main outhouse. The walls were warm to the touch. She sneaked toward the open door and peered inside. It was a foundry. A proper smelting fire was built in the middle of the makeshift space. Some of the embers had lit up where Lisabetta had disturbed them by firing her bullet, presumably in temper. Lisabetta was on her knees in front of some makeshift cupboards. She was searching for something, swearing under her breath. "Always like this at the end," Mirabelle heard her grumble. "Pah!"

She clearly didn't find what she was looking for and Mirabelle only just managed to pull out of the way as Lisabetta burst out of the building and picked her way over to a hut nearby. The door was open. "Pah!" Lisabetta said again as she gave the interior a cursory check. Then she moved on, clattering through the door of another of the little storage units. "Ah," she said delightedly, finding something she was looking for at last, "at least you are still here. Perhaps you might like to take a drive in the moonlight, yes?"

The woman was clearing her path, wiping her slate clean—this would be the time to destroy all and any evidence. If Lisabetta took Sandor with her it would be difficult to rescue him, especially if she used the chloroform. Desperately Mirabelle looked around. Back toward the car she could just make out a tabby cat picking its way across the scrub. She picked up a stone and threw it hard, hitting soft fur. The cat yowled and scrambled out of the way. Mirabelle raised another stone and fired again, this time felling a tottering pile of earth and small rocks that rolled down a small incline. It sounded as if there was someone moving near the car.

Lisabetta turned, abandoned the hut and strode back toward the road to see what had made the noise. It wouldn't take her long to ascertain that the doctor was still unconscious and there was nobody around. Mirabelle didn't hesitate. She sprinted toward the hut and grabbed the crouching figure inside.

"Come on, Sandor," she said, adrenaline pumping through her system. "We have to get you out of here." She slit the thin bonds with her flick-knife and pulled him outside. "This way," she whispered.

They headed to the rear of the foundry, crouched down and then Mirabelle peered toward the car.

Lisabetta, having found nothing awry and the doctor still out cold, was making her way back. In temper she jerked the hut door aside and then howled as she found it empty. She darted outside. The scrubland looked deserted and there was no way to distinguish footprints on the rough muddy ground. She made a quick calculation and then ran back toward the road to search for the escapee.

"People would normally make for the road," Mirabelle explained, keeping her voice low. "The other way there are only houses. She'll assume we've headed for the street and made a run for it—you'll see."

And then Mirabelle gasped. In the moonlight it was clear that the figure she'd rescued wasn't Sandor at all. The figure was female—a slender girl. A series of possibilities rushed through her mind.

"Are you Romana Laszlo?" she asked, but, before the girl could reply, Mirabelle realized that she'd seen her before.

"Who's Romana Laszlo?"

"Of course," Mirabelle whispered as it fell into place.

She checked around the edge of the wall. Lisabetta was cursing from the direction of the street. The car engine fired and the women saw the reflection of the headlights in the night sky as Lisabetta turned the vehicle and cast the beams over the scrubland. The two women fell back and froze in the darkness of their hiding place. A rabbit sat up on its hind legs, unable to move in the glare of the beam. It was difficult to breathe and impossible to move but Mirabelle realized that by creating light Lisabetta had blinded herself to the things she might otherwise have been able to pick out in the darkness. After a minute or so she seemed to have concluded that the girl had made her escape in the other direction. The beams turned back to the road and she drove away. As the noise of the engine receded Mirabelle surprised herself by thinking fleetingly of Detective Superintendent McGregor. He'd tried to stop her going anywhere near these people. Well, he couldn't get his way now. She smiled with quiet satisfaction before she spoke.

"You're one of Lisabetta's girls, aren't you?" Mirabelle kept her voice low. "The one who went upstairs with Señor Velazquez."

Delia had stayed alive because her instincts had always been good and she had always trusted them. She'd fought when she had to fight; she'd hidden when she had to hide. She'd traced the Candlemaker all across Europe and done what she had to do to get close enough to kill him. She just hadn't got away fast enough. Nonetheless she still trusted her instincts.

"Yes, it was me," she admitted, "though I'm not one of Lisabetta's girls any more."

Mirabelle checked the road—the sound of the car was fading. "We should wait here for a while to make sure the coast is clear."

They sat, listening in silence and checking in all directions, until Mirabelle nodded and the women slipped inside the foundry. The girl was filthy and bedraggled. She ran to a bucket of water in the corner and cupped the liquid in her hands, speaking as she drank. "Thanks," she said, and once her thirst was slaked she carefully washed her face and her hands.

Mirabelle looked around. There were some cans of soup on a shelf behind the door. "Are you hungry?" The girl nodded. Mirabelle opened a can and carefully laid it on the hottest embers. Then she sat beside the fire.

"Who did you think I was?" the girl asked as she sat down by the fire.

"I was looking for a friend—a man. But when I saw you I thought you might be a girl called Romana Laszlo. It was foolish of me. She was supposed to be Lisabetta's sister.

I've been searching for her but, well, if she existed at all, she's practically a ghost."

"I've never heard of her."

"I don't think anyone has. It's just, when I found you, well, I wondered."

"Ghosts can be tricky," Delia smiled. "Very demanding. Are you army? Police?"

"No. My name's Mirabelle Bevan." She held out her hand. "I work in a debt collection office."

The girl didn't falter. She took Mirabelle's hand and shook it firmly. "I'm Delia Beck."

"Your name is German, Miss Beck."

"I am German," Delia said evenly. "Well, I was."

It occurred to Mirabelle that this was the first time anyone involved with Lisabetta had admitted to their nationality. She said nothing and stirred the soup.

"Do you know where we are?" Delia looked out the door across the scrubland.

"Brighton, or just outside it," Mirabelle said. "Why did they bring you here?"

Delia lifted a tin spoon and tasted the heating soup with some relish. "They found me at the train station—I wasn't quick enough to get away. I hadn't realized she'd come for me. Stupid, of course. I'd spent the day shopping and was getting the train back to London. Then they turned up. Lisabetta was furious. At first she thought it was an accident and was just angry that I'd left. But, well, I still had the syringe in my purse. It was very quick—they put me in a car and brought me here. They were going to kill me, I expect, but I'd still have done it no matter what. I'd do it again tomorrow. He deserved to die."

Mirabelle knelt beside the fire. "You mean that you killed Señor Velazquez?" she said slowly, piecing it together. "Not Lisabetta."

"Oh, yes. That man had done . . ." Delia hesitated, her voice very low, ". . . extremely bad things. He was a monster.

Not that Lisabetta cared." Delia's eyes were clear and her voice was steady. "Will you arrest me? I'm not afraid of a British jail. Or the death sentence. It was justice and I'd be proud to die for that. Did you take part in your country's war effort, Miss Bevan?"

Mirabelle's blood ran cold. This girl was quite extraordinary. "Are you saying that man was . . ."

"Yes. He was SS. He was a Commandant. Are you going to arrest me? Civilians can do that here, can't they?"

Mirabelle thought she might sink into the ground. She'd left all this behind or, at least, she thought she had. Now it felt like standing on a precipice with Auschwitz on one side and Nuremberg on the other. She shook her head. "I only want to talk to you," she said under her breath. "I have to find out what they're doing. I'm looking for my friend, Sandor. He's a priest. Hungarian. Have you seen him?"

"No," Delia shook her head, "I've never heard that name or seen Lisabetta with a priest."

"May I say that you don't seem like a murderer, Miss Beck."

Delia shook her head sadly. "I had to," she said. "It was just him. The courts can have the rest but I lost my people . . . my family." She faltered. "If you'd ever lost someone, you'd understand."

Mirabelle shuddered. It wasn't a decision she'd ever had to take. Jack's death had been bad enough. "So, no more on your list?"

Delia smiled wryly and shook her head.

Mirabelle thought for a moment. She had the sudden realization that Delia was what Jack used to call "a door." You use the door, get the information you want and then you lock it behind you. Mirabelle wasn't going to turn in anyone for killing an SS Commandant when only a few years before she had been training and equipping people to undertake that kind of mission. Any Nazi officers left evading the courts at this stage of the game deserved whatever came their way. Jack had taught her well and she kept her eye on the ball. She'd go through the door all right. "You know what they're up to, don't you? You know what's going on. What Lisabetta is doing."

Delia nodded. "It's about washing them clean, Miss Bevan. Money. Papers. That's what Lisabetta does. She'll do it for anyone. Even someone like him. Plenty of people want to cross the new borders. Plenty of people want to get out: SS, collaborators, turncoats. I waited for him. I let her pick me up in Amsterdam and then came to London to work. I knew he'd turn up eventually. She's the best and he'd want the best. They'd never have caught him. It was up to me."

"And so you know all about Lisabetta's operation?"

"Lisabetta is very good at moving people around, if they've the money to pay her. Sounds simple, doesn't it? It isn't. But she gets them out and she'll make the trip a pleasant one—the attention of men, women or children if they prefer. Champagne and caviar. A nice painting or trips to the theater. The money makes me sick. But she washes them clean again—them and whatever they stole!"

"So she's laundering money. All the coins?"

Delia took a mouthful of soup then reached inside her shoe to draw a guinea from the lining. "Yes. Made from Nazi gold. Like this one. I took it from him. A coin for the hangman. They all have gold and loot. She legitimizes it for them. And then there are the paintings, the statues, illegal currency and God knows what else. People are nothing if not inventive when stealing the treasures of the dead."

Mirabelle's mind was buzzing. Of course that's what Lisabetta was up to. Of course. It was time to close the door. "Miss Beck, if the police catch you they will charge you. The best thing would be for you to leave the country immediately. It makes no difference whether the old man died of natural causes or not. You need to get out as soon as you can. And if you still have your weapon you need to dispose of it."

"Who are you?"

"I haven't lied," Mirabelle said calmly. "I'm Mirabelle Bevan and I work in a debt collection agency. I used to be something else. Someone else. Like you, I suppose—people are so different in wartime. No one gets to be ordinary. Not really. This is the end of your war, isn't it, though? I do hope so."

"I suppose it is," said Delia. "I've been running a bit later than everyone else."

"Well," said Mirabelle, "I suggest we clean you up and get you to a train station—a small one, this time. You shouldn't use the main stations, you know. Never. It might even be sensible to catch a bus up to town. If we get you to London, can you take it from there?"

"Yes, thank you. I have an Irish friend there who can help. I want to go to America. That was my plan."

Mirabelle picked up a poker and jabbed disconsolately at the embers as she considered. Then she noticed at one edge there was a tiny corner left of something that had been burned. It was distinctive—a buttonhole in the shape of a little cross on starched white cotton. It was Sandor's dog collar. He'd been here.

"Come on," she said, "we have to leave."

you thought you might come across some Peek Frean's while you were taking the air?"

"It's a five-pound gold coin. And a sovereign. A two-pound coin. And a guinea."

"I know. Are they yours, Miss Churchill?"

Vesta shook her head. "It's evidence."

"Ah, well, at least we agree on something. There was a lot of dodgy currency around town just before Christmas last year, I recall. These, you will be relieved to hear, are real, however. We checked. Solid gold. I understand you told the arresting officer you had taken them from a house on Second Avenue."

"Not me," Vesta said, "Mirabelle."

"I see. She did the housebreaking—you're only the fence."

"Oh, for heaven's sake," said a cold voice from behind the detective superintendent.

"He won't let me speak!" Vesta cried, delighted to see Mirabelle in the passageway outside the cell.

She looked exhausted. Still, a tendril of hair had worked its way out of her chignon and hung down her cheek, highlighting her huge eyes and the translucence of her skin.

"Ah, Miss Bevan," McGregor said. "Good morning. Of course you're here as well! Obstructing police business again?"

Mirabelle ignored the jibe. "We need to speak to you. Are you so pigheaded that you can't just listen? I walked for miles to get here and I've been waiting for almost an hour. When someone said Vesta's name upstairs, I insisted on being brought down . . ."

McGregor cast a look at the constable who had accompanied Mirabelle to the lock-up. "Well, that's most irregular for a start."

"Sorry, sir," the man mumbled.

It was too late now. "You better get back to the desk. I'll deal with this," McGregor snapped.

The constable disappeared gratefully back upstairs.

24

Advice to agents: Your life depends on your ability to tell your cover story unhesitatingly.

Whether it was the morning light streaming through the bars high on the wall or the sound of the locks scraping back, Vesta couldn't be sure what actually woke her in her police cell. As she opened her eyes blearily there was a tall man in a mackintosh standing in the doorway.

"Miss Churchill, I understand you wanted to see me?"

"Are you McGregor?"

"Yes, Detective Superintendent McGregor. And I don't normally deal with housebreaking." He was in a filthy mood. "Quite a stir you caused last night. Having them transfer you between stations. This better be worth it, young lady."

"Yes, sir. Well, I work in Halley Insurance—in the same building as Mirabelle Bevan," Vesta started.

"Mirabelle Bevan!" McGregor burst out. "My proverbial bad penny! What, are there two of you poking your noses in now? Bloody women! Is that all it is?"

"It's very important!" Vesta insisted.

McGregor interrupted. "As important as these?" He produced Vesta's coins from his pocket. "Or were these just some pocket money in case you needed a little something while you were out? A pint of milk? Or you're rather partial to biscuits, as I understand it from the night shift. Perhap

McGregor sighed. "Ladies, you have my full attention. What is it?"

Mirabelle strode into the cell and motioned toward the door, which McGregor closed. "What we've come across is dangerous information, Detective Superintendent. It was only last night I found out precisely how dangerous. So, first of all, before I tell you what I know, I need reassurance. We have to contain this information. A man's life is at stake. Can we trust you?"

McGregor sat up straight. "Is it Ben? Do you know where he is?"

Mirabelle shook her head. "Ben's the reason I'm here, though. Inside this police station, well, it's a rat trap, isn't it? There are leaks all over the place. But you knew Ben and you were kind enough to try to find him. So, I'm giving you a chance. Can we trust you?"

McGregor took off his hat. The woman was being logical, at least. "Look, I know people don't always trust the police in these parts and that working for McGuigan you might well have been exposed to some of the more unreliable elements of the Sussex Constabulary. But you two are no housebreakers, I know that. And Ben is still missing. I'm hoping this information of yours isn't just some histrionic female story. Because so far none of what you're intimating makes any bloody sense. So, yes, you can trust me but it's up to you whether you choose to do so."

Mirabelle's eyes betrayed only the merest flicker of annoyance. Then, from the bed, Vesta's voice rang out. She had snapped. "It does make sense! Really it does! Everything we're on to! Mr. McGuigan isn't missing, Detective Superintendent. He's dead in a false grave. They buried him," she said, standing up straight as a rod. Like a kid explaining a dream to her parents, the words came burbling out all at once, spilling over each other. "These people are monsters. And Mirabelle wanted to handle it on her own, but we can't. We're just two women. And this is a whole lot of trouble. Insurance fraud and all sorts. And there are all those coins. These people, they just make up other people—a complete fake identity that they can kill off if they want to—you've no idea! All for money! And now they've kidnapped Father Sandor from the Church of the Sacred Heart and they said if we went to you they'd kill him. But they are going to kill him anyway, aren't they? That's the truth. And we tried to find him last night and Mirabelle almost got caught, but we're out of leads and we can't do it on our own—I mean, that's what we were trying when your constable pulled me in, but God knows where they've got him. Lisabetta has a gun! And I'm supposed to be back at my desk in the office at one so they can phone me and let me speak to Sandor. And I'm worried, petrified, actually. I don't think you're bent. I think you're a decent bloke. Promise me you'll help because I don't want them to kill Sandor. Not after everything else!"

Mirabelle's eyes burned. "Vesta!" she spluttered. McGregor would never take them seriously now.

But, to her surprise, the detective superintendent moved across the cell and checked outside the door before closing it again firmly. "Lock this, will you?" he said to the guard through the grille. "I'll bang when I want out."

McGregor waited until the guard had moved back to his post at the end of the corridor. Then he sat down at the end of the bed. "Right, Miss Churchill, that's a lot of information all at once and I'm not really following it. Did you say Father Sandor? Because that's the priest who was reported missing yesterday by one of his colleagues at the church. How is he caught up in all this? Why don't you just tell me everything you know, from the very beginning? Slowly."

"You think you might be able to stop them killing him?"

"I hope so."

"Because they killed Ben McGuigan. They strangled him,

and it's difficult to kill a big man like that, even if you get behind him," she burbled.

"You're sure Ben's dead?"

McGregor turned to Mirabelle, in search of some sense. She nodded agreement, her head bowed. "Yes, I think they murdered Big Ben because he was onto what they were doing at the racecourse," she confirmed sadly. "It's a very long story, I'm afraid, Detective Superintendent."

"Well, let's give it a try. You couldn't do a worse job than Miss Churchill here."

Vesta sighed, frustrated, and slumped onto the mattress as Mirabelle took a deep breath.

"It's a criminal operation—clever and very complex. First of all they're involved in prostitution but that isn't where the real money is. That's only a sideline. Really they are accommodating ex-SS men, political refugees, collaborators—anyone with money who has to get out of Europe. Señor Velazquez—he was SS. He was the Commandant of a concentration camp. I don't know which one."

Vesta squealed. "You mean they were Nazis! And I walked right into it. Shit, look at the color of me!"

"Well, so far," Mirabelle pointed out, "we've only found one Nazi and he's dead, but I think there have been others. Lisabetta is at the head of it. She provides papers and more importantly a clearing house for dirty money and stolen goods. Very high end. They're laundering the money at Fairfield Road through Manni Williams. Ben was onto them. That's why they killed him. So the scam at the races isn't really about making money at all—it's about cleaning dirty currency and giving it back as a payout minus Manni's fee. And there's something going on with gold coins, too—there are gold coins everywhere. Anyway, these people come to London then Lisabetta and her team clean them and send them on their way, for a hefty percentage, of course. And now she's pulling out and we got

192 Sara Sheridan

entangled. It's the end of her operation, here at any rate. She's leaving.

"When we first got onto it Ben had an inquiry on a defaulted loan. It was fake. The whole point of it was to legitimize a payment that Lisabetta wanted to be made to a guy in London. Bert Jennings. Bert is a legitimate creditor on the estate of one Romana Laszlo. Romana didn't exist—she's just an insurance scam on a life policy. Fake lying in, fake death—everything. And Ben ended up in Romana's grave—easy for them to dispose of him that way. His body is in the graveyard at the Church of the Sacred Heart and the priest—Sandor, the guy that's missing—they kidnapped him to stop Vesta from blowing the whistle. I found the place last night where they'd been holding him. It's on Hangleton Road, on the A2036. There's a foundry there where they've been smelting gold, I expect, and minting those gold coins. Sandor was gone and the place was deserted. I thought he might have got away but if he had turned up back at the church you'd know by now, wouldn't you?"

"I'd hope so," McGregor said. "So, let's get this straight, shall we? Do you know where Sandor is?"

"No," Mirabelle shook her head.

"As far as you're aware, who last saw him?"

"Vesta and Manni—Manni was the one who kidnapped both of them, on Lisabetta's say-so. Then he let Vesta go to legitimize the claim at the insurance company."

"And who else is involved?"

"Dr. Crichton, Lisabetta—I don't have a last name—and Bert Jennings. And Manni Williams. That's all I know."

"Dr. Crichton? At the head of it? And that woman who is staying at his house?"

"No, the other way round—Lisabetta is in charge. I think Crichton fell foul of her. Last night she drugged him and she may have driven his car off a cliff along the London Road. I couldn't stop her. She's pulling out—I heard her phone London and arrange for her things to be sent down to Brighton on the first train this morning. She's going to leave the country. Soon."

"Right." McGregor held out his hand to stop Mirabelle from saying anything else. He was thinking. He stood up and paced backward and forward beside the bed. Then he turned and stared at Mirabelle. It seemed unlikely that an elegant and rather fetching woman like Miss Bevan would know about these things but you could tell straight away that she was at home in this environment. There was something impressive about her. And, his senses tingled, if what she said were true, this would be the biggest case he'd ever handled. He could shine but he had to be careful to qualify what was and wasn't accurate. Women, after all, tended toward the vibrant imagination and some of these ideas were, well, vibrant in the extreme.

There was one thing Mirabelle and Vesta were definitely right about, though. Whatever he did, he'd have to use men he could really trust. Then it came to him. McGregor smiled. For once it would be easy. Anyone he wasn't sure of he could send to Fairfield Road and then he'd put together a small team to verify Mirabelle's information. They could work down here, to start with. Out of the way. He'd only speak to the guys he knew were absolutely straight. There could be no leaks and no backhanders. Too many criminals had got away with too much in Brighton. That was set to change. And now he could prove that his men could be effective despite the corruption—the Sussex Constabulary was already miles ahead of the shambles it had been in when he first arrived.

"So," he said, "if I'm understanding you correctly, priority number one is to find Father Sandor and then arrest Lisabetta, Dr. Crichton if he's alive, Manni of course and this . . ."

"Bert Jennings," Vesta chipped in helpfully.

Mirabelle nodded.

With a stern expression McGregor banged for the door

to be opened. He called for the duty sergeant who'd worked at the station for twenty-five years—one of the few men who hadn't been implicated in the scandals. He'd suffered for it, too—McGregor had heard he'd been beaten up a couple of times for refusing to turn a blind eye.

"Simmons," he said, "I'd like the file on that missing priest—everything we've got. I need a uniformed officer to go over to the train station and find out everything that came down on the early train from Victoria by way of cargo. I want a comprehensive list. Early papers, the lot. Check out any complaints or disturbances on the Hangleton Road over the last few months. And I'll need Gourlay, Michaels and Richardson down here, please, but first everyone else can go to the racecourse. Get them on the case up there, and then we'll get cracking."

"I think you should run Lisabetta's details through the ICPC," Mirabelle said.

McGregor looked up. "Bit young," he pointed out, "but then, if this is all true, she started young, didn't she?"

"What's the ICPC?" Vesta piped up. Ever since Mirabelle had said the word "Nazis" she had sat on the bed feeling rather shell-shocked.

"International Criminal Police Commission," McGregor told her. "I suppose it would do no harm."

"I'm sure she'll have changed her name several times," Mirabelle conceded, "but you never know."

"Good idea. And we can try this other identity—Romana Laszlo—too. Who knows which name Lisabetta was using first. Simmons, could you get Gourlay to do that? And send down some tea and bacon rolls, would you? Miss Churchill appears to be on the verge of starvation, poor thing."

As the door closed he turned to the women. "Don't worry," he said. "I'll send you home soon and we can get on."

"Don't you need our help?" Vesta insisted.

"We need information, Miss Churchill, but this isn't a job for amateurs. There is no point in you sitting in the station all day."

McGregor took out a pen and paper and began to chart Lisabetta's operation. "They'd need a lot of people to pull all this off, you know. Are you sure that Lisabetta is capable of being at the head of it?"

Mirabelle nodded. "Pretty sure."

"I met her at the Grand, you know. She *cried*," McGregor recalled. "She was crying about the Spaniard who died. Friend of the family."

Mirabelle stared at him with naked derision. "You think there's a man in the background? You think that with a pretty girl there has to be. When I worked in the service some of our best spies were women. Don't guess what a woman is capable of by the front she shows you, Detective Superintendent. There may be a man behind Lisabetta, I have no idea, but there needn't be just because she's young and pretty. God knows what she has done. By my reckoning she was in her midteens toward the end of the war—looking like she does, stuck somewhere near Poland, if my reckoning is right on her accent, when the Russians rumbled through. If she got out of the country, that alone makes her very tough. No, she's more than capable of running this on her own and I'm sure the ICPC will have a file on her."

McGregor nodded curtly. He had to admit it. He'd never met a woman like Mirabelle Bevan before—she was quite remarkable. Inspiring, even.

He turned around his notebook and showed Mirabelle what he'd sketched—a charge sheet in the form of a flow chart with money coming from prostitution, sale of false papers, insurance fraud, laundering of illegal currency and valuables, involving murder, kidnapping and blackmail.

"You'll find the proof. You'll see," she said. "There are lists of missing Nazis where I used to work at Whitehall and there are agencies still looking for them. I worked on the files for Nuremberg. Velazquez will be on one of those lists. You can track him down from there."

There was a sharp knock on the cell door. Sergeant Simmons entered with a plate of bacon rolls in one hand and a sheaf of papers in the other. Behind him three men were waiting in the narrow passageway.

McGregor acknowledged them and then cast his eye over the notes.

"We're going to work down here, sir?" one man questioned. "In the women's cells?"

"For now," McGregor said sternly. "Yes."

Vesta took a bacon roll from the pile and chewed it methodically, perched on the edge of the bed.

"Looks like you're right," McGregor said to Mirabelle as he carefully checked his notes. "The ICPC is sending two officers from St. Cloud. They have a couple of possible pseudonyms for Lisabetta. Nothing arrived on the early train from London though, apart from newspapers and a couple of deliveries from Selfridges—furniture and such. Oh, and there have been several complaints over the last few months about hammering noises at your premises on Hangleton Road. Claims to be a foundry making iron railings that opened in January. Originally they were working at night. Looks like they've been at it for some time. Do you have any idea where else she might have been operating?"

"I know she was in Amsterdam, and she said she had been shopping in Paris, but she comes from Eastern Europe, though probably not Hungary, where she claims. I can't tie down her accent, but it seems more Austrian or Eastern German—maybe somewhere on the Polish border. My guess is that her background will be in prostitution—it's a way into this whole world, isn't it? It would only take one client to make her realize she can charge through the nose. She seems obsessed by money—and, well, that's prostitutes for you."

Vesta looked at her feet and Mirabelle thought she detected a blush.

"Right, well, I'm just about ready to brief everyone, I think. First priority will be to find the priest."

"We want to help, you know . . ." Mirabelle offered. "You're short-handed, and both Vesta and I would willingly volunteer."

McGregor shook his head and a dark look crossed his face. It was similar to the look Ben McGuigan had when he last left the office, Mirabelle thought. Perhaps McGregor was trying to protect her, just like Ben.

"You're two ladies," McGregor said.

"Two ladies who figured the whole thing out and handed it to you on a plate," Mirabelle remonstrated.

"You never heard of Mata Hari?" Vesta chipped in. "She's got nothing on Mirabelle. Didn't you hear where she used to work?"

"No," McGregor repeated, "and I'm sending you two home. You've done enough. You could have got yourself killed last night, both of you—housebreaking and God alone knows what else. It's too dangerous. I won't be responsible for civilians. And I need to get to the racecourse if we want to get Manni in the cells. Simmons, send these two home, would you? We'll call if we need you, ladies. And we will need you—only later."

25

X2: the counterintelligence and agent-manipulation branch of the Secret Service.

In the back of the car on the way to the Lawns Mirabelle couldn't stop thinking about Jack. He always said you couldn't predict what was going to happen for one simple reason: people. "If the universe was scientific and just left to itself, then we'd have statistical probabilities to rely on. But once people are involved it becomes much more problematic because they're erratic. People do crazy things that don't make sense."

Mirabelle had only been seeing Jack for six months and that night, back at his quarters, they had been drinking Campari. It was dreadful stuff but the whiskey had run out. Jack promised he'd cook dinner and then arrived home with a brown paper bag containing six precious eggs. He'd planned to whisk them into an omelette with an onion and some thyme, which grew plentifully in an herb box outside the window. He often came back "all thinky" from work and as he spoke Mirabelle presumed he was trying to explain some of the acts of bravery that had helped the Allies. She sipped the vivid red drink in her highball glass sparingly.

"People fall in love, you see," Jack continued with a

cheeky grin, "and then they don't behave logically. Have you ever heard of David Hume?"

She was taken aback. Jack hadn't said anything about love before. Mirabelle shook her head.

"Hume's a Jock philosopher," Jack continued as if this wasn't a landmark. "He said that you can see a thousand white swans but you still don't know that white is the only color of the swan. You can see white swans all your life, and the more you see, the more you're sure, statistically, that all swans are white. It's logical. You think you can rely on it. But all it takes is one black swan and everything changes. It's a bolt from the blue. Something you aren't expecting and you have to start from scratch. You're my black swan, Belle. I love you. And now things will never be the same for me."

She hadn't been able to speak. She'd just wrapped her arms around him and, as far as she could remember, they ended up having the eggs for breakfast the following morning.

"We're short a black swan," Mirabelle mumbled as they went up the stairs and Vesta scrabbled in her pocket for the key.

"God, I hope they get him out alive," Vesta whispered as the police car pulled away.

It was a gray overcast morning. Mirabelle squeezed her hand. The desk sergeant had promised he'd keep them informed: "All you have to do is wait by the phone, Miss Bevan."

"There's nothing for it but to sit it out now," she said, sounding downhearted, as Vesta put the key in the lock. "He seems competent enough." She checked her watch.

"I need a bath," Vesta said.

"Now that is a good idea. I think I have some bath salts. Orange stuff. It would be good to relax."

They were only just moving over the threshold when out of nowhere the man appeared. At first what was happening didn't register properly. Mirabelle felt herself being pushed forcefully through the doorway and bundled into the hall. Vesta cried out and was shoved in behind. Mirabelle fumbled for the flick-knife in her pocket. And then, in a second, they both saw with a flood of relief who the unshaven figure in worn work clothes was.

"Sandor! Sandor!"

He was safe. They flung their arms around him, buoyed up with joy. It seemed too good to be true.

Mirabelle's face flushed as she breathed in the smell of burning embers and sweat from his skin. If Sandor was alive everything would be all right. "Thank God," she whispered and she felt the tension in her shoulders release.

It was only when Mirabelle and Vesta drew back that they noticed there was another man—rough-looking and carrying a heavy bag.

"Ah, yes," Sandor grinned, proud at the reaction he'd provoked, "Waclaw helped me escape. We have been waiting here for you for hours—almost all night! We watched until you came home. We did not want to show ourselves to the uniformed officers. Just in case."

Vesta burst into tears. "I was so worried," she sobbed, "so very worried. It's wonderful to see you, Sandor."

"I'm fine, my child." Sandor comforted her, putting an arm around her shoulders. "All safe now. And I come with news for your operation."

Mirabelle shook Waclaw's hand enthusiastically. "Polish?" she asked.

He nodded.

"You're very welcome here. Come upstairs," Mirabelle said. "Follow me."

Inside, the men inspected Mirabelle's drawing room without saying a word, Vesta mopped her tears and went to put on the kettle, and Mirabelle rang the station from the telephone in the hallway. McGregor was in a radio car, the desk sergeant said. He'd make sure the message was passed on.

"Tell him that I have found Sandor. Sandor is with me. He can move straight to his other business."

"Other business? Sandy? Right."

"No. No. S.A.N.D.O.R. You must tell him straight away. It's very important."

"Right, Miss," and the policeman hung up.

Mirabelle glided back into the drawing room feeling energetic despite her sleepless night. She smiled broadly. Sandor had taken a seat and Waclaw hovered by the window.

"They were going to mount a search to pick you up this morning. I'm so glad you're safe. It took us a while to track down where you were last night and then when I found it, you were gone. We've had no sleep," she said apologetically. "I should have known that you were more than capable of making your own way."

"Ah, the British! You can always rely on the British. Just like the old days!" Sandor said delightedly.

"Not quite the same," Mirabelle replied as Vesta arrived with a tray of hot tea. "The police are not of the same caliber as Jack, you know."

Waclaw gratefully accepted a cup of tea. He looked over at Sandor, silently requesting permission to speak.

Sandor nodded. "You can trust Mirabelle. And we should get down to business now."

Waclaw hesitated for only a moment and then took a deep breath. "I need you to help me," he said gruffly. "My wife is in Berlin with our children. Two children. Boys. I will tell you everything but you have to get them out. Bring them here."

Mirabelle stared. "Berlin?" she said vaguely.

"Yes!" The man was understandably passionate. "They are in a flat near Unter den Linden. I have to bring them to the West. We are Polish and we cannot go home. We need passports."

Sandor sat back in his armchair with a contented expression. He was at peace. "Waclaw helped me escape. He is a goldsmith. He has been working for this Lisabetta woman that you are after. He will make a wonderful informant."

"My wife is Marianne Gorski," Waclaw started. He drew a crumpled envelope from his pocket. "She wrote only a few days ago. I received this. My boys are Udi and Mikhail. Please, I will tell you everything. I have proof." He tapped the bag he had been carrying. "I just want my family back."

Vesta's mouth, Mirabelle noticed, was gaping.

"Mr. Gorski," Mirabelle said gently, "I'm so sorry. I have no means to get people out of Berlin. This is a police matter now. Perhaps they will be able to help. I'm sure there must be channels of some kind but it's a criminal matter. If you give them information they may be able to put some kind of a case for your wife."

The man looked bewildered, then his eyes blazed.

Sandor stood up. "But, Mirabelle, you have so many contacts. This man helped me. He has information. Without him I'd still be tied up in that outhouse. You are obliged . . ."

"I'm not Secret Service any more, Sandor. That was a long time ago. I told you. It's a different world now."

Sandor spluttered. "What do you mean: you are not Secret Service? What nonsense is this? After all we've been through. Come now!"

Mirabelle lost her composure. "I told you, Sandor. I told you! I work for a debt collection agency. That's all. And this matter is in the hands of the police. I can refer you to them."

"And this brave young lady?" Sandor gestured toward Vesta. "I suppose she simply keeps the ledgers?"

Vesta gulped. "I work in an insurance office, Sandor," she admitted, "along the hallway from Mirabelle. I'm a clerk."

Waclaw roared. It was a furious terrifying sound, like a bull about to charge. He flung the cup of tea against the wall, shattering the porcelain.

"Marianne!" he shouted.

"Please, calm down," Sandor said. "I think that . . ."

But Waclaw had launched himself onto the priest. "You promised. You promised. You said she would help me. This is not some stupid game. My wife is stuck there. She is stuck there! She is relying on me to get her out! Police? They are useless!"

"But . . ." Sandor stuttered.

"You liar! You liar! You old fool!" Waclaw screamed. In fury he hoisted up the bag of gold and hit Sandor hard with it. The old man keeled over, one side of his face pink and bloody.

Vesta and Mirabelle rushed forward but it was too late. There was a sharp crack as Sandor hit the floor. Waclaw backed off.

"Oh, Jesus," said Vesta.

Little bubbles of spit mingled with blood dribbled down Sandor's chin.

"Is he breathing?" said Vesta.

It was impossible to tell.

"Call an ambulance," Mirabelle said. "Quickly! Go!"

As Vesta disappeared into the hallway Mirabelle moved Sandor's prone body into the recovery position. Waclaw moaned like an animal in pain and she positioned herself in front of the priest to protect him from further attack. But that wasn't what was on Waclaw's mind. He put his head on one side as if he was remembering what had happened for a second then he muttered something in Polish that sounded like a curse. "My Marianne," he said.

"You've really hurt him," Mirabelle accused him. "He's a priest, you know."

Waclaw didn't reply. He looked coldly at Sandor's prostrate frame, then with one smooth movement hoisted the bag onto his shoulder.

"Hey!" Mirabelle shouted.

But the goldsmith had already crossed the room and made for the door. She would have followed him but she couldn't leave her friend. Desperately she tried to revive the priest. "Sandor," she whispered, rubbing his hand as Waclaw slammed the front door behind him. "Wake up, Sandor. Please."

But Sandor didn't stir. He couldn't. His neck was broken, and Sandor was dead.

26

Evil counsel travels fast.

The night before, Lisabetta had moved quickly after she had seen Dr. Crichton and his Jaguar, rather satisfyingly, disappear over the clifftop by the light of a crescent moon, which was only a sliver. She picked up the bag she had packed with his stolen coins and started to walk down the country road. England, she thought to herself, really was very beautiful sometimes. She liked the calm dark glossy silence of its nights—that feeling of being the only person awake. The only person alive.

The forge had still been fiery hot. They hadn't been gone for long. Still, she knew the thing to do was simply leave it. It was always like this at the end. You got out with what you could, which for Lisabetta in this case was a lot of experience, three very healthy bank accounts in different names and different countries, this bag of coins and her clothes and jewelery from London. There was no need to go back to Crichton's house. She would simply ring. There was no need to contact Manni—he would continue if he could, launder the money and pay it into the Velazquez bank account, which, of course, she controlled. There was no need to even go back to London—Bert would see to everything there. He knew the drill. Put it on the first train

meant the second train. Send everything to the usual destination meant the last stop before wherever she was located—in
this case Preston Park station, just north of the town. Lisabetta trusted Bert. He was completely self-interested and she
had catered for that. When the insurance money came
through he'd get five hundred pounds whether she was
alive or not. It was a registered debt that would be paid
without any need for her presence. If he didn't do everything
he was told she would simply tell the insurance company the
truth anonymously—that Romana was a fabrication. She'd
lose her five hundred pounds, as well, of course—or rather
less than that, in fact. As Romana she had developed some
expensive shopping habits on account that the solicitor
would need to cover out of the estate. It mattered not a
jot. Bert would be paid and as a result he'd do whatever
she wanted. His payment wasn't contingent on her sur-
vival or her being in the country. It was perfect.

Lisabetta checked her watch. The first train would arrive in about an hour and a half and then they came every
thirty minutes. She needed to pick up her things and disappear. She'd find a city center hotel, somewhere near the
main station. She couldn't stay at the Grand this time. And
she'd need a disguise. Lisabetta enjoyed disguises. It was
like playing a game. By tonight she'd be in Southampton
on her way to the continent and then South America. Her
mind wandered and she wondered if they still made those
delicious vanilla custard tarts in Lisbon. She must stay for
a few days and enjoy the city—the nightlife in the Bairro
Alto, those crumbling regal town houses like dowagers
falling apart from neglect. Lisabetta would have loved to
be an aristocrat. A title! How glamorous. But she knew
these things were too easily traceable and in her line of business that would never do. Lisbon, she recalled, made her
feel like an aristocrat—a charming beautiful princess. She
had visited the city twice and now it was set to be her last
port of call in Europe—perhaps forever. She almost felt

nostalgic. South America, of course, was Spanish or Por-
tuguese depending where you chose—there was no advantage to one or the other as the men were broadly similar and
she spoke both languages only haltingly. She would learn.
She always did.

They want me to risk so much, Lisabetta mused. It is
enough now. I cannot do more for them.

In the distance she heard the roar of a car. She positioned herself at the roadside, drew a white hanky from
her sleeve and stuck out her thumb. The Ford stopped just
ahead and she stalked toward it.

"All right, love? You're out late!"

"Yes," she grinned. It was perfect—as if she had made a
prior arrangement. "I need to get to my aunt's. At Preston
Park. But a lift into Brighton would be marvelous."

"Hop in," the man smiled. "I'll take you wherever you
like. Want a smoke?"

"Thank you." Lisabetta quickly checked her little pistol, just in case the man tried any funny business, then she
fluttered her eyelashes and got into the car.

27

All right then, I'll go to hell.

Mirabelle stood by the window. It was one o'clock. Her hands hadn't stopped shaking since Sandor died and she kept breaking quietly into tears. It was such a shock that it hadn't properly sunk in. Sandor's body had been removed quickly, thank goodness. Though that was when she had started crying—as she'd watched them cover his body and lift him away, the tears had simply flowed down her cheeks. It felt as if her heart was breaking. Poor, brave Sandor. It made her sick—all the losses. Good men like Jack and Ben and Sandor didn't deserve to die before their time. Though she knew it wasn't true, it felt to Mirabelle like each death was an abandonment. I can't save anyone, she taunted herself. I'm useless!

After the body was gone McGregor arrived briefly and looked over their statements. He told them that the doctor and Lisabetta were missing—the staff at Second Avenue said the couple had gone to London but, unsurprisingly, so far the Met hadn't found them either at Cadogan Gardens or at Crichton's private club near St. James's. Now the force was searching the house on Second Avenue but they hadn't found anything helpful. And there wasn't any obvious crime scene on the London Road or anywhere just off it.

"We're keeping an eye on the stations, of course—here and Victoria—and I've had descriptions circulated in both locations to see if we can find either of them or the luggage. We're working on it."

Mirabelle wasn't really listening. She was finding it difficult to concentrate.

"I pinched Manni at Fairfield Road. They're holding him in the cells until I get back. He's threatening hell in a handbasket." The detective superintendent couldn't help but grin. He was enjoying this operation immensely and was particularly pleased he'd sent Robinson to supervise snagging pickpockets at work among the racing day crowd. "The ICPC officers will arrive later this afternoon. Not that we've much to offer them as things stand. They'll want to speak to you and Vesta, though, I'm sure. When you're ready."

"Here," said Mirabelle, handing over Ben's racecourse notebook, "there's a transcription of the coded figures on a sheet inside. It might help you with Manni."

McGregor smiled. "Thanks," he said, "and, Mirabelle, I'm sorry about your friend. First Ben and now this."

"That's very kind of you," she replied.

"Well, I'd better go."

Once he'd slammed the door behind him, the flat felt curiously empty. Mirabelle couldn't bring herself to sit in the drawing room. The thought of Sandor's body lying there was too much. She hovered in the kitchen, leaning against the worktop, while Vesta stared out of the window.

"It's so creepy. Perhaps," Vesta offered, "we should go into town. We could go to the office."

Mirabelle inclined her head and Vesta couldn't tell whether she was agreeing or simply about to cry again.

In fact, Mirabelle was giving up. She didn't suggest doing anything. She didn't correct Vesta or make any comment. Nor did she run over the story to see if there was anything they'd missed. Sandor was dead. Ben was dead. Just like Jack was dead. There was nothing left. She stood silently and stared at her feet.

To pass the time Vesta rolled the map out on the table-top. "I'll try to work out the bad bends between here and London. Might as well give them a hand with it, if I can," she mumbled.

What's the point? Mirabelle thought. She hadn't seen Sandor in years and it felt as if she was going to miss him every day from now on. Catching sight of herself in the glass door of the kitchen, she saw a middle-aged spinster with no connection to anyone around her. I've failed, she thought miserably. I can't save anyone, least of all myself. There are corpses everywhere. I'm the kiss of death.

Around this time, most days, Mirabelle would make her way down to the front, to dodge the deck chair fees and eat her sandwiches. That little routine with Ron, the attendant, seemed like a lifetime ago. In any case, today she couldn't face food. The thought turned her stomach. Then she realized that she really fancied a stiff drink. A dram of Glenlivet. Vesta was engaged with the map.

Taking a deep breath Mirabelle clocked her coat, which was hanging by the door, and cleared her throat. "Vesta, I think I'm going to take a walk." She headed toward the coat stand.

"You're going out?"

"Not for long."

"You're leaving me here?"

"There will be a constable arriving soon, I imagine. About the ICPC people. I need some air."

Vesta looked bereft.

Mirabelle buttoned her coat efficiently. "I can't just hang around like this. There's no point any more."

Vesta shrugged her shoulders. "So where are you off to?"

Mirabelle felt unaccountably furious. She clenched her

fist. "For God's sake! Can't you do anything on your own, Vesta!" she snapped and burst through the kitchen door, slamming it behind her. She'd drink the whole flask and maybe that would help.

Outside there was rain in the air—a dampness to match the cold, which had returned all of a sudden with the gray skies. Mirabelle shoved a pin in her hat and headed toward the sea before turning along Kingsway. The front was quiet out of town—at this time of day the racing crowds were busy at the track and the weather meant that neither tourists nor locals were keen to brave the chilly breeze that was coming off the ocean or the scattered showers that started and stopped so erratically. Only a small way along the promenade Mirabelle paused and leaned against a bollard, taking the flask out of her handbag and enjoying the sharp taste of the spirits. She didn't indulge much— just enough to let the taste pervade her mouth—and then she returned the flask to the inside pocket of her handbag. It was spitting already and getting colder. Soon the rain would start in earnest. In the meantime Mirabelle decided to stretch her legs and take her time. She struck out along the front toward the pier, punishing herself with the cold breeze and regretting that she'd lost her temper.

She hadn't meant to walk so far but once she'd started she didn't turn back. The flat on the Lawns had been her haven for months but now it felt tarnished. Touched by death. She continued almost two miles, sipping from the flask as she went and hardly noticing the streets becoming busier as she made her way into the center. At last she turned up Old Steine and westward. Here there were more people on the pavements, shoppers with umbrellas at the ready as the rain came on. She took another swig, shielded from view in a doorway. At the top of East Street the windows in Hannington's were as beautiful as usual. The doorman nodded at Mirabelle as she came toward him and without really thinking, except that it would be pleasant to get out of the weather, she crossed the threshold smoothly as if it had been what she intended all along.

Hannington's was an institution in Brighton—as good as Harrods, many people said. Mirabelle wondered about mourning clothes. It occurred to her that she would need something in black for the funerals. She hardly ever wore black, deliberately. Her only dress in the color was a figure-hugging satin evening number, which she'd bought for a reception at the Foreign Office at least five years before. Now, she decided, it was appropriate to pick up a black light wool day dress, a coat and a hat. Off the shelf would be fine. She wasn't intending to wear them ever again but there would be, after all, at least one funeral to attend and it was a mark of respect to be properly attired. Then it occurred to her that they would have to exhume Ben and rebury him again. What did one wear for an exhumation, she wondered? Did one even attend?

Taking the lift upstairs Mirabelle allowed herself another discreet shot of whiskey. It coursed through her bloodstream, tempering the pain. Upstairs she found herself in the millinery department and picked up a pillbox hat made from black crepe with a veil. Perfect for hiding any tears, she thought. She handed it to the shop assistant and, with a sigh, brought out her purse to pay. It didn't matter what it looked like, it was just a uniform.

And then, it was only a tiny thing, of course, but many of these moments, she was coming to understand, revolved on tiny things. Out of the corner of her eye Mirabelle noticed an older lady wearing a dowdy powdery-brown suit with low-heeled Venetian shoes in French navy. She was clasping a heavy-looking handbag close to her stomach and spoke with a halting accent, which had, Mirabelle noticed, very flat vowel sounds. The woman had picked out a bright red fascinator—the kind of hair ornament that a pretty twenty-year-old girl might wear to a smart party. Feathers and beads trailed down one side of the comb and three red taffeta roses grew upward from the other. It was, Mirabelle decided, a glamorous thing, but not one appropriate for a woman beyond her thirties. On this old lady it would, without question, look quite ridiculous. What on earth was she up to?

"That model is the Moulin Rouge, Ma'am," the sales assistant said.

"Most pretty," the woman cooed, inspecting it over the top of her very thick spectacles and smoothing the line of her steel-gray bun. "Yes, I think I shall have it."

"Would you like to try it on, Ma'am?"

"No. No, thank you. Just wrap it and send it on with the rest of the shopping to the Left Luggage office at the train station. I am leaving shortly—you must be quick! Your deliveryman knows my schedule is very tight—I have told him already. If you might be so kind to relay—this will be the last thing I purchase today."

The girl brought out a sheaf of white tissue paper, which she hurriedly puffed around the fascinator before popping it skilfully into a box, while the woman drew a crisp five-pound note from her old-fashioned navy handbag to pay.

"Left Luggage?" the shop girl repeated. "And your name, please?"

"Madame de Guise."

"Oh, you're French?" The girl smiled.

"French? With an accent like mine! You have no ear at all, child. My husband was French."

Mirabelle took her change and the bag with the black hat in it, without so much as looking at the girl who was serving her. Any guttural tone in my ear and I hit high doh, she thought. But, still, she surveyed the older woman top to bottom carefully and tried to concentrate on the voice. The woman was not immediately familiar, but if there was even a chance of finding out something helpful, it was worth it. Lisabetta had fooled people with a pregnancy prosthetic and clothes of a slightly different style—why not a dowdy outfit and a wig? This woman was the right size and shape—slender, in fact, for someone of her age. Mirabelle felt her blood pulsing again. It's for Sandor's sake, she told herself. Hell, it's because no one should get away with what Lisabetta appears to be getting away with.

There was something out of place, though she couldn't put her finger on it. The fascinator was certainly an odd purchase for someone of this age. Perhaps the old lady intended it as a present for some younger relation. Perhaps it was simply that this grandmother had a weakness, a fondness for glamorous headwear, although that wasn't borne out by her shabby outfit. Mirabelle lowered her eyes and stayed out of sight while carefully trailing the woman's sensible shoes down Hannington's plush carpeted stairway and through the cloud of perfume that hung around the beauty counters. Perhaps, she thought, she might just follow her and see what she could find out.

Outside in the hammering rain she followed Madame de Guise up the hill. The station wasn't much more than half a mile away and the old lady was heading in the right direction. Mirabelle struggled to keep up. Madame de Guise kept up a smart pace for someone who must surely be well into her sixties, if not older. After a few minutes, the station loomed into view and the pedestrian traffic increased substantially. The woman turned into a shabby hotel. Mirabelle checked her wristwatch. It was half past one and she was drenched.

Inside the hotel lobby Mirabelle stamped her feet and brushed the raindrops from her coat. It was clear that the accommodation here was of a far lower standard than at the Grand. The carpets were worn and the chairs in the reception area were mismatched with scuffed tables of varying heights and sizes, several of which had not been cleared. The remains of milky tea in a grubby cup put Mirabelle off sitting down. Madame de Guise had disappeared upstairs. Mirabelle approached the reception desk.

"Mirabelle Bevan," she said, "from McGuigan & McGuigan Debt Recovery."

The girl on the desk looked anxious. "Yes?"

"If you answer my questions," Mirabelle said, "I won't have to call the police."

The girl sat up straight. "Crikey."

"I need to know if you have any foreign persons staying here."

"Yes," she said, "we've got a few today. The races, you see."

"Women?" asked Mirabelle. "On their own?"

The girl pulled the hotel register toward her and looked down the pages. "Well, we've got three guests like that, I think. Is it something serious?"

"Debt recovery," Mirabelle said. "Could I see the names?"

"There's Mrs. Lawson—I think she's from somewhere funny. Must have married an Englishman."

"But he's not here?"

"No. She hasn't got up yet this morning. Do Not Disturb. I think, perhaps," the girl lowered her voice, "she *drinks*. And then there's Madame de Guise."

"The older lady?"

"Yes. Booked in yesterday. And there's a Miss Brannigan. She's American."

"Thank you," said Mirabelle. "Do you know when Madame de Guise is leaving?"

"Today sometime—one night only. She must be checking out soon. She said she was going abroad."

"Thanks."

Mirabelle drifted out of the hotel doorway, braving the showers, and crossed to the station, following the signs until she found the Left Luggage office. At the desk a boy of no more than eighteen with blond slicked-back hair was smoking a cigarette.

"Excuse me," Mirabelle said.

"Yeah." He did not stop smoking.

"I've come to check all Madame de Guise's luggage is here."

"Right," the boy said, taking a deep draw and squinting at her.

"Have the items from Hannington's arrived yet and how many pieces do you have in total?"

The boy looked over his shoulder. "I dunno. Hang on," he said and languidly disappeared through a doorway to a back office.

"Two bags, four suitcases, nothing from Hannington's," he reported.

"Do they have destination labels?" Mirabelle inquired.

"No," he replied flatly.

"What time did they arrive, these cases?"

"Dunno. Wasn't on duty and, anyway, I'm not supposed to say."

"Of course. Thank you. What time are you working until?"

"Don't finish till late. Bleeding ten."

"So you didn't do the early shift."

"Aha," the boy wagged a finger at her, "aren't you the clever one?"

Mirabelle hesitated but she couldn't think how to get any more information if he wasn't willing to give it. "Thank you," she said and turned to leave. These bags hadn't been on the first train, of course, but however they'd arrived, the police should have been alerted to them. Mirabelle hovered for a moment. Could this be Lisabetta, slipping away? She had to find out.

Buying a cup of tea at the platform café, she looked out over the concourse, absentmindedly adding sugar to her disappeared the old lady cleared her throat and Mirabelle looked up nervously.

"Would you mind closing the blinds, my dear?" she asked, gesturing toward the screens that were in place above the door onto the corridor.

"Oh," Mirabelle said, "of course."

The old lady continued speaking. "What is your destination?"

"Oh, end of the line. Plymouth," Mirabelle replied without hesitation as she pulled the blinds into place. "Where are you going?" she asked as lightly as she could. She turned back into the carriage but as she did so her heart leapt.

The old lady had pulled out a revolver and it was pointed toward her.

28

Upon the conduct of each depends the fate of all.

It was mayhem at police HQ all afternoon. Willie Walsh from the antique shop in the Twittens had been arrested, sneaking around the back garden at 22 Second Avenue with a shovel in his hands. The news that there was a missing cache of gold coins was out, and the vultures had moved in fast, seeing if they could find it before the police recovered the goods.

"It's not illegal to do a bit of gardening," Walsh tried his luck. "I don't know what the world's coming to."

"Leave it out," groaned Sergeant Simmons.

How these things got out, McGregor wasn't sure, but he was damn certain that, eventually, he'd find the culprits and indict them. He wasn't having that kind of corruption in his department. In the meantime, though, there were bigger fish to fry.

By half past two McGregor realized he had gone about as far as he could with Manni. The scumbag was holding out better than he would have expected. Even when he dropped intriguing names into the conversation Manni kept his cool.

"They're punters. All punters. You got nothing on me,

McGregor," he sneered, lighting Camel after Camel, "and you know it. I'm on the level. Legit."

McGregor persisted. He'd sent Robinson to search Manni's lodgings but he wanted to crack him before the team returned to the station—it was a matter of professional pride.

"So," he said, "you know they've scarpered then. Your mates, Dr. Crichton and the lovely Lisabetta. They've gone up to London. They've done a runner on you, Manni."

"I thought it was a free country, England," Manni retorted. "I thought if someone wanted to go to London they were entitled."

"Yes, they are. But they aren't entitled to mint forged currency. They aren't entitled to launder money through your betting stall—the racing board, you can imagine, are taking a particularly gloomy view on that one. Oh, and the insurance fraud and the kidnapping and murder, well, neither they nor you were entitled to any of that. And as it stands, Manni, you're going to be carrying the can for the whole shooting match."

"I don't know what you're talking about," Manni smirked.

"Well, let's start with Ben McGuigan, shall we?"

"Not that again. You've got nothing on me for that, McGregor, and you know it. If Ben Bloody McGuigan gets pissed and goes missing, it ain't my concern. I want my solicitor. I want Mr. Peters."

He wasn't budging and McGregor decided he'd just have to wing it. He was pretty sure that Vesta and Mirabelle were reliable or at least he hoped so.

"Thing is," McGregor allowed a slice of a smile to pass across his face, "we dug him up, Manni. Ben McGuigan."

"Dug him up?" Manni's voice faltered for the first time in the interview.

"Yes, in a grave that was marked for your friend Lisabetta's sister. A bird called Romana Laszlo by all accounts."

Manni looked considerably less cocky than he had a few seconds before.

"And seeing how when Ben McGuigan went missing he had been undercover, investigating you for a good fortnight, well, you can see that we're adding up one and one and getting a very interesting sum. You like maths, don't you, Manni? Figures are quite your thing. Oh, and we got the priest, too. We know what happened to him. So things are really coming together."

It wasn't, the detective superintendent told himself, entirely untrue to say that. They would dig Ben up and, well, they had the priest, that was certain—he just wasn't alive.

A bead of sweat trickled down the side of Manni's face. "None of that was my fault. None of it!"

"So whose was it, Manni?" McGregor was getting close now, he could feel it. It would be so easy to get carried away but he had to control himself. Get the information, the confession and see if Manni knew where they'd gone. He didn't want to feed Manni too much—it would make it easier for him to lie.

A junior officer knocked on the door of the interview room.

"Not now," McGregor barked.

"But, sir," the officer insisted.

"I said not now."

The officer considered a moment. It was only a call from uniform, after all. It hadn't seemed important—just some woman getting on a train but it definitely wasn't the woman the boss was looking for. Only some informant with a foreign-sounding name.

"Yes, sir." He backed out of the interview room. "Sorry for disturbing you."

There was no point pushing it.

"Now," McGregor turned his attention back to Manni, "there's only one way you're going to get anything less than life here. And you'll be lucky if that's all you get." McGregor drew a suggestive finger across his throat. "So, you better tell me everything you know. Because I want to find out, Manni, where the hell the others have gone. And if I don't, well, it's all going to get pinned on you, isn't it? You're in this thing up to your neck and you'll swing, Manni, you mark my words. If you don't cough up, you'll swing."

29

The Black Swan

Eighteen months before, after Jack died, Mirabelle had wanted to die. She used to lie on the floor of the drawing room at night with all the lights out, unable to sleep, and will the building to fall in on her. She had been deliberately careless when she crossed the road, waiting for fate to take its chance, just wishing that she could blot out the whole world forever and hoping that somehow she'd just die and the pain would all be over.

Now that she was faced with a dangerous criminal who had an old-style single-action revolver pointed directly at her, she felt strangely calm, and there was one thing of which she was certain: she wasn't giving up and she no longer wanted to die. Every sense in her body was heightened— she could smell coffee on the old lady's breath, feel the cold windowpane beside her as if it was radiating its chill, and hear the sound of the tracks in minute detail as the train headed west. She knew that Madame de Guise did not intend to shoot her—not immediately, anyway. The safety catch was still on. Mirabelle was familiar with the specification of this revolver and she knew there had been a lot of problems with it. The firing mechanism was delicate and, if it had been subjected to abuse over its lifetime, the spring inside could easily shift, making the weapon extremely unreliable. Though it took six bullets it was generally accepted that it was only safe to load five. One in the first chamber, then a space and four more. Mirabelle had read the firearm manual—she couldn't remember when, but she knew about it, that was the main thing. The old lady was wearing thin kid gloves, which would make the whole thing more difficult. Not, Mirabelle knew, that the gun wouldn't kill her, only that all this might buy her a fraction of a second or two if it came to the crunch.

After a moment's silence, Mirabelle decided to speak. "Well, the ball's in your court," she said quietly.

"Who knows that you're on this train?"

Mirabelle sat up straighter. "I left a message," she answered honestly. "I don't know if they got it."

"You are police?"

Mirabelle shook her head.

"Raise your veil."

Mirabelle did so.

The woman looked perplexed. "Why are you following me?"

Mirabelle gave an almost imperceptible shrug of the shoulders before she spoke. "I was right, though, wasn't I? I'll bet you have a stash of gold coins in that luggage of yours that would put the Royal Mint to shame."

"Ah, you want money." Madame de Guise seemed quite relieved. "But, of course, it is far easier just to kill you and fling you out of the train. I'm not sure you have thought this through, my dear."

"That's all you care about, isn't it? Money? That's what I heard about you."

Madame de Guise hesitated for a moment. She had no qualms about committing murder but she didn't like to kill someone before she knew who they were or what they were up to.

"It was you who broke into Crichton's house last night?" she hazarded. "It's you that Lisabetta was scared of."

Mirabelle's eyes widened. "You're not Lisabetta, then?" she said, incredulous.

The old lady laughed. "I am fifty-eight years of age. Lisabetta was in her twenties. A beautiful girl and quite impressive in her own way. You can't have met her if you are mistaking the two of us. It's quite flattering for me, I think, this mistake of yours."

Mirabelle's thoughts tumbled. This old lady, she was a black swan, she thought in a rush. The human error. The thing that couldn't be accounted for. Was this old woman the mastermind McGregor had suspected—the brains behind everything? She peered across the carriage, examining her closely.

"Ah, you think it is a wig? Makeup? Like she used?" The woman took off her hat with her free hand and pulled her gray hair out of the bun. She tugged on the strands hard. "See."

"Who are you then?" Mirabelle asked.

Madame de Guise smiled. "I could ask you the same thing, I think. You first?" She raised the gun.

"I am Mirabelle Bevan."

Madame de Guise frowned. "I don't know that name."

"And you?"

"Marguerite de Guise, for the time being at any rate. Now, I don't know what to do with you, my dear, but I tend not to kill people until I have to. So, we're going to take a journey together. Only a little journey. And then, in time, I will decide."

"You said 'was,' " Mirabelle pushed. "Lisabetta 'was.' "

"My English," the old lady dismissed the query.

"Is Lisabetta dead? Did you kill her?"

"What do you care? Be quiet. We will be there shortly."

"Where?"

cup. The constabulary were being curiously ineffective, but Mirabelle was heartened to spot three uniformed police-men hanging around the platform for London departures. The green Southern steam engines came and went regularly and the platforms were busy with weekend visitors. I need to wait and see, she thought as she sipped her tea and dunked a biscuit, sitting up as she noticed a porter's trolley laden high with bags from Hannington's moving smoothly toward the Left Luggage office. The hat box was on the very top of the pile but lower down there was a large portmanteau and a safe, as well as some smaller parcels.

A safe? Mirabelle wondered.

Madame de Guise was certainly not traveling light. Vesta wouldn't be too concerned yet, Mirabelle decided. There was no harm in staying a little while longer. Not, as it transpired, that she had to. Five minutes more and Madame de Guise herself arrived with three porters following her dowdy frame with some reverence.

Mirabelle slipped out of the café and kept at a discreet distance, lingering to one side of the Left Luggage office as Madame de Guise dealt sharply with the lazy desk clerk who continued to smoke a stream of cheap cigarettes.

"Put that out! Stand up straight!" she insisted, gesturing toward his cigarette.

The desk clerk glared at her until one of the porters chipped in with a "Come on now, lad." The boy resentfully ground his cigarette into an overflowing ashtray and pulled back his shoulders.

Then, quickly, the bags were piled high, one after the other, onto the porters' trolleys while Madame de Guise carefully checked them. One in particular caught Mirabelle's eye—a doctor's brown leather case. There was a lot of bag-gage here. Enough to contain everything she'd seen in the wardrobes at Cadogan Gardens. She squinted to check if there might be a policeman nearby but they were still over on the London platform at the other side of the station, and she did not want to lose sight of her prey. Mirabelle's heart raced. There were too many small things here that didn't fit.

"Come," Madame directed, and with a toss of the head that would have seemed flirtatious had it been performed by a younger woman, she led her coterie back towards the platforms.

Mirabelle tried to attract the attention of a policeman on the other side of the tracks. She waved and smiled, motioning him over, but the man didn't acknowledge her. With one eye on the solemn caravan now making its way down platform seven, she made another attempt, jerking up and down this time. The policeman turned away. With a sigh, she stopped a passing railwayman. "Where is this train going?"

"It's the Southern Coastal Line, Miss. The Coastway." Mirabelle looked blank, so the man continued. "Portsmouth, Southampton, Bournemouth, Exeter, Plymouth."

"When does it leave?"

"Ten to two."

Three minutes. Mirabelle dodged farther down the platform and saw Madame de Guise supervising the loading of the last of her luggage.

Mirabelle cursed silently. There wasn't enough time and she couldn't be sure. But something here was wrong. And then the old lady did it. Regally she reached inside her bag and Mirabelle saw the flash of gold as she tipped the porters, one by one, wide smiles breaking out on their faces as they doffed their hats in thanks at her generosity.

"You must take the day off now. Will you? It's Saturday. Treat yourselves." The old lady barely stopped for a moment to hear their answers before striding purposefully toward a first-class carriage to board for the journey.

As one of the porters passed Mirabelle on his way back up the platform, she called him over. "Please," she said breathlessly, "I need your help. It's that lady. The lady you were with. Will you go straight away to one of the police officers on the London platform for me?"

"Yes, Miss," the man said uncertainly. "You need a police officer?"

A guard was signaling with a flag at the other end of the train.

"Tell him that Detective Superintendent McGregor has to know—Mirabelle Bevan is on this train. The Southern Coastal Line. He has to come and help. Have you got that? And make sure he tells Vesta as well—she'll be worried."

"Yes, Miss. But that lady isn't no Mirabelle Bevan— she's a French lady, see. Can't remember the name but it wasn't that. Pretty fancy, she is."

"I know. I can't explain now. Just tell him, will you?"

The man paused, clearly waiting for a tip. Mirabelle fumbled with her handbag and extracted a sixpence.

"It's very important," she said. "Life or death. I don't want to lose sight of her until the police know. It's vital that they tell Detective Superintendent McGregor."

The man pocketed the coins, looking unimpressed after the older woman's generosity. "Right, Ma'am," he said. "Well, I'm going off now, but I'll tell the officer before I leave."

Mirabelle felt flustered. It was an odd request, she knew. "Detective Superintendent McGregor," she repeated. "And I'm Mirabelle Bevan."

The man paused. "Oh, I'm telling him you got on the train, Miss?"

"That's right."

"Shall I tell him which stop you're traveling to?"

Mirabelle rolled her eyes. "I don't know which stop. Just tell him I got on the train. This train. He'll have to figure the rest out for himself."

The guard blew his whistle.

"Right then," the porter said and opened the nearest door.

Mirabelle climbed aboard. "Any of the policemen will do," she leaned out toward him. "Go now! See that they ring it in. And tell them to let Vesta know. I'm tailing Madame de Guise, do you see? Oh, dear!"

The door slammed. The porter nodded through the glass and waved half-heartedly as if Mirabelle was completely mad and he was only humoring her. Then the carriage pulled off slowly and she lost sight of the man as the jerky shuffling of the train accelerated along the track.

Mirabelle hesitated a moment, loitering in the corridor, but realized that going into the compartment was the only way to keep an eye on what the old lady was up to. If she chose another compartment nearby she would have no way of telling if Madame de Guise changed seats or which stop she might get off along the route. She plucked her new hat out of its box and swapped it with the one she was wearing. The black veil covered most of her face, so it would be unlikely that Lisabetta would recognize her. Smoothing it into place, she carefully slid back the door, praying that the porter had delivered her message to the policeman and that the uniformed officer had the good sense to call it in quickly.

The carriage was unoccupied apart from the two of them. Madame de Guise nodded and, Mirabelle noticed, as she took the seat opposite, studiously ignored her, casting her eyes down and then out of the window.

I just have to sit here and wait, she told herself. That's all. I just have to stay calm and keep my eyes open until McGregor gets here. It's my duty. She won't do anything. She doesn't know it's me.

The houses soon gave way to fields on one side and the sea on the other, flashes of blue as the track followed its course close to the coast. As the last of Brighton's suburbs disappeared the old lady cleared her throat and Mirabelle looked up nervously.

"Would you mind closing the blinds, my dear?" she asked, gesturing toward the screens that were in place above the door onto the corridor.

"Oh," Mirabelle said, "of course."

The old lady continued speaking. "What is your destination?"

"Oh, end of the line. Plymouth," Mirabelle replied without hesitation as she pulled the blinds into place. "Where are you going?" she asked as lightly as she could. She turned back into the carriage but as she did so her heart leapt.

The old lady had pulled out a revolver and it was pointed toward her.

28

Upon the conduct of each depends the fate of all.

It was mayhem at police HQ all afternoon. Willie Walsh from the antique shop in the Twittens had been arrested, sneaking around the back garden at 22 Second Avenue with a shovel in his hands. The news that there was a missing cache of gold coins was out, and the vultures had moved in fast, seeing if they could find it before the police recovered the goods.

"It's not illegal to do a bit of gardening," Walsh tried his luck. "I don't know what the world's coming to."

"Leave it out," groaned Sergeant Simmons.

How these things got out, McGregor wasn't sure, but he was damn certain that, eventually, he'd find the culprits and indict them. He wasn't having that kind of corruption in his department. In the meantime, though, there were bigger fish to fry.

By half past two McGregor realized he had gone about as far as he could with Manni. The scumbag was holding out better than he would have expected. Even when he dropped intriguing names into the conversation Manni kept his cool.

"They're punters. All punters. You got nothing on me,

McGregor," he sneered, lighting Camel after Camel, "and you know it. I'm on the level. Legit."

McGregor persisted. He'd sent Robinson to search Manni's lodgings but he wanted to crack him before the team returned to the station—it was a matter of professional pride.

"So," he said, "you know they've scarpered then. Your mates, Dr. Crichton and the lovely Lisabetta. They've gone up to London. They've done a runner on you, Manni."

"I thought it was a free country, England," Manni retorted. "I thought if someone wanted to go to London they were entitled."

"Yes, they are. But they aren't entitled to mint forged currency. They aren't entitled to launder money through your betting stall—the racing board, you can imagine, are taking a particularly gloomy view on that one. Oh, and the insurance fraud and the kidnapping and murder, well, neither they nor you were entitled to any of that. And as it stands, Manni, you're going to be carrying the can for the whole shooting match."

"I don't know what you're talking about," Manni smirked.

"Well, let's start with Ben McGuigan, shall we?"

"Not that again. You've got nothing on me for that, McGregor, and you know it. If Ben Bloody McGuigan gets pissed and goes missing, it ain't my concern. I want my solicitor. I want Mr. Peters."

He wasn't budging and McGregor decided he'd just have to wing it. He was pretty sure that Vesta and Mirabelle were reliable or at least he hoped so.

"Thing is," McGregor allowed a slice of a smile to pass across his face, "we dug him up, Manni. Ben McGuigan."

"Dug him up?" Manni's voice faltered for the first time in the interview.

"Yes, in a grave that was marked for your friend Lisabetta's sister. A bird called Romana Laszlo by all accounts."

Manni looked considerably less cocky than he had a few seconds before.

"And seeing how when Ben McGuigan went missing he had been undercover, investigating you for a good fortnight, well, you can see that we're adding up one and one and getting a very interesting sum. You like maths, don't you, Manni? Figures are quite your thing. Oh, and we got the priest, too. We know what happened to him. So things are really coming together."

It wasn't, the detective superintendent told himself, entirely untrue to say that. They would dig Ben up and, well, they had the priest, that was certain—he just wasn't alive.

A bead of sweat trickled down the side of Manni's face. "None of that was my fault. None of it!"

"So whose was it, Manni?" McGregor was getting close now, he could feel it. It would be so easy to get carried away but he had to control himself. Get the information, the confession and see if Manni knew where they'd gone. He didn't want to feed Manni too much—it would make it easier for him to lie.

A junior officer knocked on the door of the interview room.

"Not now," McGregor barked.

"But, sir," the officer insisted.

"I said not now."

The officer considered a moment. It was only a call from uniform, after all. It hadn't seemed important—just some woman getting on a train but it definitely wasn't the woman the boss was looking for. Only some informant with a foreign-sounding name.

"Yes, sir." He backed out of the interview room. "Sorry for disturbing you."

There was no point pushing it.

"Now," McGregor turned his attention back to Manni, "there's only one way you're going to get anything less than life here. And you'll be lucky if that's all you get." McGregor drew a suggestive finger across his throat. "So, you better tell me everything you know. Because I want to find out, Manni, where the hell the others have gone. And if I don't, well, it's all going to get pinned on you, isn't it? You're in this thing up to your neck and you'll swing, Manni, you mark my words. If you don't cough up, you'll swing."

29

The Black Swan

Eighteen months before, after Jack died, Mirabelle had wanted to die. She used to lie on the floor of the drawing room at night with all the lights out, unable to sleep, and will the building to fall in on her. She had been deliberately careless when she crossed the road, waiting for fate to take its chance, just wishing that she could blot out the whole world forever and hoping that somehow she'd just die and the pain would all be over.

Now that she was faced with a dangerous criminal who had an old-style single-action revolver pointed directly at her, she felt strangely calm, and there was one thing of which she was certain: she wasn't giving up and she no longer wanted to die. Every sense in her body was heightened—she could smell coffee on the old lady's breath, feel the cold windowpane beside her as if it was radiating its chill, and hear the sound of the tracks in minute detail as the train headed west. She knew that Madame de Guise did not intend to shoot her—not immediately, anyway. The safety catch was still on. Mirabelle was familiar with the specification of this revolver and she knew there had been a lot of problems with it. The firing mechanism was delicate and, if it had been subjected to abuse over its life-

Madame de Guise cocked the gun rather expertly and Mirabelle felt her whole body tighten with fear. Those revolvers had been known to go off unexpectedly if you didn't know they shouldn't be fully loaded. For a second she thought she might not be able to breathe but then, with a shallow rhythm, she found that she could take in at least a little air.

"First stop, Portsmouth," the old lady said. "That is, if I don't shoot you before we arrive out of sheer annoyance."

Mirabelle decided she'd pushed it quite enough. She sat still and said nothing.

30

Only the dead have seen the end of war.

Madame de Guise and Mirabelle left the train at Portsmouth with Madame's luggage in tow. Mirabelle tried to make eyes at the porter despite Madame's gun being only a few inches from her side, stashed in her pocket. The man only looked embarrassed when she raised her eyebrows suggestively and he refused to look at her again all the way to the taxi.

On the backseat Mirabelle could feel the revolver jabbing into her side through both Madame's coat and her own. The old lady gave the driver instructions to go to the dock and Mirabelle felt once more as if her heart was about to stop. There was clearly a boat at Madame's disposal and Mirabelle knew well that there was no easier way to get rid of a body than to heave it over the side of a seagoing vessel. She was in the process of accepting that she was probably going to die but still she frantically kept her eyes open for a sign, a whiff of McGregor. There was none. Her heart sank and she felt tears welling in her eyes.

"Come now, dear," Madame said and passed her a handkerchief, for show.

"Jack," she whispered under her breath.

"Who is Jack?" Madame snapped, still trying to find the reason behind this elegant woman following her.

"He's my . . ." Mirabelle faltered. "Jack died. It seems a long time ago . . ."

Madame's eyes softened for the first time. "Ah, my husband also is dead. Karl was not always the best husband but he was mine . . ."

A sudden realization hit Mirabelle. "You're Mrs. Velazquez," she gasped. "Aren't you? You're the Candlemaker's wife."

"And they say that he died in a hotel room—a problem of the heart!" Mrs. Velazquez sneered. She was angry but she kept her voice low so the driver couldn't hear what she was saying. She appeared to be confiding in Mirabelle, rather than simply letting off steam. "Honestly! That man had the strongest heart his doctor had ever seen. His father and his grandfather lived until they were ninety. As if I'd swallow that stupid girl's ridiculous story. And then the hanky-panky with our money. That little gypsy tramp thought that she could play around with my family and our future because without him we were defenseless. Not true. She was a bad choice, of course, but bad choices can always be . . . reconsidered. Poor Karl, he was always stupid about women. It takes a woman, sometimes, doesn't it? To sort things out."

"They said you weren't coming for the funeral."

"I did not come for the funeral, Miss Bevan. I came to kill her and to get my money," Mrs. Velazquez hissed. "They think an old woman has no resources. No inventiveness. No direction."

A minute or two later the taxi pulled up on a cobbled dock. The driver got out and unloaded the bags as a young man came down the gangplank of a small yacht moored close to the entrance. He had a questioning look but he did not say anything, only picked up two of the bags and took them aboard.

Mirabelle looked around helplessly. There weren't any people around. It was a bad day for sailing. The weather would be enough to put off any amateurs and the mooring was full of the pleasure boats of hobbyists—small yachts, catamarans and speedboats that were tied up and out of action. This side of the dock was not used by real fishermen or the Navy—those who sailed in almost any weather.

Mrs. Velazquez paid the driver graciously, smiling all the while, and gave him a generous tip. Mirabelle took a deep breath and with her heart in her mouth decided to take this chance while the old lady was preoccupied. She took two breaths, as deep as she could, and she bolted—setting off down the mooring at a pace. Her high-heeled shoes on the cobblestones were treacherous but she knew if she got onto the boat she was as good as dead. This way Mrs. Velazquez would be unwilling to shoot her till the taxi was out of sight. There weren't any other choices.

The old lady let out a furious screech as the taxi hurtled away. But she didn't fire the gun. Instead she set off after Mirabelle, with the disadvantage of age but the clear advantage of more appropriate footwear. Mirabelle kicked off her heels. The cobblestones were slippery and cold but she could run in her stocking soles. She made it another hundred yards before she was tackled and brought to the ground by the young man from the boat who had overtaken both the women with ease when he had seen what was going on.

"*Jawohl!*" the old lady said delightedly. "*Sehr gut!*"

"You people!" Mirabelle struggled to get to her feet. "You people! Your husband did unspeakable things and all you can think about is money. All you can think about is getting away. Don't you have any shame?"

The man hit her hard on the jaw. It stung. But he loosened his grip momentarily, a stupid grin on his face and his eyes alight. Mirabelle grabbed the chance to wriggle free and launch herself at Mrs. Velazquez, and before the old lady could fumble the gun into firing position, Mirabelle had twisted her arm behind her back and removed the weapon.

"These revolvers are unpredictable, you know," she said. "They can go off quite unexpectedly. So you better be careful," she put the gun to the old lady's head, "because I've taken off the safety catch."

The man looked terrified. He motioned with both his hands to stay calm.

"Yes," said Mirabelle, "that's very good."

She was surprised at herself—holding a loaded gun to an elderly lady's head. It had been a most peculiar week.

"Did you kill Lisabetta? Have you done it?" she asked the woman.

"Yes," the old lady muttered, "of course, I did. She cheated us. These girls—they never did anything—never went through what we did. Vermin! They think they are smart. They think they can do anything. Well, for a woman who's seen what I've seen, *poof*! It's like they are made from paper—no substance. She killed my husband and cheated him just like that. She thought she was indestructible but she had no real discipline. I hunted her down and I killed her. You think that Karl was the only one who had the talent to kill people? I worked a long time for our country. I executed enemies of the Reich many, many times. One more little gypsy bitch? It was nothing. And she thought I was going to stay in the background and just say thank you, thank you so much for giving me back the tiny part of my own money she said she could get out? She thought because I am a woman and I am old I would just lie down and whimper. How would you like it if she did that to you?"

Mirabelle looked around. The dockside was deserted.

"I will give you a hundred sovereigns," Mrs. Velazquez offered. "I have them there, in her bag. They are yours. We just want to go home, my son and I."

The son's eyes burned with resentment but he held off.

"I don't want your filthy money. This whole thing is a bloodbath. I can't stand it. I'm not like you. We're going to the police," Mirabelle said. "You and I are going to move very slowly. Tell him. Tell him that if he does anything out of turn I'll shoot you and, goddamn it, I'll shoot him as well!"

The old lady spat something in German at her son.

"Right. This way."

Mirabelle guessed the harbormaster's office must be on the other side of the dock. She loosened her grip on Mrs. Velazquez and pushed her gently in the right direction but as she did the boy took his chance and bolted. He sped off down the dock toward the boat. Mirabelle ran in hot pursuit as the old lady shouted encouragement at her son, "*Schnell! Mach schnell!*"

And then, without even thinking, in a single smooth movement as if she'd been trained all her life to do it, Mirabelle aimed the revolver. Mrs. Velazquez was shouting at him to get away. To leave her behind and just get home. And then there was a crack from the gun, the man's body arched instantly and he toppled over the side into the murky water of the dock.

Mrs. Velazquez screamed. Mirabelle turned and aimed again, this time for the old lady. "I swear," she said, "it's you next if you so much as move without my say-so!" Then she walked back slowly to see if the man had surfaced, keeping her distance from the old lady and trying to control her fury.

"*Mein Sohn!*" the old woman's voice broke.

He was gone. Mirabelle's heart was pounding. "He's dead," she said, shocking herself with her own resolve, "and you'll be dead, too, if you don't turn around. Now, walk over there. We need to find the harbormaster."

They were just about to move when a car careered off the main road and, with screeching wheels, turned into the quay. Mirabelle squinted to see who was in the driving seat as the vehicle skidded to a halt beside her. She almost burst into tears as Vesta tumbled out of the passenger seat. "Oh, thank God!" Vesta barked. "We found you! Is that Lisabetta you have there? That's a great disguise."

"Not quite. And where the hell is McGregor?"

"McGregor?" Vesta asked. "How would I know? The desk sergeant rang and gave me your message. Well, I knew something was up. I mean, what would you want to go to Portsmouth for? This is Mr. Stewart—I knew he was getting delivery of his Ford this morning and, well, he's been such a sport. So we followed you. They remembered you at the train station, of course—called you an 'elegant lady' as a matter of fact."

Mr. Stewart, a burly man in his forties, emerged from the driver's side of the vehicle.

"Are you ex-forces?" Mirabelle had never felt so grateful in her life.

"Air Corps. Want me to take that gun?"

Mirabelle felt a sudden wave of nausea overcome her. "Yes, please. And we need some police officers. I really don't feel well."

"You don't eat enough," Vesta lectured. "I bet you ain't eaten anything at all today."

"Oh, Vesta, stop fussing!" Mirabelle heard herself say. She felt woozy. "Here," she said, thrusting the revolver into Mr. Stewart's hands. "Watch Mrs. Velazquez."

And the next thing she knew everything went black and she passed out on the cobbles.

When Mirabelle woke up, the boy's sodden body was laid out on the quayside and the police had arrived. The old lady was crying. Inconsolable, her hands were cuffed and soggy makeup was dripping off her chin. As she passed, she threw Mirabelle a look of sheer hatred. Mirabelle could hardly blame her.

"Well done, Miss Bevan," a man in uniform said as he passed her a cup of tea, "that was a pretty plucky show."

But Mirabelle felt like crying. She wasn't proud of what had happened—she'd never wanted to kill anyone but there simply hadn't been a choice.

"I'm sorry," she said to Mrs. Velazquez, "but he was trying to get away."

The woman looked away, eyes burning.

Mirabelle turned back to the policeman. "There's a body somewhere—she killed a woman in Brighton this morning sometime. Brighton police are looking for the woman but they don't know she's dead, if you see what I mean. Her name is Lisabetta."

"We'll look into it, Miss Bevan."

"Come on, Mirabelle." Vesta took her arm. "We better get you home. The officers here can finish everything. Those foreign cops—the ICPC fellows—are coming over. Remember?"

Mirabelle raised her head. "Right. That's good. It's just such a mess. It's a horrible mess. Thanks for coming to get me, Vesta." It felt good to have someone to lean on.

"Sure thing." Vesta smiled proudly, looking more mature than usual. "It was my responsibility and I couldn't shirk that now, could I?"

31

Love is a reciprocal torture.

The trees outside the morgue were in blossom and fallen petals clumped together over the ground around the entrance, held together with mud and drizzle. Dressed in black, Mirabelle looked composed. She took a deep breath as the sergeant opened the door for her to go in. It smelled, unsurprisingly, of antiseptic. The sergeant signed the paperwork and motioned her through.

On a trolley, under a bare lightbulb, Lisabetta looked tiny—like a broken china doll. Her glassy eyes were bloodshot. Her carefully painted fingernails were broken where she had tried to fight off the Candlemaker's wife. She seemed older, somehow, now she was still.

"Yes, it's her."

"And you've no idea of a last name?"

Mirabelle shook her head. "No one does. Where did you find her?"

"Station Hotel," the sergeant said. "In her room."

"How did she die?"

He lifted the sheet to expose a gunshot wound to Lisabetta's chest. "Pathologist reckons the shot took her by surprise. She was fighting someone off but she didn't know there was a gun. She was booked in as a Mrs. Lawson."

"Oh," Mirabelle said faintly. "Do Not Disturb."

"And the old lady confessed the crime to you?"

"Yes, she did. Hasn't she said so?"

The sergeant shook his head. "Hasn't said a word. She's a tough old bird."

"That's the competition for you," Mirabelle said, and she smiled. If Jack was anywhere, he'd be with her now. And he always called them the competition. The Jerries.

"Come on." The sergeant motioned her away. "The Super said to drop you over at the Sacred Heart."

McGregor stood in the rain over the grave. The team had erected a tent before they started digging and Father Grogan had blessed them. Now they had almost excavated the whole thing, a shade off six feet down. It wouldn't be much longer. Mirabelle stood to one side, dabbing her tears with a handkerchief. As the spade hit the coffin lid she flinched visibly and McGregor went to her side. Her skin looked very pale but he couldn't be sure if it was the effect of wearing such a dark color or if she had blanched. In a way, he thought, whatever it was, the color suited her. It highlighted the warm hazel tone of her eyes.

"Are you going to be all right, Miss Bevan?" he whispered.

Mirabelle nodded silently. It was best not to faint, of course, though with the visit to the morgue and now this, it was turning out to be a challenging day. She took a few deep breaths. She had wanted to be here—had insisted, in fact—and she mustn't make a fuss.

"I'll be fine," she said. "Honestly."

The first of the team jumped down into the hole, covering his mouth and nose with a handkerchief before opening the coffin. McGregor moved forward to get a better view. "It's him, all right," he said as Father Grogan sprinkled some holy water into the grave.

It was set to be a long week of funerals. Crichton's body

had washed up near Bournemouth, identified initially by the very expensive and distinctive driving gloves he had been wearing, of which, the housemaid said, he had been extremely fond. His face had been bashed on the rocks until it was almost unrecognizable. Lisabetta's body would be released for burial now she had been formally identified.

Mirabelle had surprised herself—she wanted to attend all the funerals. "Just to be sure, I suppose," she'd said.

"You've been very brave," McGregor said kindly. "A rock, quite astonishing."

Mirabelle breathed deeply. Being here in the churchyard felt like the most difficult thing she had had to do in a long time. She wasn't sure if the memorial mass that was planned for Sandor the following day would make things better or worse but, one thing was certain, she'd rather face down Mrs. Velazquez again than have to attend any of the formal services that were planned. She didn't think she could cry any more than she had over the last few days. The loss she felt was profound and the sense of her own responsibility worse.

"I wish . . ." The rest of the sentence disappeared from her mind as a woman with a bunch of daffodils in her hand came out of the side door of the church and walked along the main path through the graveyard.

McGregor met her, barring the way.

"I'm sorry, Ma'am. I'm afraid there's police business here. The churchyard is out of bounds."

"Oh," she said, staring, Mirabelle noticed, directly into his eyes, "I didn't mean to pry . . ." She paused, waiting for him to introduce himself.

"Detective Superintendent Alan McGregor," he said, right on cue.

The woman smiled. She was neatly dressed and wearing immaculate makeup.

"I come every Tuesday at this time, Mr. McGregor. Father

Grogan will vouch for me. I'm Mary Duggan. My husband is buried over there. I only want to leave the flowers on his grave. Yellow, you know, was his favorite color."

Mirabelle shook her head. Jack's favorite color was red, the color of blood. McGregor she noticed, however, seemed entranced by the widow. There was something quite pretty, even vulnerable, about her as she stared up at him with her wide blue eyes.

"If you don't mind my accompanying you, I'm sure it will be fine to leave the flowers, Mrs. Duggan."

"Please, call me Mary. Jack was in the detective force, in a way, during the war. He worked in Whitehall. I never really found out exactly what he did but you people do such a wonderful job. It's so terribly lonely without him."

Mirabelle couldn't believe the woman was peddling that line. Jack had hardly seen his wife for the last ten years of his marriage—they had, by mutual arrangement, kept separate households. Mary had been utterly uninterested in what Jack was doing—not that he could have told her about it, anyway—and only seemed concerned about the latest round of cocktail parties and spending the money he earned. If it hadn't been for the twins they would never have seen each other at all. The idea that Mrs. Duggan missed her husband seemed very unlikely.

But McGregor had fallen into step with Jack's widow who picked her way delicately along the path, her black patent stilettos sparkling in the gray light. At the grave Mirabelle heard the woman giggling at something he said. "You must call on me, Detective Superintendent. I make a wonderful venison stew—it's a recipe that my mother handed on. She was a Forbes, you know, very Scottish, very proper. From Nairn. It would be delightful to have a man to cook for again, I must say. Will you come on Friday?"

"Well, that's very kind of you, Ma'am . . . Mary," he corrected himself.

Mirabelle felt her color heighten. At least, she thought, she didn't feel like fainting any longer—more like kicking Mrs. Duggan and her bloody daffodils right out of the bloody churchyard and back home to her bloody venison stew. People were such a sham, sometimes. What was she doing here, flirting and giggling, while Ben was being taken out of the ground? McGregor should have known better.

The men had heaved up the coffin and maneuvered it onto the pathway before filling in the hole. It had been decided not to use the burial plot for anyone else—it would remain vacant for all time. Who, after all, would want to be buried in a spot with such a checkered history? Perhaps they would erect a memorial but all that was for later. Ben's box landed on the gravel with a bump and the men turned immediately to shovel in the soil and close the hole.

Mirabelle heard the familiar click of Vesta's heels on the path behind her and turned to see her friend clutching a huge magenta umbrella, almost falling as it was caught by a gust of wind.

"Spring storms, Mirabelle. Sorry I'm late. You holding up?"

Mirabelle nodded and looped her arm through Vesta's slightly damp raincoat.

"This came in." Vesta pulled an envelope from her pocket. "It's the payment from the solicitor. Bert Jennings's money for Romana Laszlo's death. No one told them! After all that!"

Mirabelle smiled sadly. She crumpled the envelope and flung it into the grave where it was covered immediately by a clod of damp earth.

Vesta looked down into the hole. "Yes, you're right, I guess."

At the other side of the graveyard McGregor walked Mrs. Duggan to the gate and held it open for her, chatting pleasantly.

"There's another reason I'm late," Vesta admitted. "Mr. Halley's back. Never seen him so furious. I made him tea and toast but it didn't calm him down one bit. I think I'm out of a job."

Mirabelle shifted her gaze from the flirtatious conversation that was clearly underway on the other side of the churchyard—details over timings for Friday night and if the detective superintendent preferred a martini or a sidecar before dinner, no doubt.

"You got fired?" she said.

Vesta shrugged. "I hated insurance, anyway. I'm not sure how I'll ever get back to normal life, really. After all this, I mean, I hardly feel like anything normal. I was listening to *The Archers* on the radio last night and all I could think was why doesn't anything interesting happen? I can't believe they canceled *Dick Barton*. I loved that show."

Mirabelle smiled. "Normal life. What is that?"

"The thing is, I was wondering . . . you know, if you might be interested . . ." Vesta continued.

"Oh, yes," Mirabelle cut in, "I was wondering about that, too. Do you think we could keep Ben's name on the door?"

"It's only fitting. And we could be partners? I mean, I'd be a junior partner, obviously. Because you, well, you're just amazing."

"Sixty-forty." Mirabelle held out her hand.

Vesta shook it. "But next time I'll be damned if we have so many bodies. That's all I have to say."

"We're going into debt collection, Vesta. I worked for Ben for eighteen months and not one single person turned up dead."

"Debt collection *and* investigation then," Vesta insisted. "We got skills."

"Well," Mirabelle smiled, "you certainly proved that you've got potential. That's for sure."

The hole was half-full now and the coffin had been re-moved in an unmarked hearse. The police insisted on per-forming an autopsy before Ben could be reburied. It was a procedure that Mirabelle had felt was quite unnecessary, but the law was the law.

"Well, that's that," she said.

"Come on." Vesta took her arm. "Let's get out of here."

It took ten minutes to make it back to the Lawns. Vesta had decided she would have to throw away her shoes—they were squelching in a most unattractive fashion and the sole had come away. "Well, at least we won't have to deal with that idiotic policeman any more."

"Absolutely. We won't. Ever again." Mirabelle trotted smartly up the stairs, drawing the key from her pocket. Vesta grinned. There was a gold sovereign hanging from the fob, swinging from side to side. A drop of rain ran down the face and dripped off, making it look even shinier.

"Mirabelle! How could you?"

"Oh, don't worry, Vesta. I think we're due a little me-mento, don't you? I had one made for you, too. Lucky pen-nies. Now, do I take it that you might be ready for a spot of lunch?"

AUTHOR'S NOTE

The quotations and misquotations used to open each chapter are taken from the following sources: "*Suspicion*: a feeling that something may be possible" (generic dictionary definition); "Better a diamond with a flaw than a pebble without" (Confucius); "There are a thousand ways to go home" (Rumi); "HA HU HI: I am going to Paris" (radio code used by double agent Eddie Chapman); "Chickenfeed: information intended to attract and puzzle the recipient" (SOE operation manual); "Curiosity is one of the forms of feminine bravery" (Victor Hugo); "All war is deception" (Sun Tzu); "True friendship can afford true knowledge" (Henry David Thoreau). "All knowledge begins with experience" (Emmanuel Kant); "He is a hard man who is only just" (Voltaire); "There is no such thing as accident; it is fate misnamed" (Napoleon Bonaparte); "Let wisdom make you a good gamester" (Francis Quarles); "Never was anything great achieved without danger" (Machiavelli); "There is no sinner like a young saint" (Aphra Behn); "He who would search for pearls must dive below" (John Dryden); "*Friendship*: a state of mutual trust and support" (generic dictionary definition); "Ratissage: a counter-espionage manhunt" (SOE operation manual); "The only thing to do with good advice is pass it on" (Oscar Wilde); "As a man is, so you must humour him" (Jean Racine); "Common sense is not so common" (Voltaire); "Blowback: the unintended consequences of covert operation" (SOE operation manual); "It takes two to speak the truth" (Henry David

Thoreau); "Where there is a mystery, it is generally suspected there must also be evil" (Lord Byron); "Death is not the worst that can happen" (Plato); "Advice to agents: Your life depends on your ability to tell your cover story unhesitatingly" (SOE operation manual); "X2: the counterintelligence and agent-manipulation branch of the Secret Service" (SOE operation manual); "Evil counsel travels fast" (Sophocles); "All right then, I'll go to hell" (Mark Twain); "Upon the conduct of each depends the fate of all" (Alexander the Great); "Only the dead have seen the end of war" (Plato); "Love is a reciprocal torture" (Marcel Proust).

ACKNOWLEDGMENTS

It may take a village to raise a baby, but hell! it takes an army to produce a book. Happily *Brighton Belle* has had strategists, generals, collaborators and even the odd foot soldier.

First of all, I have to thank my parents, Kate and Ron Goodwin, without whose boozy lunches I'd never have had the idea at all. Dad's fabulous reminiscences of Brighton and London in the 1950s were inspirational so a big thanks to him and also thanks for being patient with the late night phone calls about how to give change in old money. Next up is my agent, Jenny Brown, who takes ideas and runs with them. I couldn't do without Jenny's upbeat attitude no matter what—she's a have-a-go heroine (my favorite sort) and I'm very grateful to her for all she's done. A huge thank-you (and a bottle of bubbly at least) is due to crime writer Lin Anderson who gave me abundant expert advice about how to write in a new genre. Such generosity, Lin, thank you. Then there is the team at Polygon who know a lot about publishing *and* know what they like. These two wonderful attributes do not always go together but when they do it's impressive. Thanks for taking on the book and running with it—I hope both Mirabelle Bevan and I do you proud. And last of all a big thanks to everyone who took an interest—my friends online and off, my daughter, who patiently helped me research the ins and outs of 1950s fashion, and my husband, Alan, who though not a Secret Service agent, as far as any of us are aware, shares many qualities with the love of Mirabelle's life, Jack Duggan—a girl has to find inspiration where she can.

Sara Sheridan
Edinburgh

QUESTIONS FOR READERS' GROUPS

1. Is it history if it's in living memory?
2. Was rationing good for the country?
3. We don't know a huge amount about Lisabetta—what do you think happened to her during and just after the war?
4. At what point, if any, is it right to stop hunting war criminals?
5. Did advances in forensics put an end to the amateur detective?
6. Is Mirabelle Bevan "curiously British"?
7. How did the post-war landscape differ in 1918 and 1945?
8. Without the 1950s, could we have had the social changes of the 1960s?
9. Would you have let Delia go?
10. How different is the racism Vesta encounters to the racism she would encounter in British society today?
11. What is the fascination of a female detective? What can they bring to the genre?
12. How does historical crime fiction differ from contemporary crime fiction?